G.H. FRYER

Jacket design by Naomi Pickett. Jacket portraits by Alexander Krivitskiy and Dylann Hendricks

First Edition: October 2023

ISBN: 979-8-9861578-8-7   (Hardcover)   979-8-9891474-1-0   (eBook) 979-8-9891474-2-7 (Paperback)

This book was independently published and adheres to industry standards set forth by the Independent Book Publishers Association.

This one's for you, munchkin.

Also By G.H. Fryer

Contemporary Murder Mystery
The Arsenic Box

ROT

Prologue

FEAR HAD TEETH AND snapped at Katherine's heels. She ran through the woodland, her red cloak snagging on branches. The pit in her stomach told her that the demons were close even though she couldn't hear them. Too frightened to look, she continued running. Branches whipped at her ivory skin, twigs crunched beneath her boots, and the chaotic rhythm of her heartbeat pounded in her ears.

She needed a spot to breathe and to think. She spotted the broad trunk of a nearby spruce and crouched behind it. It was at least a century old and generous enough to hide her petite figure. Lady Katherine Ainsley slipped her back against the rough bark and pulled her knees to her chest, making herself as small as she could. Her breath ragged, she fixated on slowing her breathing and tried futilely to calm the terror of those monsters. She wondered if she would ever love this place the way she once did.

After closing her eyes, she let her head fall against the tree. If only this was a frightening nightmare, she thought, but all her senses were shouting at her. She'd once read that you couldn't smell in a dream, so she inhaled and the sharp tang of pine and sap filled her senses. Her eyes opened. The complex ironwork bracing the panes of glass framed the midnight stars above. This place was magical. It was breathtaking to conceive that someone had grown a forest within the barriers of this extravagant manor, but magic could be terrifying as well as beautiful. It was ironic that she would fight for her life in this place. She wouldn't have met Lord Brahm if it weren't for her insatiable curiosity. Despite her fear and weariness, she smiled at the memory.

A flurry of wings breaking free from a nearby tree startled her. There could only be one reason birds had burst from their roost. The monsters were close. She wondered how much longer Lord Brahm needed to set his trap. It wasn't so long ago that she believed demons were merely a story told by priests to reinforce the consequences of misbehavior. She hadn't contemplated that the black-eyed creatures were actually real. Katherine strained her ears to catch any hint of her pursuer's location. Nothing. Damn them for being so quiet, she thought.

When a twig snapped, her body twitched. Her heart stopped, and the downy hairs on her arms stood on end. The sound was so near that she could've reached out and touched it.

Fear anchored her to this spot. If it weren't for the veins in her slim neck pulsing with the rush of blood from her pounding heart, she could have been a statue. She wanted to run, but she couldn't seem to force her body to move. Gentle pressure tapped on her arm tentatively. Her mouth opened wide, and her eyes bulged. Pale fingers crawled across the fabric of her cloak, reaching and stretching to wrap around her arm. When her eyes met the owner of the hand, she saw her own petrified face in eyes as black as a witch's scrying mirror.

Katherine didn't wait for death. She threw herself out of the way, getting tangled up in her cloak. Somehow, she managed to get to her feet and was already in motion. The red of her cloak whipped behind, signaling her location to anyone watching. They had found her, so there was no point in remaining quiet.

She ran. She ran as fast as her legs could take her, fighting against the branches of the trees grasping at her. The coldness from the demon's touch infected her skin, and despite her haggard attempt to flee, her skin grew cold. The trees reached out for her with their cadaverous fingers, and she became tangled among them. Katherine clawed at the clasp of her cloak.

The little noises escaping her lips matched the sounds of a frightened animal.

Finally, the clasp of her cloak released, and she freed herself from the tangled woods around her. The trees cast long frightening shadows in the night, and she tripped over roots as she tried to evade their claws. Iron and glass shielded this impossible forest. The light of the stars in the velvet sky twisted through the panes of glass, dimmed and diminished, unable to reach her. She wished she could see them clearly, to find some comfort in what she knew was her end. She didn't want to die, but fear soured everything. Her legs were weary, her lungs burned, and still, she ran. Then the forest gave way to stone, and she fell into the open space at the center of the magnificent woods.

Her hands slapped onto the Venetian mosaic floor. She was back where she'd started. At the center of this garden of sorts was a massive orrery. The intricate glass ceiling gave way to open sky here to celebrate the mechanical representation of the solar system built on such a grand scale that it towered over her. Its gears were perfectly shaped, metal moving against metal seamlessly, quiet as a whisper. The celestial bodies danced with each other in a complicated pattern woven in the heavens. The orrery at the very heart of the garden was beautiful and awe-inspiring. It reminded Katherine of her smallness in the universe.

She ran along the edge of the orrery's reach, waiting to see what she knew was just around the other side. There he was. He worked furiously.

"My lord," she called out, but her voice was haggard and raspy from her exertions.

Lord Brahm had set up a makeshift easel by setting the large canvas against one of the many statues sprinkled throughout the garden. It looked as though an angel of mercy had spread her wings over the artist to shield him from his enemy. She could use an angel of mercy about then.

Lord Brahm's unique gift was the only thing standing between her and the horror of those black eyes. She had seen the proof of his ability, the way he wove magic into the very paint and created worlds. Those worlds existed beyond the canvas. They moved of their own accord. If she hadn't seen it with her own eyes, she would never have believed it. He was a patient artist, always preferring to allow his subjects to take shape gracefully. It was possible to believe miracles could exist, but scientific advancement made that harder and harder to believe in. There were those who believed that magic and miracles were merely natural occurrences that we just didn't understand the science of yet. She used to be one of them.

She prayed for one of those miracles that night. Usually, the handsome Lord Brahm was charming and collected. They would spend their days together walking this magnificent forest, and during the evenings, they read in the library, enjoying conformable silence and properly steeped tea. She would catch him staring at her from over his book, and it brought a smile to her face every time. Their courting had been slow and gentle, and she was looking forward to seeing what the future held for them. Katherine would be lying if she denied being attracted to the healthy sprinkle of silver throughout his dark hair, or that his rich chocolate eyes were a mirror of her own, though the wrinkles at the corners of his eyes when he smiled, belied his years. She ached to touch him, for him to touch her. She longed to be his muse, for him to capture her beauty with his magic.

That night, though, he paid her no mind. She rushed over to him, reaching for something familiar, remembering that she was cherished and worth saving. He flinched at the sudden movement and lowered his shoulders when he saw it was just her. His tailored suit was smeared with crimson and gold, pitch and aubergine. He grasped her upper arms, the paintbrush forgotten, and smeared paint across the sleeve of her dress.

"My lord, please tell me you are almost finished," she begged. His eyes met hers and saw the truth in them. He loved her.

"I'm working as fast as I can. There just isn't enough time." His voice was rich, laced with a melodic accent of his homeland. She had never traveled to New Zealand, but he had shared such wonderful stories of the place with her. His eyes were sad, and it broke her heart to see him this way.

"I don't know how long I can keep away from them," she said.

"I know. I'm sorry for all of this."

Katherine knew it was the truth, but she was so tired.

"What do you need me to do?" All she had to give was herself. He pulled her in close and placed his lips on hers. A kiss out of courtship was a scandalous affair, but she didn't care. She'd been daydreaming of his kiss for ages. His body pressed into her own, and for a moment, they were not two lovers, but one person, one shared love. When their lips parted and her eyes opened, tears were running down his face. She didn't understand.

"You've given me everything I need to trap these demons forever," he whispered.

She looked at the painting, which was propped up against the statue. Paint was splattered everywhere, with chaotic drips and streaks on the statue and the ground. She had never seen a painting like that before. The textures, layers of color and light, gave it such realism Katherine thought she could have reached out, touched it, and fallen inside the canvas.

Instead, her blood ran cold. There was no point in him loving her. He had sealed her doom. His arms held her tightly. For the first time since they met, she wanted nothing to do with him. He was going to curse her. No love could survive that.

She stared in horror at the beautiful painting of herself. The red cloak practically moved in an invisible breeze. Her face was hidden, but one of her hands was reaching to draw down the cowl. It was simply the most exquisite portrait, and she hated that she loved it. If she didn't do something right then, it would also be her prison. Katherine tried to pull herself away from him. She needed to destroy that painting. She didn't want to die. She didn't want to be forgotten. That was worse than death.

"I'm so sorry, my love."

She watched this strong, stoic man practically plead for forgiveness, but what could she do?

"I needed a living soul to bind them to their prison. You are the kindest person I've ever known. I'll find a way to release you, I promise."

But the damage had been done. Her fate was sealed. She would be imprisoned in that painting along with the demons hunting her. Katherine pushed herself away from him, stumbling back, right into a pair of icy hands.

"Your promises mean nothing to me," she said.

Katherine Ainsley released her fear. She brought her petite figure to its full stature and raised her chin defiantly. Lord Brahm flinched at her words as though she slapped him. She wished more than anything that he might renounce his path and choose her instead and his lips parted as though he wanted to say something, but he let the tears roll down his cheek in silence. With one last look at the only woman he had ever loved, held by the beasts with black eyes, he turned away from her. He reached over and, in a quick decisive stroke, signed the painting and her fate. She screamed for him to stop, but the magic had been completed.

Lord Benjamin Brahm stood before the painting. He faced the portrait, which was nearly as tall as he was, that he had started within days of meeting Lady Katherine. He'd been smitten with her at first sight. She was charming, intelligent, well-read, and exquisitely beautiful. He wanted to keep her for himself. He ached to see her skin as fair as porcelain, her brown hair so dark that without light it looked black.

Before him, a mysterious woman in a red cloak stood in the grand foyer of a brooding Gothic manor, but the pain of grief and betrayal was all he could see in the portrait. Her beauty was forever captured on the canvas, but lurking in the background, hidden just beyond the twisting banister of the stairs, waited the demons this trap was made for.

His fingers released the brush, letting it fall to the ground. His knees buckled, and the shame of what he'd done swept over him. Burying his face in his hands, he wept for the loss of the only person he ever loved. He would spend the rest of his endless days alone.

1

Violet Brennan sat on a bench at the rail station waiting for the beeline to pull in. Her sketchbook open on her lap, she drew her mom sitting next to her. Spring in Colorado was indecisive at best. Some days were hot, and others were full of wind and snow. The late May morning was chilly, but the afternoon would probably be stifling. Crisp clear skies overhead cast a glow to the side of her mom's face that made her skin look like pure gold.

Violet had only been sixteen when her mom was diagnosed with Alzheimer's. She'd done everything she could to ensure she remained her primary caregiver. Nothing else in her world mattered more than her mom and her art. Her dad had died before her mom got sick and it had been just the two of them for a while. Whenever she got a break from her work schedule, she took her mom to the Denver Art Museum. Before her mom got sick, it was one of their favorite places to go.

The last couple of years had been hard since she worked her ass off to graduate high school early while handling a couple of jobs to keep a roof over their heads. Violet was thankful for a few supportive neighbors in their building who had helped watch her mom when she had to go to work. Currently, she was working several odd jobs like pet sitting and freelance graphic design work to help pay for her mom's medical bills. It wasn't an easy life, but it was days like today that made it all worth it.

Her mom didn't have much of an attention span these days, and she was constantly needing help with simple tasks. They lived on the third floor of their apartment building, which had posed more than a few problems whenever her mom got it in her head to go on one of her walkabouts. The disease had progressed differently than the doctors had predicted, and while many people with Alzheimer's would get mentally stuck at different points in their lives, it was unusual for someone to regress to a childlike state. The doctors couldn't explain it, and there was nothing they could do but try different meds to keep her stable. It was up to Violet to do the rest.

She would wake up early to have a few minutes of quiet and coffee before their daily routine started. All the little tasks of helping her mom filled her days. She would bathe and dress her, make meals, and even read her bedtime stories. Violet didn't really know a life other than this, and as long as her mom was happy, everything was worth it. While their days normally blended together with habits and routines, that day was a treat.

Violet got her love of art from her mom, and they spend a whole day checking out new exhibits and old favorites. They would sketch the other patrons as they meandered through the exhibits, comparing their drawings. It was also one of the few places where she could take her mom these days, where she would remain calm and actually enjoy herself.

Violet looked up from her sketchbook and smiled. Her mom was sitting perfectly straight with her hands folded neatly in her lap. Violet pretended for just a moment that her mom was healthy and back to her usual self, but as the train pulled into view, her mom's feet tapped against the ground.

"All right, Mom, you ready?" Violet asked as she stuffed her sketchbook into her backpack and lightly grabbed onto the hem of her mom's cardigan in case she ran after the train.

"It's here!" her mom exclaimed. "It's here."

Violet let herself relax a little. Together, they waited on the platform as the B-line pulled in. The crowds weren't as bad as they could've been, but that's because Violet purposefully waited for the morning rush to pass before heading out. It was hard enough to manage her mom normally, but intense crowds pushed her out of her comfort zone. But so far, that day was turning out perfect.

Her mom clung to one of the poles mounted throughout the compartment, and Violet sat in a nearby seat. She liked to give her mom some freedom to just experience her surroundings, but she had to be close enough to keep an eye on her. The train rumbled through industrial districts and blocks of low-rent apartments. Well, as low as the rent got around here. Eventually, the downtown skyline grew, and the arts district of Denver engulfed them. Violet might not be able to fill her life with as much art as she wanted to, but she did what she could. Besides, the museum itself was a piece of art. It had been designed by a famous architect. The unusual angles of the building were supposed to be inspired by the jagged peaks of the nearby Rocky Mountains, but they reminded Violet of giant shards of glass jutting out of the ground at odd angles. She supposed there was some truth to that adage that art was pain.

The train deposited them a few short blocks away. Before long, they had paid their admission and were walking into the closest exhibit, *Modern Women/Modern Vision*. It was a wonderfully diverse exhibit, but her mom's distraction made her a little sad. Her mom normally would have loved this, but in that moment, she ran through the exhibit laughing and skipping, a child trapped in an adult's body. Violet followed her mother around, taking in the art that she could.

The white walls of the museum were like a blank canvas ready to host the exhibits. Each room was a surprise. The harsh angles mirroring the exterior of the museum held vastly different exhibits. Black and white drawings crawling across the floor, walls, and ceiling inspired children and families to chart their adventures through the museum. A neon pink sign and irregular popping of flash bulbs welcomed them into the Old Hollywood experience. There was a room full of Old West landscapes, a room of indigenous pottery, and a display of bronze-era weapons that caught the light in ways that kept her mom enraptured.

Violet followed her mom out of a Roy Lichtenstein exhibit full of massive canvases covered in paintings that resembled the old newspaper comic strips in fashion and style. It was amazing how much depth you could create when simply using bold dots of color. She wished she could've spent a little while longer admiring the pulpy art, but her mom was on the move. The Lichtenstein exhibit emptied into a little courtyard with some benches and a few potted plants drowning in light from the towering skylights overhead. Across the courtyard was the entrance to another exhibit that caught Violet's attention, sucking her in like a black hole.

The courtyard of white walls and ivory floors washed out by the bright light from above couldn't seem to reach beyond the threshold to a magnificently forbidding exhibit boldly titled *Gothic America*. Pillars of black stone and painted brick reaching up to the ceiling to create parapets and flying buttresses welcomed visitors into a world of brooding sincerity. Cobblestones had been painted on the floor, creating a path that crouching gargoyles guarded. The severe snarls on their faces were wonderfully gloomy. The path curved beyond the entrance of the exhibit, and Violet couldn't see what was beyond. It was all simply enchanting. She wanted to explore every dark corner of *Gothic America*, but her mom was already padding along toward another corridor. Violet ran to catch up with her mom, her head twisting around to get one last glimpse of the curious display.

"Well, hello there, Mrs. Brennan," a familiar deep voice declared.

Mark Walsh was a burly security guard who'd been working at the museum for at least a decade. His hairline was disappearing, his belly was expanding, and his bulldog jowls were always intimidating until you got to know him. Violet watched her mom's face light up in a big goofy smile. Walsh had taken the time to get to know Violet and her mom, offering a sympathetic ear when Violet was stressed out. His friendship with her mom was silly and wonderful, and Violet was grateful for that.

"Mark!" Violet's mom proclaimed loudly as she ran up to the giant man for a hug. "It's museum day."

"I can see that. What did you do with Violet?" Walsh said, their conversation echoing down to Violet.

"She's toddling over there by the scary place," her mom said with a shiver.

The security guard's deep laugh rumbled softly through the echoing space. "Not a fan of that one, are you?"

She shook her head. Violet stifled a laugh at the childlike response. Walsh gave Mrs. Brennan a tight hug but shot Violet a side-eye of concern. "You're looking a bit tired, young lady. How've things been?"

"Good, Walsh. The new medication seems to be helping with the mood swings, so things have actually been going great."

"Glad to hear it. Have you had a chance to get some time for yourself lately?" Violet scrunched up her face. "I see. Why don't you let me take your mom around for half an hour, give you some time to yourself?"

"Aw, Walsh, that'd be awesome." She gave the burly man another hug. "Thanks," she whispered.

"Ah, you know me, just a big ole softy over here," he said, guiding her mom away from the dark exhibit and Violet. "Mrs. Brennan, there's a new exhibit over this way, and I think you're going to really like it."

"Really?"

"Promise," Walsh's low voice said, "it's all about coloring. You even get to color on the walls."

Her mom squealed in delight at getting to do something so forbidden. Violet listened to the two friends talk, their voices dimming as they passed around the corner and out of sight. She waited a few minutes just to make sure her mom wasn't going to come running back, which happened on occasion. Eventually, Violet relaxed a little and took a deep breath, soaking in the silence. Only then did she turn around, and with unrestrained curiosity, approach the brooding entrance to *Gothic America*.

2

Violet stood at the threshold, holding her breath. She loved art. She especially loved art that stepped into the shadows. Human nature was violent and cruel, and when an artist could capture that and turn it into something beautiful, well, that's what hooked Violet. She stepped through the entrance and the lighting changed. The washed-out brightness of the neutral courtyard behind her disappeared, and the cool dimness of the space ahead rustled around her like an autumn breeze. The walls here were still white, but massive sconces mounted on the walls mimicking firelight cast shadows everywhere. Violet couldn't help but smile. The space had been transformed into something resembling Victorian England but with a touch of the American West to it all. Elegance mixed with darkness, culminating in luxurious, eerie shadows. She was comfortable in the shadows. Maybe it was because her life had been so difficult. After all, she had seen the cruelness of the world early on, but she felt at home here.

She approached one of the gargoyles crouching along the path. Its gnarled claws gripped a sign.

Gothic American is a genre of art and literature celebrating humanity's love of the perverse and macabre. *Gothic American* often includes supernatural elements, such as beasts, ghosts, and deformity to expose the corruption underlying the golden fantasy of modern civilization.

Not wrong, she thought. The cobblestone path led her past the ugly gargoyles and to each collection. She admired the portraits of stately lords and ladies set against backgrounds of ancient manor houses and gardens that looked like they'd eaten many of their visitors. The collection of pulpy Gothic noir book covers and illustrations for macabre poetry thrilled her. The deeper into the exhibit she went, the more she forgot about the outside world and her responsibilities.

The light on each collection was clean and simple in order to showcase the art, but the guests looking at the art lingered in the shadows. It was like peeking through a keyhole and getting just a tease, a glimpse of something special beyond. Although the exhibit space wasn't particularly large, the meandering path and the engineered lighting made the exhibit feel much bigger than it was. When Violet reached the end of the exhibit, something caught her attention. Just before the exit, she saw a man working at an easel.

One gargoyle along the path gripped a sign explaining that an artist was onsite doing live paintings. She loved watching other artists at work. There was something special about sharing an artist's space and energy. It was a surreal experience to watch an artist as they put paint to canvas. The lights were brighter here, perhaps to give him enough light to work with in the moody atmosphere of the exhibit.

She approached the artist from behind the canvas, so she couldn't see his artwork. Violet slowed, clearing the edge of his workspace, and was about to give the canvas a look when the artist, who was sitting on a stool, glanced up and gave her a gracious smile. He was an older man, perhaps in his mid-to late-forties. His ashy brown hair was flecked with streaks of grey and swept stylishly back and out of his face. His dark eyes were keen, and she felt as though he saw her immediately. Not the way that everyone else saw her. The rest of the world saw her as just a lazy punk, like the rest of her generation. There were a few, like her neighbor, Mrs. Widawski, that knew her situation and saw her as something more, but none of them saw her for what she wanted to be, an artist.

His penetrating gaze wasn't his only characteristic that caught her off guard. The artist was dressed in a clean black suit with a crisp white clerical collar showing his faith. Violet tried not to feel too awkward in her torn-up, faded black jeans and vintage Bowie T-shirt.

"I'm sorry," she stammered. "I didn't mean to disturb you." She fidgeted with the strap of her leather backpack hanging on her shoulder.

"Not at all," the priest said as he straightened his posture. What was his accent? It could be Australian or South American, maybe. She wasn't great with naming accents, but wherever he was from, it was surely an exotic place. "How are you liking the exhibit?" He asked, but it took her a minute to register.

"What?" She stammered before realizing that he'd asked her something. "Oh, the exhibit, it's really great!"

"Isn't it just perfectly dreary?" he replied, but the way he said it drew her in. She had to check herself. What was she going to tell Walsh? Sorry I'm late, I was just lusting over an artistic priest! Nope, there was no way she'd admit to that.

So, she smiled. He gave her a quizzical look as though he were appraising her. "You look as though you might have a good eye for this sort of thing. Why don't you step over here and give me your honest opinion?"

"Me?" she asked in disbelief. Violet wasn't used to being on the receiving end of compliments. She tried to run her hands nervously through her hair, but her fingers got tangled up in the charcoal pencils she stuffed into her bun for safekeeping.

"Yes, you." The corner of his mouth lifted in a curious smile, and her pulse quickened

"Okay," Violet gushed. Violet wasn't usually the bashful type. She didn't have the time to be timid when it came to taking care of her mom. Early on, she'd learned that wallflowers got ignored. After spending so much time in hospitals and treatment centers, being the only advocate for her mom, she knew that someone had to speak up, ask questions, and be curious, especially about procedures and medications. But in this scenario, she couldn't quite explain her timidity. Her cheeks felt hot, and she hoped to God she wasn't blushing.

She stepped into his personal space and tried to ignore the fact that he smelled clean and slightly earthy. Was he wearing cologne? She couldn't tell. All she knew was that he smelled amazing. Violet could feel his eyes on her and tried to ignore his gaze as she turned to face the canvas.

She wasn't sure what she was expecting, but this wasn't it. The image before her was haunting. A lonely gravel road flanked on either side by an uninviting forest led to a brooding Victorian manor built of stone and shadow. The manor looked as though it had been abandoned, empty, but its opulence preserved. Behind it all, a storm was building. The artist's skill with color and brush was so impressive that the clouds appeared translucent where lightning traced a path through the gathering storm. Despite the brooding image, she couldn't help but notice details that made her smile. A black cat stalked its unseen prey in the tall grass, running along the edges of the road. A yellow glow behind a curtain in a single window of the manor made her realize the house wasn't empty. She wanted to reach out and touch it all.

"Your technique is amazing," she said.

"Thank you," he answered. "Would it be too much to ask to see your work?"

The request caught her off guard. Her head whipped around, and his face was intimately close to hers. "What?" she stuttered. That curious smile of his grew a little more.

"I'll admit that I'm fairly good at reading people, and you, my dear, are very obviously an artist."

"Um, yes," she said, straightening herself and stepping back from the hot priest. "Oh, oh sure."

She dropped her backpack off her shoulder and opened it enough to rummage around and pull out her most recently drawn-in sketchbook. Violet nervously handed it over to him. Since Violet didn't go to school for drawing, she wasn't accustomed to other people seeing her work. He accepted it and set his brush down on his traveling palette before opening her sketchbook.

While he examined her drawings slowly and carefully, Violet didn't know what to do with herself, so she enjoyed the view. Although his hair was graying, it was lush and just long enough that she could imagine running her hands through it. It took everything she had to not let those thoughts run rampant. She was pretty sure it was a sin to crush over a priest.

He looked up from one of her drawings. "Who's this man? You've drawn him several times."

Violet leaned forward, looked at the page her sketchbook was open to, and smiled sadly. "That's my dad."

The priest must've seen the change in her. "How long has it been?"

"A few years now."

"I'm sorry. I know how it is to lose someone you love," he said, and she believed him. His velvety brown eyes met hers, and she saw the same sadness.

"Who was it for you?"

"A woman who I was very much in love with."

A funny look came over her face. Violet couldn't connect the idea of a priest and the passion of a lover in her mind.

Admittedly, she wasn't very good at hiding her thoughts, and he actually laughed at her. It was a melodic laugh, gentle and rich. His eyes sparkled with genuine amusement. "I wasn't always a priest."

"I'm sorry." She wanted to grab her sketchbook out of his hands and run away from embarrassment, but she couldn't move. "About your lady, I mean." She knew nothing she could do would ease his own sadness. He gave her a smile, which showed his understanding that neither of them could do anything to make the sadness go away. His face said the *thank you* that his lips didn't say.

"You know, you're very good," he said, tapping on the open sketchbook. Violet looked down and saw that it was open to the sketch she had started of her mom when they were waiting for the train. "You have a good eye for angles, and even in such a raw sketch, you've captured so much of the individual."

"Thanks."

"You know, I host some drawing classes at St. Mary's. Maybe you could stop by. I think you might enjoy the experience."

"That would be great, but it's hard for me to get any free time, with work and all."

He looked up at her. She gave him a look that she hoped was apologetic. How was she supposed to get away from taking care of her mom and her jobs, all so she could go feel like a real artist for an hour? She couldn't, so she had no reason to get her hopes up about it.

"Well, the invitation is open to you anytime. We meet Tuesday nights at eight-thirty, right after the A.A. meetings." He closed her sketchbook and handed it back to her. "You are welcome anytime. I'll keep an easel open for you."

"You shouldn't make a fuss about it. My schedule is pretty crazy." Violet took her sketchbook from him, their hands brushing lightly. In that moment, she felt something, not quite electric, but some invisible connection between them. She didn't have time in her life to worry about fate or destiny, but maybe she was supposed to know him. Maybe they were supposed to meet. Violet brushed the thought aside and stuffed her book into her backpack before hoisting it on her shoulder.

"I should probably get going. My mom will worry if I don't meet up with her soon."

"I'll walk with you if you don't mind," he said, standing up and smoothing out the non-existent wrinkles in his immaculate black suit. He was taller than her, by several inches, and she had to look up to meet his gaze.

"Um, all right."

He stepped away from the easel and bowed his head in some sort of antique chivalrous gesture. As she joined his side, something flickered at the edge of her vision. She could swear that she saw something in his painting, a reflection of light, or something like it, but when she faced the painting, nothing there could reflect light. The oil paints were still wet, but that wasn't enough for what she thought she saw.

Violet scrunched up her face at the incongruity but shook it off. Together they walked along the cobbled path, talking about their favorite artists and pointing out their favorite gargoyles, and by the time they exited the exhibit, a broad grin had stretched across Violet's face. She enjoyed hearing his impression of the melancholy exhibit and was amazed at how comfortable she was talking about art with a priest. This was definitely an experience she hadn't seen coming.

Walsh was waiting for them in the sterile little courtyard between exhibits, her mom standing next to him with her hands folded in front of her and her hair a little messier than she remembered.

"Mr. Walsh," the priest said to the burly guard.

"Mornin', Father Benny."

"Mom, you look like you've been up to no good," Violet said, then gave a smile to Walsh.

"She got a little overexcited for a minute there, but all's good, Violet."

"Thanks for watching her, Walsh."

"It's my pleasure," he said, giving Violet another of his big bear hugs. "You two keep safe."

"We will," she said, with her face buried in his chest.

"All right, all right, you're gonna turn me soft," Walsh exclaimed. When she pulled away from him, he winked.

"It was a pleasure to meet you, Miss Violet," the priest said as she took her mom's arm and guided her away from the men. She turned back to see the priest and the bull of a security guard standing side by side like comical chaperones. Her mouth made some awkward attempt at a smile, but she was feeling strange about the whole encounter.

"Come on, Mom, let's go check out the rest of the museum."

"The crayons. Let's go see the crayons again."

"Okay, Mom." Violet laughed. "Let's go see the crayons."

And just like that, all the small tasks that made up Violet's life distracted her again. The strangeness of her day forgotten like a passing shadow.

3

THE SUN WAS DROPPING below the mountains to the west, and Violet could tell her mom was exhausted from the adventures of the day. It was barely eight o'clock, but Violet smiled as she tucked her mom into bed. Her mother wriggled as her head sank into the pillow. Violet turned out the nearby lamp and went to close the door, but she stopped to look at her mom. A soft line of light cast across her mother's face from the crack in the drapes.

For just a moment, she remembered what life was like when her dad was still alive, her mom was happy, and she actually felt like she had room to be a kid. She wished she could go back in time. She wished she could hug her dad one more time. She wished everything could be different, the way it used to be. Her eyes filled with tears, and she roughly wiped them away as they dripped along the curves of her face. Hearing her mom's breathing shifting subtly into that soft rhythm of the sleeper, Violet closed the door softly, careful not to wake her mom.

She leaned against the wall just outside her mom's room and squeezed her eyes shut. It was hard to keep regret and bitterness out of her thoughts. There was no possible other life for her other than this one. This was all there was. Most of the time she accepted her life, but at the museum that day, she had a taste of what her life could be like. She could do so many things instead of taking care of her mom, but here she was.

Her hands clenched into tight fists, her knuckles blanched, and her face burned. Violet's body bent, practically curling in on itself. She opened her mouth and, without making a single sound, let her body scream. Her head shook, her hands flew out in front of her as though she were a wizard casting a curse, and her rage spilled out of her in invisible waves coursing across the small apartment, through the walls, and out to the world. When she had finished her silent scream, her knees buckled, and she collapsed on the floor.

Violet lost track of time during her wallowing. By the time she raised her head and wiped away the last of her tears, the room had grown dark. The sun had set, and the streetlights were blinking to life. The crappy little apartment was dressed in shadows with small pops of color from the neon shop signs outside. She picked herself up off the floor, grabbed her back-pack, and went out onto the small balcony.

The air was crisp, the warmth of the day already dissipating. She stood there on the little concrete balcony with the wrought-iron railing and accompanying fire escape. The collection of industrial buildings and old apartments spread out around her. Neon lights blinked and faltered, casting rainbows of color onto the streets. The rusted shells of abused cars and beat-up parking meters absorbed it all. Colorado was an arid state, and moisture was few and far between. Rather than the colors and lights glistening off the still surfaces of puddles in the streets, they shimmered in heat waves radiating off the asphalt.

Violet let her backpack slip off her shoulder and it landed softly on the ground. Violet's head fell back, and she took in a deep breath. The cool air filled her lungs, icing down the ragged emotions just beneath the surface. She felt her own comfortable gravity returning to her. She didn't allow herself to give in to despair very often, but she knew from experience that if she bottled everything up, bad things happened.

Her shoulders relaxed, and her breathing calmed. The city didn't care if she was having a meltdown. It simply turned and churned, chewing up everything and everyone in its path. Violet leaned on the balcony railing, her elbows absorbing the remnants of the warmth of the day through the metal, and she looked out at her world. A couple of kids ran down the street throwing profanity around like a football. Ambulance sirens cycled through in the background like a familiar ambiance.

She'd come out here to draw. Drawing always calmed her when life was too much. Her art was essential to her survival, as necessary to her as an inhaler to an asthmatic. But now, her backpack lay momentarily forgotten, and she let her thoughts get carried off in the haze crawling through the city. A few blocks away, a steeple breached the canopy of jagged buildings. St. Mary's Cathedral wasn't one of the larger churches in the city, but it had been around forever. Its solitary bell rang out twice a day, once at noon and once at midnight. The neighborhood of impoverished citizens, all of whom lived below the poverty line, set the rhythm of their days by the tolling of the bell.

Headlights from a car coming down the street cast beams of bright yellow light that highlighted a small figure making its way down the sidewalk. Mrs. Widawski was a tiny woman. Her pin-straight jet-black hair brushed her shoulders when she wasn't wearing her customary ponytail. Violet couldn't help smiling when she thought of the woman, a contradiction of stereotypes from her obvious Vietnamese heritage and her kosher lifestyle. Her husband died over ten years ago, but Mrs. Widawski was fiercely independent and one of the most caring individuals Violet had ever known.

The petite woman carried a couple of large paper grocery bags on her way home. She lived a few doors down the hall from Violet and her mom and, since she was retired, could often watch her mom while she ran errands. Violet paid her for all her time, and over the years, Violet had come to appreciate Nguyen Widawski's honesty and compassion.

"Young lady," the petite woman hollered up from the street, "come let this old woman into the building."

"Yes, ma'am," Violet called back. She left the little apartment quietly and ran down the stairs at the end of the hall, popped out in the dingy foyer with the buzzer door and the mailboxes, and held the door open for Mrs. Widawski. She reached over and took one bag of groceries from the elderly woman, and the two of them mounted the stairs to the third floor in silence.

They stopped at the plain door marked with simple numbers, 308, and the older woman unlocked the door, letting them in. The widow's apartment was identical to Violet's in layout, but that was all. The furnishings were older, the walls were decorated in more traditional art and prints, and the nearby piano—Violet didn't want to think about how she managed to get the piano in here. Her piano was old but well-loved. It was dusted regularly and played frequently.

She helped put the groceries away and was about to leave when the pictures on the sideboard next to the door caught

Violet's attention. The framed photos showed Mrs. Widawski and her husband. So many moments had been captured, and only she knew the stories behind each one. It was a secret kept between lovers, between companions.

"What's that face for?" the widow asked with a disapproving scowl on her round face.

"What?" Violet said, scrunching up her face.

"Don't deflect, young lady," Mrs. Widawski threw back. "That shit won't work on me.

"Language, language!"

"Come on, give it to me."

Violet picked up one photo and stared at it. "Do you miss him ever?"

"Every day," Mrs. Widawski answered. Violet wiped away a tear slipping down her cheek. Damn these tears, she thought. She didn't want to let herself go, here. She didn't want Mrs. Widawski to see her like this.

"Look at me," the older woman said. No, that wasn't right, she ordered. Her voice wasn't cruel or demeaning, but it demanded obedience.

Violet turned to face the woman and only found kindness. "I tried to draw him the other day and couldn't remember the way he wore his hair. I couldn't remember the color of his eyes." She squeezed hers shut against irrational anger welling up inside her. "I couldn't draw him, Nguyen." Her eyes popped open, and the tears flowed freely. "I couldn't even draw my dad!"

"It's all right, Violet."

"It's not all right, Nguyen. Mom isn't capable of remembering any of it. I must remember him for her."

"That's ridiculous," the older woman scolded. "You are only human. Don't be an idiot and hold yourself to some unattainable standard."

"I don't know what to do."

"You don't have to do anything other than what you are doing. She is happy. You're allowed to be happy too." Mrs. Widawski wrapped her up in a fierce hug, and all Violet could do was sink into it. Her own mother wasn't even aware that she had a daughter, but here was this woman who used to be a stranger offering her the love that she needed.

Violet looked over the woman's shoulder and out the balcony doors. The night lights of the city twinkled. Mrs. Widawski pulled back and took a long, hard look at Violet. She frowned, and Violet couldn't help but snort out a laugh.

"What?" Violet asked indignantly.

"I was about to ask you the same thing," Mrs. Widawski said.

Violet shook her head slightly. She didn't want to talk about it even though she should talk to somebody about it. Mrs. Widawski followed Violet's distracted gaze and turned to look out the balcony doors. "Go."

"What?"

"Go. I said, Go!" She squeezed Violet's arms and spun her around towards the door to the apartment. "I'll watch your mother."

"But Mrs. Widawski—"

"Nope, let's go," she added as they moved out into the corridor.

"Nguyen—"

"Enough. I don't know what happened today, but you need to spend a little time focusing on yourself." With that, Violet and Mrs. Widawski shuffled down the corridor just a few doors until they came to the one marked 312. Violet's nerves were rattled, and her hands trembled, but she opened the door and ushered the widow into the small apartment.

It was quiet. Violet stood in the dim light, conflicted, torn. There were times like then when she wanted so badly to just run away. She wanted to be free, to just be a kid. But she couldn't. There was no one to take care of her mom, and she refused to have her institutionalized. Her shoulders drooped, and her instinct to run faded. This was her life. What she really needed to do was turn out the remaining lights and go to bed. She'd feel better in the morning.

"But you shouldn't—"

"Nonsense, whatever you're going to say will be utter nonsense, so don't waste my time and keep it to yourself."

"But—"

"That's enough. Go somewhere. Anywhere," Mrs. Widawski said in a way that did not brook talking back. Violet simply sighed. There was no winning against the tiny woman. "I will stay here until you get back. Don't worry about your mom. Just go."

"Thank you, Nguyen."

"Yes, yes, yes, enough already. Get out of here."

"What if—"

"If I get tired, I'll just sleep on the sofa," Mrs. Widawski said. "Now go," she added gently.

Violet walked out onto the balcony where she'd left her backpack and picked it up before leaving the tiny apartment and entering the corridor. Mrs. Widawski moved to close the door, offering Violet a sympathetic look just before the door shut.

The corridor was empty. Half the overhead florescent lights had burned out, and the remaining ones flickered feebly. The carpet was from the eighties, and most of the doors could use a fresh coat of paint. It wasn't a nice place, but most of the people here were genuinely good. Maybe Mrs. Widawski was right to kick her out.

She pulled her backpack onto her shoulder and walked down the hall towards the stairs. While the floor technically had an elevator, it was unreliable at best. She reached the stair-well, which was the most industrial section of the building. Violet squinted at the gray walls stained with graffiti, for the only lights were floodlights tucked behind wire cages. The bottom of the stairs emptied into a grungy foyer lined with mailboxes on either side. Violet pushed her way out the heavy doors and into the cool night air.

A velvet black sky was draped over the city. The lights of the city washed out the stars, but the moon was bright and hung overhead like part of a kamikiri paper doll theater. It shone brightly on the church steeple in the distance. Since it was Tuesday, Violet wondered if the hot priest would be teaching his art class. She knew better than to turn back. Mrs. Widawski wouldn't let her back in after such a short time. So, without overthinking it, she set off for the small church.

4

THE ATMOSPHERE OF THE city at night was tangibly different. Florescent light from the streetlamps overhead cast an amber glow over everything, and the shadows were deeper. Violet crossed the street and headed for St. Mary's, careful to step around the homeless people nestled in the shallow doorways of the closed businesses. Sirens wailed in the distance, and dogs barked. This part of town wasn't the safest place for a girl to walk around at night alone. A personal alarm dangled from her backpack by a carabiner, and she reached for it every minute or so.

An awkward punk decked out in black leather burst out of a nearby tattoo parlor, and Violet shrunk into herself, hoping he wouldn't notice her. As usual, she had no such luck, and his cat calls echoed in the street. She picked up her pace.

St. Mary's was a small chapel with big aspirations, but the broad oak doors with iron hinges and aging stone facade gave it a foreboding aura. The streetlights couldn't seem to penetrate the craggy shadows of the little chapel, and Violet thought it would perfectly fit in with the museum exhibit. As she mounted the stone steps, the surrounding neighborhood was empty and quiet. She started to feel stupid for coming all this way, for what? For a chance to see a hot priest?

"Ah, this is so dumb," she snarled. "What are you doing, Vi?" She turned on the spot and descended the stairs. "Oh, nothing, just being a creepy stalker."

The doors of the church burst open, and a collection of somber people spilled out. Violet whirled around in time to see a red-faced construction worker give her a skeptical look, his gray eyebrows tugging up.

"Looks like you missed the meeting, little sister. Better luck next time," he called out to her as the people split off in different directions.

"I'm just here for the food, man," she called out sarcastically.

"You might be able to catch yourself some stale donuts if you hurry."

Violet turned around to see who was offering stale donuts and found herself staring at a serious-looking nun. Violet's mouth hung open stupidly.

"Um, no thanks, ma'am,"

"If you're here for the art class, it starts in fifteen minutes," the nun offered.

Violet climbed the stairs nervously. "I was actually here to see Father Benny," she said, hoping she remembered his name right. "He said he was here on Tuesdays."

The nun looked down at Violet as if she were peering at her over spectacles. Despite the disapproving look she shot Violet's way, the curmudgeonly nun seemed to deem Violet as tolerable. Violet thought the woman probably looked at all young people that way.

"He is usually here on Tuesdays to guide the free art class, but he is still at the museum helping them with-," she paused, her mouth pursing with distaste, "*an exhibit*." Violet couldn't help but hear the nun's distaste at the mention of the exhibit. Apparently, anyone using art for ungodly reasons was not high on her list. Violet couldn't help but give the nun a look of shock. The nun simply huffed at her. "You are welcome to join the group this evening. I can have someone set up an easel for you."

"That's not necessary. I'll just try to meet up with him some other time."

"Perhaps there's something I can help you with?" The nun's expression softened slightly.

"Thanks, but I'm good." Violet wasn't ready for a Christian conversion session. Evangelists were all over the place in the more run-down neighborhoods of the city. There was always someone who wanted to proselytize around her. The nun took the hint and tucked her hands into the pockets of her gray pinafore. The starched white-collar shirt didn't move beneath it when she bowed her head slightly and turned around to head back inside. Violet stared at the nun's back until she disappeared into the mysterious depths of the church. She'd never been inside a church, and she wasn't ready to break that streak.

Violet descended the stairs and headed home. It was probably for the best since she didn't know what she'd say to Father Benny, anyway. At the end of the block was a bus stop. The plexiglass box encased a dreary metal bench. The plexiglass was the color of urine, stained from sunshine and time. Crude jokes and the initials of lovers from long ago were carved into its yellowing surface. Ugly flickering fluorescent bulbs threw a circle of unattractive light around the bus stop.

No one else sat underneath the covered bus stop, so she flopped down on the bench and stared out into the night, letting her thoughts drift away. Before long, a beam of light stretched out in front of her on the street, and one of the buses running through the night had pulled up to the stop. The doors hissed open, and the driver offered her a smile.

She had nothing better to do, and she was pretty sure Mrs. Widawski would consider it too early to come home. What the hell, she thought. So, she stepped up onto the bus and sat behind the driver.

Other than her and the driver, only one other person sat on the bus. Violet looked down the length of the aisle and stared at the small figure sitting with her legs tucked under her. She wore a purple hoodie and a braid pulled over one of her shoulders. The girl couldn't have been more than nine or ten, so what was she doing here all by herself? The window at the back framed the little girl in blackness and neon.

The night unfurled behind the bus, and Violet realized she'd been in this part of town already. If it were the middle of the day, she'd tug on the signal string running the full length of the bus above her head, but since there was practically no one else here, she reached around and tapped the driver on the shoulder. He pulled the bus to a stop about a block away from the museum, and she jumped onto the sidewalk. Before the doors hissed closed, she gave a firm look to the driver.

"Make sure she gets home safe," Violet said. Through the closing doors, he gave her the oddest look. What was his problem? she thought. The bus rolled away and Violet took one last look towards the back of the bus, but the girl was gone.

Gone? How was that even possible? Violet stood there with her mouth open, wondering if she'd imagined it all. Eventually, she shook her head, stuffed her hands in her pockets, and walked the last bit of the way to the museum, which was hard to miss in the night.

Floodlights tucked into the landscaping shot broad beams of light up toward the sky, exaggerating the sharp angles of the museum. The arts district was busy with traffic, but the museum was oddly silent and still. Its jagged edges loomed out around the surrounding buildings. The library across the street and the annex building next door, all seemed smaller and insignificant. She wondered if the museum was even still open, but the doors were wide open so she let herself in.

Certain places felt completely different at night. She'd once left her portfolio in her locker at school, and her mom had taken her to pick it up, for she needed it for a project she was working on for a final. Violet still remembered the feeling of being in some horrible alternate universe. Likewise, at the museum, the lights were all still on and it didn't look any different other than being empty, but she couldn't shake the sense of being watched.

The registers at the ticket counter all said that they were closed, and the velvet ropes that would normally guide patrons into neat lines at the gift shop were all blocked. Each step she made seemed to echo off into oblivion, bouncing off all the odd angles of the museum.

Was this even legal? Was Walsh going to show up and throw her in cuffs just for being here this late? The doors were still open, though, so someone had to be there. Well, the damage was done when it came to her making poor decisions, so she went for it and headed deeper into the empty museum.

Eventually, Violet stood in front of the entrance to *Gothic America*, the exhibit where she had met Father Benny. Her heart thrummed erratically against her ribcage, and her cheeks grew hot. She shook herself free from her nervousness and stepped into the brooding exhibit.

It was just as she remembered it. The giant sconces flickered with artificial candlelight, the gargoyles waiting along the path with grotesque patience. However, when she approached the easel, the artist was nowhere in sight. The canvas reflected some of the ambient lighting, the oils still fresh. Resting on his travel palette with its adjustable tripod legs was a cup of tea. She could just make out the steam curl off the surface and breathed a sigh of relief knowing he was nearby.

Violet looked around but couldn't see him, so she inspected his work more closely. She stepped directly in front of the canvas and let her eyes wander around the composition. The individual strokes had been blended so well she could hardly see them. In fact, his technique was so impressive that it looked almost photorealistic. The storm clouds building in the darkened sky seemed to pulse with lightning from within. She could practically feel the wind blowing the tall grasses lining the gravel road.

The longer she stared at the painting, the more she thought she was going crazy. It wasn't just that his skill and technique with paint and brush gave the impression of movement, of motion in the grasses, but she could swear the blades actually moved. The motion was so subtle that she got a small knot in her stomach and the feeling that she'd been here before, something like déjà vu, but more tangible.

She bent forward, leaning in so close to the canvas that she could finally discern his meticulously blended strokes of paint. The cat was stalking its prey, its black slender tail sticking up above the grass and twitching in agitation. Wait, did it just actually twitch its tail? It wasn't possible. Violet rubbed at her eyes and then looked again. Just as her eyes focused, a bolt of lightning pierced the tumultuous sky and lit the canvas up.

Violet jumped back, eyes wide, hands curled into her chest as though something could jump out of the painting and hurt her. This was definitely not possible, but she couldn't look away. Her eyes squinted, looking for any other sign of something happening that definitely shouldn't happen. That's when she saw it. She found her nerve, stepping close to the painting and bending forward to look at the cat. It was closer to the frightening manor off in the distance. She was certain of it.

Everything in the painting moved. Unlike in a film where everything moved at the speed of life, this was softer, the movements more like something out of a dream. Violet couldn't help but think of the sultry voice of Fiona Apple and her exquisite lyrics. Everything about the painting was "slow like honey and heavy with mood."

Somewhere in the depths of the culminating storm, a flicker and flash of lightning illuminated the churning clouds. Her eyes grew wide as she watched the bolt of lightning coalesce and cascade through the layers of clouds, streaking subtly across the surface of the painting until it came to the forefront of the canvas. A bolt of lightning breached the surface of the painting and zapped her finger in a bolt of blue static electricity.

"Ow!" she yelped as she pulled her finger back to nurse the pain away. It was in that moment that soft footsteps approached her in the distance.

"Ms. Violet?" The rich melodic voice she'd been hoping to hear sent her pulse racing. "Is that you?"

She turned away from the curious painting and smiled at the sight of him, but then her world went black.

5

It was a moment of sublime weightlessness. She could've been floating in a calm ocean at night. But the peace didn't last long. An invisible string cinched around her intestines and pulled her down into the suffocating pit below the surface of the sea. She knew, even in her confusion, this place was dangerous. It was full of creatures wanting to devour her. She flailed in the darkness, grasping at air, reaching for anything in the darkness to slow her descent. But there was nothing she could do.

She had no sense of direction, of up or down, like Alice tumbling down the hole after the White Rabbit. Her stomach twisted, then the sickening sensation was followed by the sharp lurch of wakefulness. Her body jolted awake so abruptly that her muscles nearly cramped up on her. She had no idea what had happened or why she'd been asleep in the first place. Her eyes were unfocused, and her head ached. The vein above her right eyebrow thrummed with the beating of her heart. When she stretched out her arms, dirt and gravel fell from them.

"What the hell?" she said aloud, but her confusion was just the beginning. Violet was not where she should be. She should be, well, she wasn't really sure where she should be. Her last thought was of Father Benny. The sound of his voice calling out to her with gentle curiosity drifted through her mind. There was something unusual about him, but she couldn't quite put her finger on it. Maybe it was just that he was a priest. She'd never met one in person. All she knew about priests she learned from movies and television and was probably wrong.

What had she been doing?

The painting! The painting had been moving. Her day had dissolved into chaos, but she was certain she hadn't imagined that. She didn't understand how it could be possible, but it was real. The way the grasses had blown in waves against the backdrop of the storm. Lightning had burst across the canvas from within the clouds, casting an eerie glow that shifted like her mom's moods. That didn't explain how she had gotten here, though.

Where was *here*, anyway? Realizing she was lying on a gravel road, she pulled herself up and took stock of her surroundings. Tall, tangled grasses grew along the sides of the road and led off into broad fields that met at the feet of a brooding gnarly forest, which could be straight out of *Lord of the Rings*. The road ahead was empty and dark, with no moon hanging in the night sky. Her hair whipped around in the wind, so she had to keep pulling it out of her face. Ahead, a powerful storm was building behind a massive creepy old house. Behind her, the road ran off into infinity.

I am in the painting! she realized. Somehow, Father Benny's imagination created an alternate reality. A drop of rain smacked her on the forehead, signaling she was going to have to seek shelter soon, and unless she wanted to navigate the super freaky forest, then the only option was the spooky house at the end of the lane. She had no idea how she managed to fall into Father Benny's painting, but there was no denying where she was. She wrapped her hoodie around her and crossed her arms to shield herself from the oncoming weather. Putting one foot in front of the other, she leaned into the rain and made her way toward the house.

Violet peered up occasionally from beneath the rim of her hood and looked out at the blustery landscape. It was as if life had fled this place ages ago, but a flutter in the tall grass proved her wrong. Something was following her. Small tumbleweeds bounded across the path like a gaggle of geese crossing the road, and against the velvety blues of the night was a flick of black.

Just above the tips of the grasses bending in the wind was the tail of a black cat. She remembered it from the painting.

She couldn't help smiling at the thought of it hunting after its prey. Cats were mesmerizing to watch. There never seemed to be any fear in them, just an exaggerated sense of predator and bravado. They believed they were the superior species and traveled through their short little lives regally confident in that belief. What are you hunting? she thought.

Violet continued along the road, the cat like a constant shadow. Her hands were cold, her face numb and raw from the wind and rain, so she picked up her pace. The only sounds in her ears were the howling gusts of wind and her boots crunching on the gravel road. Finally, she was close enough to the house to see a flickering light behind the drapes in the windows.

She broke into a jog toward the short set of steps leading up to the foreboding giant doors. Before ascending them, she glanced out into the grasses waiving frantically in the storm, expecting to find the whipping tail of the black cat, and nearly jumped out of her boots when she saw the cat staring directly at her from the edge of the road.

Shit, she thought.

She considered taking back every nice thing she'd ever thought about cats. She tilted her head to the right, and the cat mimicked her gesture. Violet tilted her head to the left. The cat did the same. Was she reading too much into it? Totally. She snorted.

Violet turned away from the cat and ran up the stairs. Rain poured off her face and her hoodie was drenched, but despite the twist in her stomach trying to warn her from danger, she looked around with excitement. She was someplace new, surrounded by things that couldn't possibly exist. It was impossible to fall into a painting; the universe didn't work that way. But here she was, prepared for anything.

She raised her knuckles to the door, but before she could give it a knock, a *clunk* thudded behind one of the double doors and it swung inward. Violet wasn't prepared for what greeted her on the other side.

6

Ben sat on one of the decorative brick ledge planters spread out around the museum to break up all the modern surfaces and infuse a little greenery into the area. The museum was technically closed for the day but he'd convinced Walsh to let him stay longer, so the front door remained unlocked. He enjoyed the night more than anything. During the day, the world was washed out amongst all the light and cacophony of society. Televisions blaring vulgar commercials, horns honking, and the incessant noise of traffic—it all cluttered his mind. They made it hard to focus on his job during the day.

He'd been working at his easel all day, and his back was screaming at him. With his leather-bound sketchbook balanced on one knee, he sketched a homeless man making a nest for himself beneath a nearby sculpture. The black sky was draped over the city, little pinpricks of sparkling diamonds piercing it, the stars twinkling and winking with their secrets. Henry loved the night most of all because it revealed the truth in everything. People dropped the lies, and the garish glow of neon lights emphasized every chip, every crack, every wrinkle.

Ben ran a hand through his graying hair. He was old, much older than he looked, and had seen many things in his lifetime. He'd watched the world change, yet, as his graphite pencil scratched along the toothsome surface of the paper, he recognized that some things never changed. The wealthy would always do everything in their power to remain wealthy, while every creature beneath them rotted away in abject poverty. He added some deeper shadows to the man's face. Ben looked up to check his reference and saw a small shadow flit across the street.

Shadows were the necessary contrast to light. Where too much light washed out the truth, shadows clung to the dark side of everything. They never lied. Shadows could never be anything more or less than what they were, unless they were more than a shadow. Some shadows were monsters, primordial creatures born of humanity's fear. Fear of death, fear of loneliness, and even the fear of the monster beneath your bed could congeal to form real monsters. But like everything else in the cosmos, there always had to be balance. He was a part of that balance. This was why he understood some shadows were more than just a shadow.

He waited patiently as the city breathed around him. A streetlight flickered, and he squinted his eyes at it thoughtfully, remaining still. The public library across the street from the museum was empty at this time of night, so no one else noticed that the sconces flanking the entrance burned brighter, impossibly bright. The cosmos required balance, and the balance to unnatural shadows was unnatural light. Well, that, and him of course.

Ben continued to watch for the shadow as he closed his sketchbook and tucked his graphite pencil into the inside pocket of his jacket. There you are, he thought. A small shadow scurried out across the green lawns of the library where the light should have washed it away. From here it looked round and nimble, like a large raccoon. Ben knew better what they were really like. He hadn't come across one of these in a few years and worried a nest of them was growing.

Violence had accelerated in certain areas of the city. Union Station was particularly plagued with a growing homeless population and increased drug-related crime. It had previously grown into a modern hot spot where twenty-somethings could share every detail of their day with a backdrop worthy of the current popular social media sites. Currently, most people kept clear of it unless they were feeling brave, or stupid. He would have to look into it after he dealt with this creature. But for him to do that, he would have to get a better look at it. He needed to see its true form.

Keeping an eye on the shadow, knowing that if he even blinked he could lose sight of it, he unbuttoned his jacket and slipped the leather book into a secret pocket he had sewn into all his jackets. He would be foolish to be caught without some way of working his craft.

The shadow across the street remained still. They weren't particularly known for their patience, so it must have been working. That didn't bode well. Light from the headlights of the bus approached, causing the shadow to twitch toward the light. Ben watched it as it crept across the lawn. Its form stretched out, elongating, morphing, then it tilted its head upward, catching a scent.

Ben swore as the bus rumbled down the street, blocking the creature. By the time it had passed, he'd lost sight of the small deadly shadow. He stood up and looked across the street. What he found in its place made the fine hairs on the back of his neck prick up.

Standing on the sidewalk directly across from him was a small human figure made of pure shadow. It was the sort that would absorb any light aimed at it and never flee. He couldn't see the creature's eyes from here, but he didn't need to. He knew what he would find. It had been nearly a century since he'd battled one, and he didn't relish the fight. While some shadows were monsters, others were more than that, worse than that. The world was full of monsters, created naturally by the primordial hate and greed of humanity. But some were carefully crafted, with patience and purpose. An ache in his shoulder that never faded away was his constant reminder that he was not infallible.

Why was it here? He supposed it could be here for him. The last time he'd tussled with one, it had let slip that they were not independent creatures. A mind was working behind the machinations. The shadows weren't just mindless eaters; rather, they were working towards a goal. Ben didn't know what that goal was, but at that moment, just before the creature tried to devour his soul, it snarled something at him. "Regele Monstrilor," it said. "He is hunting you." In their shadow form, they were not the most elegant speakers, but when they smiled, it could make even the most stalwart heart shutter. He remembered its smile, spreading slow and wide, lips curling away from its long black teeth dripping with saliva. The beast had laughed in a grotesque inhuman voice, as if it were chewing on glass. He had tried to glean more from the creature, but in the end, Ben dispatched it to the only place he knew of that would allow it to die. His mind gnawed on those words more often than he would prefer to admit. *Regele*

Monstrilor, the king of monsters in Romanian. *The king of monsters, he is hunting you*. It was not something he would forget anytime soon.

Without seeing its eyes, he could not see what the shadow was focused on, so Ben remained still to avoid the creature's attention. Time ticked by, and ordinary shadows lengthened, stretching out across the ground, crawling up walls. The shadow figure standing across the street remained motionless for a long while, but the head of the human-shaped shadow twitched unnaturally as it caught a scent off the gentle breeze running through the streets of downtown Denver.

Something moving along the peripheral edge of his vision alerted him to someone approaching on his side of the street. The shape of the creature twisted and contorted as it lengthened itself out toward the passerby. It was preparing for the hunt. If he let this creature get away, an innocent life could be stolen. His pulse quickened. The pupils of his dark eyes widened. It was time to work.

In the space of a single heartbeat, the chase was on. Ben heard the familiar sound of the museum doors opening and closing. The beast launched forward and reverted to its shapeless form. It moved impossibly fast, but Ben knew this game. He sprinted in pursuit. Despite his being closer to the entrance of the museum, the beast reached the door first and slithered through the gap in the closing door like a sentient oil slick. *Shit*, he thought. This one was unusually fast.

Ben bolted, letting his strong legs carry him. He pulled the door open and crossed the open area leading to the stairs before the door closed. The museum lights were still blazing, and the shadow was easy to pursue. The inky blackness contrasted against the white walls and odd angles. Up the stairs, around the corner, and through the exhibits. He chased the creature as it hunted its prey. He wondered what about this person had caught the creature's attention. Maybe he'd get a chance to ask it before he sent it to its doom.

The creature slowed down, and Ben hung back. He didn't think it had noticed him yet but couldn't be sure. He hid behind the closest corner to where the creature had suddenly stopped moving. His ears caught the soft sound of footfalls leading away from the creature. Whoever it was, they didn't seem to be in any kind of rush. Who would come to the museum at this time of night, he thought, other than himself, that was?

The shadow slithered around the corner into the next exhibit, and Ben followed. They were making their way toward the *Gothic America* exhibit. His exhibit. The knot in his stomach tightened. He hoped it didn't mean anything, but he knew better than to ignore coincidence.

Beyond the ominous entrance to the exhibit, the space was dark and moody, with simulated candlelight still flickering throughout the space. He placed a hand over the breast of his jacket, subconsciously checking that he still had his pencil and sketchbook. His only weapons against the nightmare creature were right where they should be. So, with one foot placed before the other, he entered the haunting exhibit.

In here he could follow more closely. The curves and twists along the path concealed him from his foe. He proceeded cautiously, for he'd been caught unaware before and didn't relish a fate worse than death. As he maneuvered around one of the last bends along the cobbled path, he spotted the shadow. Here it was larger, bolder. It savored the flickering dance of light and dark. It moved and morphed in ways that made the human mind ache with wrongness.

There! He lunged forward to surprise his enemy. What he found stopped him dead in his tracks.

"Miss Violet?" Why had the girl returned?

The shadow creature had caught up to its prey. It had stopped just a few feet behind the young woman. Why had it focused on her? he wondered. He'd let himself become dangerously distracted. He watched in helpless horror as the shadow beast lurched and shuttered, taking on its more deadly form. It contorted into the shape of a small human child made of shadow and death. It unfolded its limbs, reaching out toward its prey. Toward Violet.

Ben's stomach lurched, and bile bubbled up the back of his throat. He was too far away to help. Violet turned towards his voice. She smiled at him, unaware of the danger standing right behind her. The moment their eyes locked, a warm curious smile spread across her young rosy lips just as the beast was mere inches from reaching her.

And then she was gone. One second, she was there, and the next, she was nowhere. The beast pursuing her shrieked. Ben slapped his hands against the painful sound, like grinding glass and gore. The grisly noise made his ears hurt and his mind shrink in protest. The creature melted into shapelessness and oozed away.

He should have pursued it. It was an impossibly dangerous creature to let remain free. More ominous thoughts tumbled through his mind. How had the girl simply disappeared like that? She wasn't connected to the painting in any way. The power of the painting couldn't have worked on her. He let the creature go, almost a forgotten thought already. The girl was unprepared for what was coming for her. He didn't know how he could have let this happen, but he didn't know how he could've prevented it, either.

Ben raked both his hands through his hair. The pain and sorrow for what he had unintentionally done were already eating at him. He had to know how this could happen. Would he be able to undo the damage? To his knowledge, no creature had ever returned from there, so why would he expect her to find a way?

A moan of anguish slipped past his lips. He'd just sentenced that young woman to a terrifyingly painful death.

7

The massive door opened, and for a second, Violet thought it had opened all on its own. This was, after all, a creepy painting universe, and she wouldn't be surprised if the brooding manor was haunted.

She dropped her gaze and stared at a child. A young boy, maybe no older than eight or nine, looked up at her with the same entitled curiosity as the cat. His clothes made him look like he stepped out of the past with tweed trousers, a button-up collared shirt, and a matching bow tie.

"Hello," she said.

"Hello, miss," he greeted her in return with a small bow of his head. "Please do come in from the weather."

The young boy stepped aside, and Violet accepted his invitation.

Violet stepped over the threshold and into a magnanimous foyer. Maybe that wasn't the right word for it. Foyer seemed too small a word for the grand space she found herself in. The young boy stood beside her, patiently waiting with his hands folded neatly in front of him.

"Um, thank you," Violet said. "The weather out there is crazy."

At this, the young boy tilted his head again. Little weirdo, she thought. She looked at her feet. Water and mud from the storm outside was dripping off her, making a huge mess on the polished wooden floor. "Oh, sorry about the mess."

"Don't mind him, he's just being impolite," an unknown voice said.

Violet turned around to see a young girl standing right behind her. She appeared to be about the same age as the boy. She was wearing a long dress that barely whispered across the floor. Her raven hair was plated ornately in two long braids on either side of her head, and her dark eyes were inquisitive but confident. Violet hadn't possessed that confidence at her age. The world always seemed so big and scary. She used to be afraid of monsters and bogeymen. Growing up, she knew the world was a scary place, but the real monsters were just horrible people and bad luck.

"What a state you are in," the girl said with absolute sincerity. "We had better get you out of those wet clothes." The girl took Violet by the hand, her touch sending shivers up Violet's arm. The girl's hand was cool to the touch. Violet supposed she'd been expecting the girl to be warm, but so far, all she'd experienced of this world was coldness.

The girl led Violet into the great hall. Two curving staircases flanked the expansive space, and off to one side was a hallway that led off into infinity. Or at least that's what it looked like to her. The walls were papered in rich damask, all the woodwork was lacquered in onyx, and the only lighting came from sconces flickering with candlelight. After a short distance, all she could see were shadows.

Violet let her gaze follow the sweeping curve of the staircase. Doors led into mysterious rooms. The sconces outside the doorways were lit, too, but like everything about this place, it wasn't enough to chase away the shadows. To the other side was a massive stone fireplace. The hearth was so big you could fit the kitchen in her apartment in it. Arranged neatly around it was a Victorian sofa and a couple of formal reading chairs. The fire crackled joyfully in defiance of the shadows all around.

The young girl escorted Violet to a sofa and turned to the boy.

"Will, please fetch some blankets. I shall get the tea."

The strange little boy sauntered off in one direction and the girl in the other. Violet sat in front of the roaring fire, dripping wet and shivering, but she yearned to get a look at the place. The woodwork was exquisite. It bent into peaked arches at every doorway like a cathedral. Violet thought that if you filled the great hall with several dozen church pews, you could have held Sunday mass here. The high walls had windows tucked into them with views of the storming, tumultuous sky outside.

Violet hadn't realized how quiet it was until she grasped that the noise of the storm couldn't penetrate the walls of the manor. She had no idea why, but for some reason, that thought frightened her. If something were to happen to her here, would there be anyone to hear her, anyone to help her? She wondered if time moved the same here as it did back home. Would anyone notice she was missing?

"Mom!" She needed to get back home to her mom, but she didn't know how to get home or where home even was compared to here. She bolted up off the sofa and whirled around in a panic, only to be confronted by the children.

"Are you all right, miss?" the girl asked.

"Honestly, I don't know," she sputtered. "I have no idea where I am, no idea how I got here, and I really, really need to get home."

"There's no sense in worrying about things that you cannot affect, miss."

The girl was right after all, but it didn't make Violet feel any better. She couldn't even think about what would happen to her mom if she wasn't able to get back home. And that terrified her.

"For now, miss, you should sit and get warm while we find you some dry clothing," the girl said with authority. Violet sat obediently, but her skin crawled. She understood the words coming out of the girl's mouth, but there was an unusual quality to it that rubbed Violet wrong. It was nothing big and scary. There were no red flags or blaring alarms, but the shiver threatening to run along the length of her spine was enough.

"Evelyn?" the boy asked. Violet had almost forgotten that he was there. The girl seemed to be the one in charge around here, or so she thought. The boy stood by while the girl set down the tea tray she'd been holding on a nearby table. His arms were full of blankets, and his eyes were full of unrest.

"That's a pretty name," Violet said as her teeth chattered. It was freezing in here despite the blazing fire.

"Thank you, miss. This is my brother, Will."

"Lord William Sable," the boy said with earnestness and bowed, "and my sister, the Lady Evelyn Sable." Evelyn curtsied.

"Aren't you a little young to be lord and lady of the manor?" Violet joked, but it was obviously the wrong joke. The boy's expression changed. His eyes clouded over, and his eyebrows cinched together.

"Our circumstances are not fodder for your imbecilic attempt at humor," the little lord said. Ice crystals bloomed in her veins, their sharp edges cutting her from within.

"Brother, be nice to our guest," Evelyn countered. The look he gave her could have killed, but it didn't seem to faze the girl. "I'm hungry, and I don't need you spoiling supper."

The silence between the two children was brief. An entire conversation was had in that moment, heavy and laden with so much history she wasn't privy to. Violet didn't understand what was going on. Her body shivered again. This time not from the cold, which was penetrating her wet clothes. She shivered at some unseen threat.

"I'm so sorry, Will," Violet stammered. "I didn't mean to be rude."

Will turned his chilling gaze toward Violet. "You will address me as, my lord," he declared softly yet menacingly. For such a small individual, he laced his voice with much venom.

"Don't be such a troglodyte," Evelyn tossed out before taking the blankets from her terrifying brother and tenderly wrapping them around Violet. Evelyn's hands brushed against Violet's skin.

Evelyn finished wrapping the last of the blankets around Violet and straightened herself, taking a good long look at the drenched and bedraggled woman in front of her. She nodded with satisfaction.

"You'll be warm in a jiffy," the young lady of the house announced.

Violet wasn't so sure about that. She watched the girl going about her soothing ritual of making a cup of tea. She handed the cup to Violet with all the reverence of a miracle cure. "Tea will put you right as rain," Evelyn said, her voice a little bird song in the night. Violet didn't believe her, but she accepted the cup, anyway. "Now, you sit tight and warm up while I go find some dry clothes for you to change into."

Violet watched the precocious girl walk away with more elegance than she could muster on any given day. She was wondering if she had not merely fallen into a painting and another world, but if she had slipped into the past too. Nothing was modern about the two children. Their mannerisms, their clothing, everything about them spoke of a time long forgotten.

Soft tendrils of steam from the tea twisted in the air. The fire crackled and popped while her young hostess was quickly swallowed up by the impenetrable shadows of the house. Violet brought the cup of tea to her lips and took a tentative sip. The hot tea slid past her lips and down her throat, warming every part of her. The gentle scent of Earl Grey warmed her freezing heart. She felt like the melting icicles hanging from the fire escape of her apartment after spring would come and warm everything up.

"Wow," she said out loud. She hadn't really meant to, but it was hard to deny the life-changing experience of having a properly made cup of tea. She wanted to hug the cup, but she settled for wrapping both hands around it and pulling it toward her heart. Violet's eyes fluttered closed, and her thoughts drifted. She wanted to be back on that bench at the station, drawing her mom in the morning sunlight. An icy tendril reached through her memories and touched her.

Violet's eyes snapped open to see little Lord William staring at her. His face was unreadable again and his posture seemed relaxed, but she was pretty sure he didn't like her much. He had passed judgment on her, and it wasn't favorable. This entire situation was unreal, but until she had a better understanding of where she was and what the hell was going on, she couldn't do much about it. She gave the cup a tip in his direction with a wink and a nod, an acknowledgment of his blatant staring. If she was going to piss off the little lord, then she was going to do it by being her true self, sarcasm and all.

She sipped the tea, stared longingly at the fire that couldn't seem to warm her, and waited. She didn't have to wait long. A few minutes later, Evelyn returned with a small pile of clothes and a pair of shoes. Violet's stomach flipped. The amount of lace in the small stack of clothes was alarming. She wasn't really a lace kind of person. Jeans and a hoodie were more her speed, but she remembered she didn't have a lot of options as a wave of shivers wracked her body.

"Come along, miss," Evelyn declared. Violet obeyed, following her across the broad empty expanse of the great hall and up one of the sweeping staircases. She took in the haunting architecture, the sweeping arches, and every tiny detail carved into the wood banisters. Once upstairs, Violet realized the shadows seemed to follow them. It was like driving down a road less traveled at night. Without the bright streetlights to wash away the shadows or the comfortable garish glow of neon coming from nearby businesses, the only thing to see was what the headlights of the car illuminated. Darkness swallowed everything outside the periphery of light. What happened in the shadows when no one was watching?

"You may use my room to change," the young lady of the house asserted. The girl laid out a long gown across the bed next to a pile of undergarments and a pair of shoes. Her brother, never seeming very far away, lurking just outside the door. "We'll be just outside when you are done."

The door closed softly behind them, and Violet was by herself once again. She marveled at the room. In so many ways, the house felt straight out of a scary movie with the endless night, foreboding storm, and creepy children. Her senses were screaming at her, though. So many things were wrong with this place that her mind couldn't keep up. Where were the children's parents? They couldn't possibly live here all alone. She didn't know how she knew that; she just did. And this house, well, it was something else entirely. It was old, really old, but the doors moved silently, and the floors didn't creak. Violet was sure that she could move around freely without ever having to worry about making a sound.

The bedroom was more welcoming than any other part of the manor she'd seen. She wasn't sure if it was just because the room was smaller or because it felt lived in.

It wasn't a small room, but it wasn't overly large like the cavernous hall downstairs. The four-poster bed was neatly made, but the dolls on the bed were well-loved. Little touches here and there proved this space belonged to a young girl, but it was unlike anything she'd ever experienced. There were no posters on the walls proclaiming the newest neon cartoon characters. No oversaturation of pink or purple. The walls here were covered in the same dark luxurious wallpaper that lined the walls out in the corridor.

She turned to look at the gown on the bed. Violet couldn't remember the last time she wore a dress. Then her face scrunched up with the realization that she *did* remember. It was at her dad's funeral. That was the last time she'd worn anything other than her daily uniform. She looked down at her clothes. She definitely didn't fit in. Violet let her hand run across the forest blue fabric, and she sighed as she touched the luxurious texture. She'd never come across fabric that felt this amazing. Everything around here seemed to be much the same. It was all organic and exquisite. There was art and patience in the making of everything here.

The modern world she came from didn't treasure quality. It worshipped the bottom dollar, and the cheaper you could earn it, the better. For the time being, she was stuck in this secret world and didn't know what it was going to take to get back to her mom. The only option was to adapt to her new circumstances. She undressed, peeling off the layers of her drenched clothing. The undergarments lay as though their previous occupant had simply dissolved into nothingness, waiting patiently for the next tenant to arrive.

8

VIOLET STRUGGLED WITH THE buttons and lace. The gown and underclothes were unlike anything she'd ever worn, but eventually, she tucked her slim frame into the beautiful blue gown.

She opened a few drawers in the nearby dresser and inside were just linens and some clothes. On the low surface of the dresser was a carriage clock that didn't seem to work, a silver tray holding a beautifully ornate silver hairbrush, and some jeweled hair combs. Other than that, it was mostly bare. What else could a little girl need, anyway?

A massive oak wardrobe rested in the far corner of the bedroom. Violet opened the doors, and a full-length mirror was mounted on the inside of each of the doors. She examined herself and was taken aback. She looked downright respectable and not even remotely like herself. Her hair was still piled atop her head in a messy bun, but she couldn't do much about that. She shrugged. It wasn't likely to get any better.

When she opened the door, she nearly screamed. The two children were standing side by side, right there at the door, reminding her of a macabre pair of Victorian portraits, or more accurately like the creepy twins from *The Shining*. Violet's skin crawled at the sight of them. They seemed paler in the dim lighting. The dark wallpaper seemed a little darker than before too. Had it always been this dark? She couldn't tell. The house was made of shadows, growing darker or lighter with its mood.

"Yes, that will do just fine," Evelyn said. Violet wasn't sure about that. She was so far out of her element that she had no basis for making any judgments.

"If you say so."

"I do, thank you very much," Evelyn retorted. Violet stepped out into the hallway. Candlelight flickered against the walls. Shadows stretched and danced, reaching out to the three of them standing in the hallway. The hairs on the back of Violet's neck bristled, and her spine stiffened. She was twitchy. Everything in this place made her skin crawl. There was nothing here but too much space and the pair of super strange children. It was all just a little askew and her brain was malfunctioning, trying to set it right.

"Well, what should we do now?" Violet asked.

"I want to play a game," the little lordling declared.

"What did you have in mind?"

His eyes squinted, and then a smile slid across his face. Violet had a sudden inkling that she should be frightened, but she couldn't bring herself to be frightened of a child. There were plenty of things to be afraid of, but if you didn't know it was there, how would you know to fear it? A shadow behind Violet stretched out, reaching longingly towards Violet, but William glared at it until it receded.

"Not now," he hissed.

"Okay, then, maybe later," Violet offered.

"How about hide and seek?" he asked.

"Sure, I guess," she stammered. Indecisive much, she thought irritably but shrugged it off. "I haven't played that game since I was little," Violet said, mostly to herself. William grabbed his sister's hand, and the two broke out into a run. In a heartbeat, they were gone, swallowed up by the shadows. "Um, okay, I guess we're playing now."

Silenced filled the air. Violet stood there in the hallway alone, her ears fighting to hear anything. She couldn't even recall the sound of the children's feet on the floor as they ran away. The only morsel of sound was that of the faint giggle echoing from the children. She counted.

"One. Two. Three," she said slowly, loudly at first. It was wrong to speak so loudly in such an empty space. Her voice echoed throughout the manor, coming back to her ears different, distorted. "Eleven. Twelve . . ." It didn't even sound like her. It was a different voice, almost, with unique inflections. It was darker and deeper.

"Twenty," she whispered. "Ready or not, here I come," she shouted, then lowered her voice. "This place is going to be the death of me, I'm sure of it."

Violet picked up a small lantern on a nearby table. The oil in the burner sloshed slightly as she settled it. The glass chimney protected the flame against the breeze when she moved down the corridor. Shadows retreated from the light as she moved, at least the shadows she could see.

Behind her, other shadows didn't run away. They stretched out, each one melting out of the natural shadows like sentient oil slicks. They twisted and writhed, strangling each other to be the first to taste the new guest. Always just a breath away from having what they've been starved for. Among them, something lurked, something that even the shadows were afraid of.

In all of Violet's favorite stories, the setting was just as much a character as anyone else in the story. Alongside Frodo and Aragorn was Fangorn Forest, dark and mysterious, and full of magic that even wizards were afraid of. *The Turn of the Screw* introduced her to Flora and Miles but also to Bly Manor. Maybe that's why this place was so easily able to crawl beneath her skin. If any place could be haunted by the past, it was most certainly this place. She wondered if it had a name. Every haunted house had to have a name.

"I think I'll call you Priestly Manor," she asked the house in a soft voice. It seemed fitting since none of this would exist without the talent of Father Benny. "What do you think of that?" She took another step, and the floorboard beneath the woven rug groaned. It was the first sound to prove this place was real and not her imagination. "I'll take that as a yes."

She could see the landing to the stairs ahead. Lightning from the storm outside occasionally lent extra light to the dark interior. The first door on her right was directly across from one of the grand staircases that descended into the great hall below. She lifted her eyes skyward, and the Gothic vaulted ceilings spread out over everything like veins, with intricate carvings in the wood hiding their own secrets. Violet followed the veins of wood, noticing that none of the woodwork ended abruptly. It was all elegantly connected.

The glass doorknob was cool to the touch but twisted smoothly. Everything here felt old, like it had been here for centuries, but it all worked like it was new. Violet opened the door slowly. Every room here was empty, but she couldn't help but feel like there were half a dozen pairs of eyes always watching her. As the door swung inward, she leaned her head in. It was empty for the most part.

Violet stepped into the bare room. This room differed great-ly from the one she'd changed in. Evelyn's was furnished, not just with actual furniture but with memories. It reflected the personality of the girl who spent her time there, who dreamed and played there. This room was vacant of furnishings and memories. There was no rug, no bed, and no dresser. The singular window was bare, with no drapery. Violet padded across the bare floor to the window.

She sucked in a sharp breath in awe. She hadn't known what she expected to see. Clouds billowed, climbing high into the sky in a boiling mess. Bursts of lightning chased each other across the sky. But it wasn't the storm that caught her off guard. Stretching out beyond the manor was a greenhouse. Cathedral spires jutted up to the sky, intricate latticework holding the massive sheets of glass together in what Violet could only describe as a glass castle.

The rain ran off the glass of the greenhouse in sheets. She got so close to the window that her breath fogged it up. She wiped away the fog to stare at the magnificent creation just outside. Violet didn't have a green thumb, but she appreciated everything green. Through glass and fog, Violet could see the hint of greenery just beyond her reach. The mist twisting up off the ground and the clouds dropping low shrouded part of the greenhouse, making it seem as if it stretched on forever. She'd have to find a way to get in there with her sketchbook.

A familiar noise tickled her ears. Violet couldn't place the sound, but she knew she'd heard it before. She turned away from the fantastical greenhouse outside, letting her hand slide away from the window. It was only then that she realized the room wasn't completely empty. A single painting hung on the wall opposite the window. It's no wonder she didn't see it right away.

Violet approached the painting, the game of hide and seek forgotten. Staring out of the painting directly at her was a black cat, poised and alert. The cat sat on a front porch, a black door behind it. A small placard attached to the bottom of the frame titled *Dorian*. There was no signature from the artist, but something about the background of the painting looked more modern than anything here. It made it seem out of place.

She stared at the cat. The cat stared back. She wanted to touch the painting, but as her fingers hovered above the canvas, she hesitated, remembering the last time she did something she ought not to have. Violet pulled her hand back. She would have to rely on her other senses to tell her more. The gravelly voice of her high school art teacher tumbled around in her head. "You must see the artist's work with every sense. See it with your eyes, yes, but see it with color and sound too." She straightened her back and took a step back, leveling her eyes with the cat's.

There! she thought. It couldn't have been her imagination, not after what's already happened. She was sure she saw one of the cat's whiskers twitch, actually twitch. And then she heard the sound again. This time, it made perfect sense. The comforting sound of the cat's purr emanated from the paint and varnish—a soft, reassuring motor, matching her pulse's rhythm. "Hello, Dorian," she said. The cat continued to stare at her. "My name's Violet. It's a pleasure to make your acquaintance." Almost imperceptibly, the cat lowered its lids and bowed its head.

She stumbled back away from the painting instinctively. "No way!" There was no one to hear her, but she couldn't restrain herself. She approached the painting again, this time with unfettered curiosity. Violet didn't get the chance to lean into her curiosity back at the museum, but here. Here, she had nothing but time, well, that and a couple of super creepy siblings. Sooner rather than later, those kids were going to wonder where she was. She needed to get back to her game of hide and seek.

In a flurry of silk and lace, she whirled around back towards the door. "Sorry, Dorian," she muttered from over her shoulder, "got to go." Just before she stepped out into the hallway and the painting would become lost to sight, she stopped. Violet turned to the painting and the cat. She didn't know how much of this was just her imagination and how much of it was just the most amazing impossible magic, but as she was stuck in the spookiest mansion possible, she'd have to hedge her bets. "Hey, Dorian," she started. She waited, but nothing happened. "Do you think you could watch my back while I'm here?" Nothing. "Well, if you could, that'd be great. Thanks, in advance, cat."

With renewed energy, she left the room, shutting the door behind her with more force than she'd intended.

"You should not have done that."

Violet spun around and found William standing behind her with a frown etched on his young face.

"Sorry, I didn't mean to slam the door."

"Maybe she didn't hear it," Evelyn said. Violet spun the other way. Where had they come from? The hallway had been empty just a second ago. The three of them stood together in the empty corridor, listening. Violet didn't understand what there was to be afraid of, but she also didn't realize someone else was in the house, although she should've expected it. She felt a little dumb about that too. Of course someone had to watch over the children.

Quiet filled the space like a tidal wave bulldozing across the shore. No one moved. No one spoke. Violet didn't dare breathe. Somewhere in the deep dark of the manor, a door opened. William and Evelyn each grabbed hold of one of her hands and burrowed into her as close as possible. She didn't know who was coming, but when the scariest kids she'd ever met were frightened, well, it just wasn't good.

"Who is she?" Violet whispered.

"She's our governess," Evelyn whispered, her voice shaking.

9

BEN STOOD NUMB IN a caricature of motion. The girl had fallen into his painting like so many creatures before her. How could that happen? There was no intent, he hadn't painted her into it, yet it sucked her in. The beast he'd been in pursuit of was long forgotten. His only thought was of the girl and the hellish place he'd unwittingly sent her.

His stomach knotted with shame at his carelessness, but he broke himself free of the shock and approached the painting. Ben needed to see if anything differed about this painting compared to his others. He'd been painting for centuries and didn't understand how something like this could have happened. As he approached the easel, something crinkled beneath his shoe.

Ben bent down and picked up a piece of paper from underneath his foot. The thick cold-pressed drawing paper must have fallen out of the girl's bag when she slipped into the painting. He straightened his back and admired the skill of the artist again. She didn't sketch with small timid strokes. Her lines were long, smooth, and confident. Ben didn't know who the woman in the drawing was, but she was attractive. Her hair was pulled back into a simple ponytail at the base of her neck. Her complexion was smooth, and there was an aura of light around her.

He could just pick out some features of the face to know that this must be the girl's mother. Their jawlines were similar, as were their cheekbones. Ben recalled seeing the other woman and his heart ached at the realization of the struggles the girl endured. He didn't know much about the girl, Violet, but he knew that she'd met grief; he'd seen that in her eyes. Would someone miss the girl? He wasn't sure her mother was capable on her own. He needed to find out.

Ben put away his paints and carefully pulled a canvas tarp over his painting. He didn't need anyone else falling into that image while he was away, at least not until he figured out what was going on. He looked at the drawing in his hand. It was incomplete, but the amount of detail, the raw emotion etched with every charcoal line and smudge of shading, said every-thing. Whoever this woman was, she was important to Violet. He would start with that. He'd leave the exhibit in search of a stranger he'd only seen in a fleeting moment.

Fortunately for him, the first person he saw was familiar and friendly. Ben stepped into the open expanse of space at the entrance of the museum just as Mark Walsh was pushing his way through the front doors. He stopped in his tracks with a look of surprise on his round face.

"Father Benny?"

"Walsh."

"What are you still doing here?" The genial security approached him after he recovered from his shock.

"I didn't mean to startle you. I'd made arrangements earlier to stay and continue to work when the place was quiet."

"Oh, well, that sounds fine," Walsh said. His face was a little red, and his eyes subtly darted off to the side, to where he'd just come from. Ben hoped it was just the aftereffects of startling the man, but it was hard to ignore that he was focused on something else. He was more than happy to be proved wrong. Whatever was bothering Walsh would have to wait, though. Ben needed information about Violet, and he knew the security guard would help.

"You're a good man, Walsh," Ben offered.

Mark Walsh visibly relaxed and gave Ben an easy smile. "Thanks, Father."

"You know, you are just the man I need right now, as a matter of fact."

"How so?"

"I had a great conversation with that very talented young woman earlier today, but I'm afraid she dropped this at my exhibit." He showed the security guard the drawing. "It seems rather personal, and I'd love to give it back to her."

"That's one of Violet's drawings. I'd recognize her stuff any day," Walsh said. His face brightened, and he practically bounced like a proud papa. "She's a great kid, you know."

"I got that impression. She also seemed like maybe she could use a friend every now and then."

"Not wrong there. She's had a rough life. I'm sure she'd be grateful if someone returned one of her drawings."

"Any chance you know where she lives?"

"Already on it." Walsh reached into the pocket of his uniform shirt and pulled out a tiny notepad. It appeared comically small in the burly man's large hands. Ben waited patiently as the security guard wrote something down, ripped the page out of the little notebook, and handed it to the priest. Ben noted the address. "You know it?"

"Can't say I do."

"You know the Lost Penny Apartments?"

Ben thought about it. He'd heard of the place, but he had never been there. It didn't have the best reputation. It was an old relic of a hotel from the twenties, the architecture was a bespoke art déco, but it had been neglected for a very long time.

Currently, it was a haven for the strange and outcast. Decent folks didn't go there. Ben nodded.

"It's just down the block from the Penny," the guard added.

"Thanks, Walsh," Ben said. He patted the gentle giant on the arm and turned to walk away.

"Oh, hey, Father Benny?"

"Yes?"

"You all done here tonight?"

"Yes," Ben admitted. He had bigger problems to worry about than finishing a painting in solitude. "I'm done for the night."

"Great, thanks. I'll finish locking up after you."

Ben stepped out into the cool night. As he walked towards the parking garage, he saw the silhouette of the security guard backlit by the bright glow of the museum lobby. He couldn't shake the feeling of something amiss. The day had started so benignly, but after chasing down a shadow beast for the first time in many years and watching Violet fall into his painting, he couldn't deny the right to acknowledge his fear. He didn't fear many things, but he knew where he'd inadvertently sent that girl and it wasn't a very nice place. Making matters worse was the idea that a shadow was after the girl. It had targeted her specifically, but why?

Twenty minutes later, he still couldn't clear his mind as he parked across the street from Violet's apartment building. In the rearview mirror, the street stretched out behind him. The block was quiet, and the streetlights that still worked dropped circles of harsh fluorescent light down on the sidewalk. In the distance, he could see the glow from the pink neon sign of the Lost Penny. When all this was done, perhaps he should give that place a visit. Who knows what mischief was going on behind those doors? he thought.

He got out of the car and smoothed down the wrinkles on his black suit. Ben checked that his white cleric collar was straight and approached Violet's apartment. He wasn't certain what to expect when the door opened, but the petite Jewish woman of Vietnamese descent was not it.

GENTRIFICATION HAD NOT MODERNIZED the neighborhood yet. This was where people lived when they were just surviving. A commune for the forgotten and neglected, this neighborhood had no giant planters overflowing with brilliant flowers and lush greenery. There were no electric scooter stations or mega-chain coffee shops. Here, the bus stops weren't clean and brightly lit.

Just down the block, one of the old bus stops had deterio-rated, an ugly monolith of decay. The plexiglass surrounding it was stained yellow from decades in the sun. Etched into the tarnished surface were the initials of long-forgotten lovers sur-rounded by vulgar profanity painted in garish graffiti. Within the imaginary protective confines of the bus stop was a long metal bench bolted to the concrete beneath it. The florescent lights installed on the bus stop's ceiling flickered. Nothing was wrong with the lights; it was just difficult for any sort of tech-nology to work properly when in proximity to a natural source of power like that of the handsome man sitting patiently on the bench.

Domn Dehanie thought of himself as a very charming man. Well, he used to be a man. Currently, he was something else entirely. His dark hair was cut short and buzzed on the sides. He wore a two-day-old beard, and his brilliant blue eyes were usually enough to get him most things he desired. The lines across his brow and the soft crow's feet at his eyes were the only hints of his age. But much like the man he followed here, he was much older than he looked, much older.

He waited patiently on the bench. Domn Dehanie was dressed in black denim, and the buttons of his black shirt were open just enough to seduce but not enough to be labeled a douchebag. His sleeves were rolled up. After all, he had work to do.

Domn watched with satisfaction as the priest entered the apartment building down the block. The corners of his mouth pricked up. He loved it when everything worked out as he expected. A shriek of animalistic pain broke the silence of the neighborhood. It could have been the loser in a nearby catfight or a wounded dog crying out for help, but the guttural quality of it pricked his attention. His brow furrowed, and he tilted his head like a curious cat to listen to the night.

Clinging to the dark spaces between the streetlights and neon signs, a shadow that wasn't a shadow lurched and slithered. It moved with the wet sound of gristle and bone grinding against the pavement. Domn leaned forward. He recognized that familiar sound and his heart broke. Twitching against the bright flickering fluorescent light, the shadow beast from the museum oozed into the shelter of the bus stop.

"I am so sorry, my child," Domn soothed, his voice laced with his lyrical Romanian accent he refused to forfeit over the centuries. "Come here, child." He opened his arms, and the grotesque shadow beast crawled up the man's leg, revealing the shapeshifting gristle within. "Tell me what you've seen."

The beast slid across Domn's chest, melting against his bare skin. It seeped into his veins, his ears, down his throat, and into his eyes. His beautiful eyes, blue-gray as an oncoming storm, turned black as coal. His back arched slightly, finding pleasure in this sort of embrace. This unique connection between master and beast was more than physical, though. Thoughts and feelings were shared as well. The master and beast shared everything in that tender moment.

"Here, child, let me help you," Domn said. With the gentle wave of his hand, the struggling lights of the bus stop relinquished their fight, and darkness enveloped the sheltered space. The beast pressed itself out of his chest just as measured heavy footsteps approached. The beast howled and snapped, its jawing coalescing and dissolving with disturbing fluidity. "Shh, it's all right. I don't much like him either, but he has been exceptionally helpful."

The beast slithered back down Domn Dehanie's body. In the safety of the dark, it pulled itself upright, into the form of a child, a child with eyes so black they stood out against the darkness of the night. The beast took its place between its master and the owner of the approaching footsteps. It stood like a wary sentinel when Mark Walsh stepped out of the ambient light of the city night and into the oppressive dark space.

"Domn," Walsh said.

The beast opened its mouth to speak, and the hissing of its voice twisted with the wet gristle sound its corporeal body made when moving. "You dishonor Regele Monstrilor with your callousness." It was a sound that belonged only to nightmares, and Walsh was visibly disturbed by it, which made Domn smile.

"Sit, Mr. Walsh, and tell me that everything is going according to plan."

10

Violet stared down at the angelic faces of the children. Evelyn's face had gone pale, and her eyes bulged with fright. But it was young William who startled her the most. His youthful face was full of anger. She didn't have siblings, but she could imagine how angry she'd be if someone frightened her sister like this.

Behind her, the stairs creaked as loudly as a freight train. Fear was like that. The quietest things could evoke the most terrible sensations. Whoever was approaching, the children were not happy to see her. Her heart skipped and stuttered in reply. She didn't want to turn around. She had enough of her own nightmares to deal with. Violet wasn't prepared to meet someone else's nightmare.

Her hands shook, and her brain was having trouble focusing. All Violet wanted to do was run. But she couldn't. She didn't know what kind of danger was approaching and lacked the power to stop it. Like the hint of a lullaby being sung from far away, it wafted closer and closer. Violet was the only barrier standing between that unseen terror and the frightened children.

The children were a mirror of sorts. Her fear reflected back at her. Their little bodies trembled. She couldn't leave the children to fend off this nightmare by themselves. Based on the children's widened eyes, Violet knew it had reached the landing.

"Children?" the nightmare queried. The voice was beautiful and elegant but cold. Violet couldn't put the sensation into words, but everything about the voice felt wrong. It held no humanity behind it, no compassion. The inflections were just barely off-key. She remembered watching a documentary about a song that basically went viral back in Victorian times because it was played entirely in the flat range of keys and drove people to commit suicide. That's what the voice behind her reminded her of: wrongness. Violet tried to not let her fear show as she slowly turned around to greet the frightening woman behind her.

But nothing could have prepared her for what she faced. Standing at the landing with one hand still resting on the banister was a vision of the most sophisticated creature she'd ever seen, in real life or her wildest imagination. The governess wore a long corseted Victorian gown. No, it wasn't quite Victorian, but something near it, maybe more Edwardian. Her gown had luxurious textures of fine lacework and beading, and the long sleeves and high neckline covered most of her skin. Her perfectly smooth ivory skin would make the hottest influencer envious. The woman's dark chocolate hair was ornately arranged atop her head. It was all overwhelmingly beautiful, but none of that mattered.

Covering the woman's face was an intricately carved porcelain mask. It wasn't like what you'd see for a masquerade ball, but it struck Violet as something you'd find on a vintage porcelain doll. Even from where she stood, Violet could see the exquisite detail of the shape of her lips, the curves of her doe-like eyes. The pupils, lids, and even lashes were finely carved in every way. It was flesh turned to stone.

"Hello there, dear," the governess said, "I apologize for not greeting you sooner." The woman glided toward Violet, revealing more detail in the mask. Violet's body shivered without her consent as the flickering candlelight cast the mask in relief, and even the clean eyebrows framing the mask's eyes were carved in individual hairs.

"Um, no worries," she stammered, wishing she didn't sound so stupid. "I-I didn't mean to disturb you." The mask was a work of art that made her want to weep just seeing it, but it added to the wrongness of everything else. The governess's voice wasn't muffled behind the mask. It carried clearly across the space even though there was no opening for the mouth.

"What sort of hosts would we be to just leave you out in the weather?" the governess said. As if the man behind the curtain recognized his cue, lightning from the storm raging outside splashed light into the candlelit corridor. "I can see that the children have at least managed to find some dry clothes for you."

Violet's mind threatened to break right there and then. There were no holes for her eyes to see through the mask. How could the woman have seen what she was wearing?

"Yes, ma'am." What else could she say?

"Children, it is time for bed," the governess commanded.

"No," William said.

"Now," she replied, her voice barely a whisper. Iciness had crept into her already chilling voice. Apparently, it was the sort of tone that brooked no retort. Evelyn and William shared a knowing look before they followed the governess's orders. Violet wished she understood their communication. There was no sense to anything about this. It was as though she'd opened a book in the middle and just started reading. She didn't know any of the backstory or who the players were. The most frightening part of all was that she didn't even know what kind of book she'd picked up. Was this a supernatural thriller or some gruesome horror?

As the children walked past the governess, the woman turned to follow them, and it just looked wrong. Violet's brain glitched as she watched the governess smoothly follow the children to a room further down the hall. William opened the door and entered. Before Violet could get much of a look, the governess turned around to face her.

"Please wait out here," she said. "You, too, Evelyn." Then she slipped into the room and closed the door behind her.

"I hate that." Evelyn pouted.

"What?"

"He's always the first to be put to bed." Evelyn crossed her arms with a huff. "One of these days, I'll get my turn to be first."

"I'm sure you will," Violet said. She hoped it came across as supportive, but it was probably as empty as this house. "Hey, Evelyn? Is there anyone else in this house that I should know about?"

A clouded look briefly drifted across the young girl's face. It was a simple question that she didn't really mean anything by. Her sarcasm had gotten her into trouble on more than a few occasions, but before she could say something else, a soft

THUMP came from behind the closed door. Both Evelyn and Violet turned towards the curious sound.

"I don't think William is being very nice to her tonight."

"Does that happen often?"

"More than it should, I suppose." The young girl gave a rather grown-up sigh. Violet turned to face the girl. Out here in the hallway, Evelyn didn't seem particularly scared of the governess. Had she read the signs all wrong? She was starting to feel more and more like Alice in Wonderland. Up felt like down, and down felt like sideways.

"So, what's the deal with the mask?" Violet asked, hoping she could avoid an awkward conversation about it. But of course, that was when the door to William's room opened, and Violet found herself once again face-to-face with the governess. She was rather petite, Violet noticed.

"Your turn now, Evelyn."

"Yes, ma'am."

The governess led the way back down the hall to Evelyn's room, where Violet had changed out of her wet clothes.

"Please wait here for me, I'll only be a moment," the elegant woman said to Violet, and once again, she stood in the corridor with a closed door between her and the answers she needed. Violet leaned back against the wall opposite the girl's room and closed her eyes. There could be a chance that she was just dreaming. Although, if she were, she should probably talk to a therapist about it. Behind her closed eyelids was the comfort of blackness. No sound penetrated her thoughts, and the tension in her muscles softened a little. If she thought hard about it, she could imagine the familiar comfort of her blankets being pulled up to her chin.

But then a door opened, and her eyes opened. The governess softly closed the door to Evelyn's room behind her and turned to face her. Violet watched as the woman tilted her head to the side.

"What?" Violet asked.

"You seem to be taking your new circumstances rather well."

"What do you mean?" Violet asked. While she couldn't see the woman's face behind the mask, she was eerily certain the woman was smiling at her.

"Come with me. I have just the thing." The governess hooked an arm through Violet's and bent her head in close. Under other circumstances, they might have looked like besties confiding juicy morsels of gossip between them, but these circumstances were darker and far more dangerous than gossiping teenagers. "My name is Katherine, Lady Katherine Ainsley, to be precise."

"Violet, Violet Brennan."

"It is a pleasure to meet you, Violet," the governess said as she guided them towards the stairs.

Standing at the landing and staring into the vast space of the great hall framing the massive front doors, Violet could imagine Katherine as the lady of the manor. The seclusion, the storm, the shadows that moved of their own accord, it all came together as some ominous set waiting for the curtains to rise and the show to begin.

They descended one of the grand staircases. Violet noticed something she hadn't before. From the stairs, she saw a door tucked tidily in the woodwork just beneath the curve of the other staircase. Lady Katherine seemed to know where she was looking.

"I don't ask much while you are here," she started, "good manners, of course. And that you allow me a modicum of privacy."

"That's your room?"

"Yes."

"Privacy is something I don't get much of, so I understand." Katherine turned her masked face to Violet and bowed her head almost imperceptibly. Violet didn't understand where the children's reaction to her had come from. She was well-spoken and elegant, and other than the mystery of what was hiding under that mask, she couldn't reconcile her own visceral reaction to the woman she was speaking with. "Lady Katherine?"

"Yes, Violet?"

"You haven't asked me why I'm here or how I got here."

"I know how you came to be here. We have all been brought to this place in the same manner."

"The painting," Violet breathed.

"The painter, more so than the painting, my dear."

"The painter?"

"There is great evil out in the world. Some evil is coarse and grotesque and, as such, quite easy to recognize," the governess said. Lady Katherine's grip on Violet's arm tightened, and her fingernails bit into her flesh. "Some evil, however, is rather good at disguising itself."

They walked past what Violet expected to be a mirror but was surprised when she saw it covered in black paint. The gold frame surrounding the black surface unnerved her.

"I can't imagine the priest being evil."

"A priest, you say?"

"Yeah, the artist was a priest," Violet said with a strange, dreamy look.

"Ah, I see," Lady Katherine acknowledged. "Even a priest can be attractive."

"Ugh, that obvious?" Violet scolded herself. The governess patted her hand.

"It has been quite a while for me, but I still remember the flush of attraction," she said wistfully. "It's a human desire and very primal."

They continued in silence, past the door leading to Katherine's room and down a long corridor until they came to a set of emerald green lacquered doors. It was striking against the midnight blues and velvet aubergine decorating the rest of the house. The paint was old, having been patched and touched up over the years.

Lady Katherine reached out and opened the door. She stepped aside and let the space beyond welcome Violet in. Violet's eyes grew wide, and her lips parted at the unspeakable beauty waiting for her just beyond.

11

As Ben walked down the corridor with tattered carpet and peeling wallpaper, he heard pieces of the lives of those living through the thin walls and behind each aging door, lives that were as frayed as the carpet beneath his feet. He had seen humanity rise from the ashes only to crumble again, but every time, the call for progress was always to the detriment of those less fortunate. It wouldn't change any time soon.

He found the door to Violet's apartment as per the directions Mark Walsh had given him. While Ben was not unaware of how late it was and was worried about frightening people unnecessarily, he also knew that any mother worth her salt would be pacing frantically if their daughter was not home when they should be. The woman he saw with Violet at the museum was not well, though, and he didn't know yet how that would fit in with the puzzle he was trying to piece together. He didn't know the relationship between Violet and her mother, but he understood the emotions behind the drawing he still held in his hand.

Ben knocked. He waited. Standing in the empty corridor in his black suit and white cleric collar, he listened for any hint of movement behind the closed door. Soon enough, he recognized the sound of steps making their way to the door. The peephole clouded over, and he wondered how he would be perceived. It wasn't often that a priest showed up at your door near midnight. He didn't suppose folks would think it a kindly visit.

The chain on the door slid away, the lock clicked out of place, and then the door opened. Father Benny found himself looking down on a petite woman of Vietnamese descent. The wrinkles crosshatching her face and the silver streaks in her otherwise black hair gave her age away.

"Can I help you?" she asked. Her eyes focused on the cleric collar at his neck. Her hand reached for the delicate pendant hanging around her own neck, a star of David. The woman was a contradiction against modern stereotypes, and he admired her for the choices she'd made in her life. He didn't know her, but he knew already she held principles within her that she would not allow the world to tarnish or diminish.

"Yes, ma'am, I met with a young woman at the museum today, and she accidentally dropped this." He handed over the drawing.

"That's one of Violet's all right," the woman said as she accepted the drawing. Ben wasn't sure how much to tell this woman who was very obviously not Violet's mother.

"I know this is unusual, but I was wondering if I could speak with her?"

The petite woman looked at her watch and then back up to him. She didn't need to know that he was several centuries old or that he hunted shadows for a profession. So instead, he offered her a small apologetic smile. She opened the door all the way and stepped aside so that he could enter.

The apartment was small and run down, but it was tidy and welcoming. The living room was tiny, with an equally small kitchen attached to one side. On the other side was a bathroom and a closed door he assumed was a bedroom.

"She's not home right now," the woman said, closing the door behind him.

"Is her mother home?"

"She's—unavailable."

"I'm sorry to have imposed. It's just that, well, she seemed a little lonely."

"You're not wrong there," the woman said. She pointed to the empty place on the couch as she sat down. He accepted the invitation. "She's a lonely girl."

"The woman in her drawing?" Ben bowed his head towards the drawing still in her hands. "I assume it's her mother, by the love she put into it."

The woman frowned slightly, and he couldn't help but notice her eyes dart to a closed door on the opposite side of the room. There wasn't much to the small space. The living room was crowded with only a few pieces of furniture: the couch, a couple of end tables, and an old channel-back chair with a small stack of bedding and a pillow resting on the cushion. Well, that and the artwork and collection of family photos hanging on the walls.

"She's a good girl, smart too, but—" The woman hesitated. "No one so young should have to care for their parents, not like that. It's not right."

"I am so sorry. I didn't know that circumstances were so dire for her," he said, but he was curious. What was this young woman's life truly like? Had he rewarded her noble efforts to survive a cursed life with something even worse? "I am so sorry, I don't mean to be rude. My name is Ben. Most people around here call me Father Benny, though."

"Nguyen Widawski," the older woman said curtly. It was not out of any grievance towards him, he knew this, but rather more that she was angry at a world that would cause this much grief for such a young person.

"If you'll pardon my curiosity, that's an unusual given name," he asked.

"It's not my given name. I honored my husband by taking his surname when we married. I wear my family's surname to continue to honor my own heritage."

"I see," he said with a nod.

"What parish are you associated with?"

"St. Mary's."

She nodded. "She's not some starry-eyed kid who expects the world to be fair, you know."

"I understand, but certainly it can't be quite as bad as that?"

"Her father died several years ago. She loved him very much." Ben smiled at that. "My husband and I have been friends with her parents for a long time. They are all good people, but when he died—when he died something in her mother just broke."

"Broke?"

"The doctors say it's Alzheimer's, but I think it's more than that."

"Her heart broke," Ben said. He knew that feeling all too well. The woman snapped her gaze up at him, searching for the truth behind his understanding.

"Her heart broke," Nguyen agreed. "You know this personally, yes?"

"Yes."

Nguyen leaned in closer. "The woman in that room"—she waved an angry arm towards the closed bedroom door—"she is nothing more than a shell of the woman she was. She has retreated into her own mind, to be in a place where she doesn't have to deal with this horribly cruel world." She clenched her fists. "She ran away in the only way she could think of and left her daughter to pick up the pieces."

"Violet cares for her all on her own?"

"Yes. I mean, she has me. I help as much as I can, but that poor girl works so hard to make sure her mother is happy, to make sure her mother has her medicine, but it is tearing her apart." Nguyen leaned back in a huff. Ben wondered how long she'd been holding that thought in. This was the blessing and the curse of the cleric's collar. People opened up to you. They shared their joys with you, but they also shared their grief and grievances with you. And he'd be the first to admit that in this shattered world, they were all a part of, far more grief than joy was going around. Ben looked at the slightly crumpled drawing in the woman's hand.

"She should be going to school," he said.

"She should be doing lots of things. Going on dates, going to school, making the same mistakes we all do when we're that age."

"Instead, she has to be a parent to her own parent." Ben sighed. The knot in the pit of his stomach tightened. What had he done to that poor girl? The two of them sat in silence, each absorbed in their thoughts about what should have been.

Nguyen Widawski shifted slightly as the silence between them stretched out. "Father?"

"Yes?"

"Can I ask you something?"

"Anything."

"When you spoke with Violet, was she—did she seem okay?" The older woman's eyes met his, and he recognized the pain of concern. It clouded her dark eyes and added years to her aging face.

"She just seemed lonely," he replied. "Is something wrong?"

Nguyen reached again for the comfort of the star hanging from the thin gold chain around her neck. Her forehead wrinkled up in thought, and her lips parted in fits as she searched for the right words.

"No, nothing specific."

"But you're worried about her?" he offered, to which she nodded. "Is there something I can do to help?"

The woman turned her head away. Ben couldn't tell if she was hiding her face from him or something else but felt a secret lurking just beneath the surface. The more he learned about Violet, the more intrigued he became. There was far more to this young woman than he had thought at first. He needed more information, though, and he hoped this woman would give it to him. It had been a long time since he'd needed to coerce knowledge from a creature. He didn't relish the task, but if it meant trapping one more beast, well then, he'd do whatever he needed to.

The petite woman wiped her hands on her trouser legs and then stood up abruptly, crossing the small space in only a few steps. Supporting the television was a squat little table with a few drawers in it. When she opened a drawer, he saw the usual collection of movies, a few family photo albums, and some books. Nguyen pulled one of these books out of the drawer and stared at it for a long time before bringing it to him.

"She's such a talented artist," she said as she handed the book to him, "but I worry that she might be afraid of her own abilities."

Ben's hand was hanging in midair, caught in the act of accepting the book, but the woman's words caught him by surprise. It wasn't every day that he heard the very words of his own heart spoken out loud to him. He accepted the book but continued to study the woman.

"What do you mean?" he asked.

She sat down and tapped a bony finger on the book in his hand. "Her father died several years ago."

"You mentioned that."

"What I didn't mention was how strange his death was."

Ben felt his brow cinch in confusion. "What do you mean?"

"Patience Brennan, her mother, was always Violet's biggest fan. She took her to the museum regularly, and to art exhibits around town."

"Not everyone has that kind of support these days."

"No, they don't," she agreed, "but her father was always very proud of her too. He is what you could call the strong but silent type. He didn't have much to say, but what he did say was thoughtful and weighted." She looked Ben in the eye and smiled warmly at the memories. "Get a few beers into the man, and he wouldn't shut up about how proud he was of his daughter."

Ben smiled at that. He'd met a few truly good men in his life, and Violet's father seemed one to be counted among them.

"She lived a charmed life?" he asked.

She nodded. "Shortly before he died, Violet had come over so excited because her dad had agreed to sit for her, so she could draw him, you see. He wasn't the sort of person who liked having his picture taken, and he definitely didn't like to be drawn."

"But he wanted to support her and her passion?"

"Yes, and he did, he sat for her." The woman's expression clouded over with the memory, her words catching slightly on the grief. "The last picture in that book is of him."

Ben opened the book to the last page, which was fresh and unused. He realized young Violet had abandoned this sketchbook after the death of her father. He flipped back until he found the drawing that Nguyen wanted him to see. It was a simple portrait but full of light and color. The image spoke of everything that the young girl couldn't put into words. The man was handsome in a rugged way. His jeans were baggy and worn at the hems. He was a blue-collar man who worked with his hands and found pleasure in the simple things. This was the sort of man who found his own pleasure in caring for his family.

Ben looked up from the image of the man relaxing in a chair with a glass of bourbon or whiskey resting against his lips. The chair was the same as the one in this very room. The antique channel-back chair held more than a little sentiment for Violet. He wrinkled up his face as he stared at the pile of bedding folded neatly on it.

"Nguyen?"

"Yes," she answered, her voice barely a whisper.

"How many bedrooms are in this apartment?"

"Just the one, Father." She didn't hide her thoughts from him. She understood what he was asking. Violet worked hard to care for her mother, a mother so disabled by grief that she was unable to care for her child. Violet lived in this small apartment with her mother, whom she gave up everything for. Her reward for this beautiful devotion to her family was to sleep on the sofa and forfeit her dreams. And atop all of this, he somehow managed to send her to a place worse than hell. Ben ran his fingers along the edges of the drawing. He didn't want to smear or spoil the image itself.

There, in the lower right corner, was the girl's scribbled signature, the simplest proof that an artist had declared the piece to be complete. He didn't sign his work very often. Because of his particular skill, to sign one of his creations was to lock the door, to throw the deadbolt of a prison cell for creatures bent on devouring the souls of this world. An awful thought burned in his mind.

"How long after she drew this did her father die?"

12

Violet was awestruck. When Lady Katherine stepped aside to allow her admittance to the room, she wasn't prepared for what awaited her. An impossible vision of greenery and life in a place that she was starting to think was barren greeted her on the other side of the doors. Everything else that happened to her was momentarily forgotten. She stepped into the arboretum with wide-eyed wonder.

The loneliness of being so far from home and her mom was forgotten. The isolation of this improbable mansion stuck here in the middle of nowhere was forgotten. The two strange children, out of place and time, all of it forgotten for the briefest of moments. This amazing garden tucked away behind some doors in a painting from the mind of a priest was simply too much for her to comprehend. She'd completely forgotten about this place she'd seen from the window until then. So, she simply let herself experience it.

Lady Katherine took her arm once again and guided Violet along a pathway of stone and tile laid out to encourage visitors to wander. Vines crawled up every surface. Dew and mist conversed across the glass walls, their conversations twisting and winding around each other.

"I-I think I saw this place from one of the upstairs windows," she finally managed to say.

"It's my favorite part of the manor," Lady Katherine answered wistfully. It was the first time Violet noticed any real emotion behind her words. She turned to look at the woman at her side. Katherine's head was tilted as she admired the plants all around them. She had a long, slender neck and perfect porcelain skin. Where the woman's skin met the exquisite mask, Violet couldn't see any scars or blemishes. She wondered what was hiding behind that mask.

"I can see why," Violet said. They fell into an easy silence as the governess guided them along winding paths through the arboretum. The garden was vast, and at every step along the way, there was something new to discover. Periodically, they came upon some open seating areas. At one of these, Lady Katherine sat down on a stone bench, and Violet joined her.

"If you sit here for just a moment, you can make out a bird's nest in that honeysuckle vine," the governess said in a soft voice. Again, Violet was struck by the tenderness in her voice, but there was something else hiding behind her cordial words.

"Lady Katherine, are you all right?"

"Yes, dear, I am fine. Just a little tired, I suppose."

"Is there anything I can do?"

"No, no, don't you worry about it. Tending to the children can sometimes rob me of energy, but I shall recover." The governess gave Violet's hand a gentle, reassuring pat. Every time their skin touched, Violet felt a strange sensation, something like static electricity, but colder. She stared at the governess. She was perfect in every way. So, what was hiding beneath her mask? She wished desperately to see the face beneath it, but she was also frightened to know. You could never unsee something and sometimes, those things could haunt you for a long time.

She remembered the day her dad had died. Both she and her mom had gone to bed hours ago, but her dad had wanted to stay up and finish watching one of his television shows. He was a simple man in some ways and not in others, but when it came to his after-dinner routine, he was predictable. He would settle into the navy-blue chair that used to belong to his grandmother, turn on the television, and sip on a Manhattan. It was his favorite treat after a long day at work.

"Are *you* all right, dear?" Lady Katherine asked. Violet turned to face the woman, always caught off guard by the emotionless expression of the mask. Violet wiped away the hot tears that had arrived without permission.

"Yeah, I'm fine."

"I am certain that you are not fine," Lady Katherine said, but she didn't push. Violet hadn't spoken very much about the death of her dad to anyone. Her mom's grief was hard to be near, and it had been up to her to take care of things while her mom wasted away.

"I was just thinking about my dad," she started, "and the day he died."

"I am so sorry, dear," Lady Katherine said. Violet believed her, but the woman didn't move to embrace her as other people did. She was grateful for that. All the hugs and handshakes she endured from the people at the hospital, from the funeral, and every time she ran into one of her parents' friends while she was out. It was all overwhelming. It was too much. But the governess gave her the space to feel and not be burdened by anything else.

"I miss him, but I don't really get time to think about him. I'm usually too busy to worry about anything other than me and Mom."

"Is it just the two of you now?"

Violet nodded.

"I can't imagine how difficult it is for you, but I hear that it is easier for a woman to make her own way in the world these days. At least that is some comfort."

Violet looked at her curiously.

"I've been here for a very long time. When I first arrived, it was rather unseemly for women to work outside the home. Unless, of course, you were a governess," she said with a little bow. "We were responsible for managing the estates that our men collected, but we were expected to do it while being soft-spoken, well-dressed, and perfectly mannered." Lady Katherine's words rubbed Violet the wrong way. "You bristle at those restrictions."

"I don't think I could live like that."

"You and me both," the governess said with an elegant scoff. "I wasn't very well-behaved. I read too many books and have always had a curious mind." She sighed.

"I'm sorry?"

"In my time it was unseemly to be a curious woman. I suppose when it comes down to it, I am here because of my curiosity."

"Me too, I guess."

"How do you mean?" Lady Katherine asked. Violet told her about the museum and the exhibit. She told the woman about the priest and the painting. Violet shared her crazy story with the only person she could. When she finished her tale, she was breathless. She hadn't realized how pent-up she'd been. Her new companion sat in silence for a long time, and Violet wondered if maybe she'd gone too far in telling her everything. She must sound like a lunatic.

"No wonder this has been such a frightening experience for you," she said at last. The woman rearranged herself. "I, at least, knew something of what this all was."

"Um, exactly what is all of this, anyway?"

"It is a prison."

"What do you mean, it's a prison?"

"This placed was designed to keep monsters locked away," the governess explained, "forever."

"But why are you here, then?"

"Faith in the wrong person, I suppose."

Violet wanted to shake the woman. How the hell could she be so calm about being stuck in a prison? No way, not Violet. She had to find some way out of here. She needed to get back to her mom. In the meantime, she'd have to get used to being here while she tried to find a way out.

"As prisons go, it's not horrible, I suppose," Violet said, but it was apparently the wrong thing to say. The governess's body tensed up, and she stood up faster than Violet could react. She had to run to catch up with her. "I didn't mean to upset you," Violet called after her, but the woman kept walking, around the curving pathway and beneath arches of wisteria and honeysuckle. Then the governess stopped dead in her tracks at a massive clearing at the center of the arboretum. Violet stumbled to a stop next to her, with much less grace.

"Whoa," Violet said.

"It's the heart of the garden," the governess said. Violet couldn't help but notice that her voice had returned to that icy emotionless tone and, with it, a sense of danger. She rubbed at her arms as her hairs prickled up. "At least it was the heart of the garden when I last saw it in truth."

"I don't understand."

"He was not capable of painting something that didn't exist. Every painting he made was of something that actually existed."

"Wait a minute." Violet's brain was going to explode. "Are you telling me that all of this"—she waved her arms around emphatically—"exists somewhere in the real world, the outside world, I mean . . ."

"I understand what you mean," she replied impatiently, "and yes." The governess stepped into the center of the garden. Surrounding the central clearing was a collection of Renaissance statues of men and women, all arranged like the stone circles of Scotland. Beautiful, cold sentries all turned inward with their faces lifted to the sky. It was paved in stone with lines of gold and the occasional mosaic star, which was all beautiful in its own right, but Violet's eyes drifted toward the massive sculpture placed at the center of everything. An enormous yet shallow round pool had been erected to serve as the plinth for a massive stone sculpture of the solar system. Cords of steel bent to connect the planets with their moons. The whole feature towered over everything.

"It's an orrery," Violet said with childish wonder.

"And this place is called the Orrery Garden." Lady Katherine stepped up to the shallow pool beneath the orrery and sat on the ledge. "It was this feature that drove me to visit this place."

"I can see why."

"You see, I am very well-read and have always been intrigued by science. There was a fabulous rumor running around that an eccentric lord had commissioned an orrery of immense size. Of course, he was also a recluse, so no one knew if the story was true."

"You just had to find out, didn't you?" Violet couldn't help but smile. She knew the pull of curiosity. It's one of the reasons she's so drawn to art. You never knew what you were going to find, but you knew you'd find something new.

"I did. I traveled the country and met with many great minds. Eventually, my interest in the orrery spread far enough to garner me an invitation to see it in person." Lady Katherine recounted her story with coldness, as though she were telling someone else's story. "Lord Brahm was gracious, polite, and very well-mannered. He showed me the orrery and many other things." She turned her masked face to Violet. "I wish you could see it as it was then. It moved with the night sky."

"Wait, it moved?"

"Indeed. It was a glorious thing to see. The low rumble of stone and steel mixing with the rippling water was rather soothing, and I would come here every day to write in my journal."

"Why doesn't it move now?"

"I do not know why. Perhaps because this place is only a shadow of its real-world counterpart." Lady Katherine seemed to drift off through her own memories, but Violet saw one of her hands twitch slightly, as though she were remembering the act of writing in her journal. "In the evenings, after supper, Lord Brahm and I would retire here to the garden. I would read and enjoy a cup of tea while he would paint."

"It's a kind of therapy."

"Hm?" the governess asked.

"Painting, or for me, it's drawing. I can forget about everything crazy going on in my life even if it's just for a few minutes."

"You are an artist?" Violet nodded. The governess grew still, impossibly still. For the longest time, she didn't say anything. If it weren't for the vein pulsing in her neck, Violet would've believed she was just a statue.

"Curious," she said eventually. Although Violet wasn't sure she was speaking to her.

"What?" Violet asked, but the governess ignored her. The woman stood up in one smooth motion and walked around the celestial centerpiece. Her arms hung casually at her side, but her fingers worked at some invisible puzzle. Violet got up and silently followed her. She didn't understand anything of what was going on, but she recognized the touch of inspiration and didn't desire to disturb her.

Lady Katherine circled the massive stone and steel orrery, but her attention was on the statues, one in particular. Violet rose to her side and looked upon the white statue. That's when she saw something that wasn't supposed to be there.

"Is that blood?" Violet asked, studying the flecks and smears of red across the otherwise pure white stone.

"It is paint."

"Paint?"

"This was where I last saw Lord Brahm. He was caught in the rapture and frenzy of his craft. The paint was flying off his brush. I had never seen anything like it." The woman knelt in front of a red smear in the shape of a hand on the stone tile. Lady Katherine caressed it. "All these years I have hoped that he died in painful agony and that this is where he met his demise."

Violet froze. There was more than just ice in her words. Leaching into every syllable was pure malice. At first, she thought this might have been some Bronte-esque tortured romance, but there was no love lost here. Violet knew that if the governess had her own way, she would reap Lord Brahm in a shower of pain and gore.

13

The walk back through the house was cold and uncomfortable. Violet had wondered why the children were so frightened of her. The mask she wore certainly played into her own fears of the unknown, but this was something more. The volatile nature of Lady Katherine was terrifying. She didn't know how to read the woman, especially when she couldn't see her face.

"I suggest you get some rest, dear Violet," the governess said without emotion. "I think you will need it before too long."

Too afraid to argue, Violet followed the elegant nightmare of a woman back through the garden and the house and up the stairs, only to stand at the door of the empty room with the cat portrait and the window looking down on the garden.

"Good night," Violet said, but the woman had already turned her back on her and was walking away. Violet stood alone in the dark shadowy corridor thinking about how little rest she was going to get lying on the floor of an empty bedroom. Was the corridor getting darker? Maybe Lady Katherine's steel trap of a heart was sucking up all the light, Violet thought. She grasped the glass doorknob and gave it a turn. As she pushed the door open on its eerily silent hinges, she snorted indelicately. "At least I'll have the cat for company."

But she stumbled to a stop at what greeted her on the other side of the door. She didn't understand how, but the house seemed to have prepared for her. It welcomed her with a room fully furnished. What was once a mostly empty room currently contained an oversized and overstuffed bed with a massive ornate headboard. There was also a low bureau with a mirror and a small stool. Unlike most of the other mirrors she'd found in the house, this one hadn't been painted over. In its mercury-silver reflection, Violet saw the large portrait of the cat hanging over the headboard. The house had welcomed her into its fold, and she wasn't sure if she should feel gracious or concerned.

Behind her, the corridor was dark. No candlelight flickering against the antique wallpaper, no light of any kind. She could barely make out the chair rail molding running the length of the hallway. It was simply a black void framed by the open door to her new room. That can't be good, she thought. So, Violet did the only thing she could do. She closed the door. On her side of the door, an old iron skeleton key sat comfortably in the lock. She wondered if the house was trying to tell her something. Did she need to keep her room locked? Better safe than sorry. She turned the key, and the lock gave a satisfying click as it engaged.

Violet stepped farther into her new room, fiddling with the key. There was a comfortable-looking reading chair tucked beneath the window, and resting on its tufted cushion was her backpack. With everything that'd happened to her that day, she'd completely forgotten about it. She practically ran across the rather large room, flung herself into the chair, and pulled her backpack up to her chin like it was her stuffed animal. It was all she had from before and didn't realize how deeply she needed a connection to her life outside of this strange experience.

The backpack smelled like home. It felt like home. And when she opened it up and saw her sketchbook and tin of pencils, well, she shed a few tears since no one was watching. What the hell was she going to do? How was she going to get home to her mom? She had a million questions tumbling around in her head, but she had to admit that this place was intriguing too. Violet felt guilty enough for abandoning her mom, but she felt even worse because, on some level, she wondered if she could learn to enjoy this place. Nope, this place was just a little too weird for her, and she wasn't really excited about Lady Katherine. That woman was more than a little terrifying.

Her mind raced, with all her thoughts tumbling over each other, and she had to admit that she was tired. Violet stared longingly at the bed in front of her and shouldn't have been surprised to see a nightgown had been laid out neatly for her. Had that been here when she first came in? She couldn't remember. The house seemed to have a mind of its own.

Violet pulled herself up and made her way to the bed. She picked up the nightgown and held it up to the light. The white fabric was soft as air, but the gown went down to the floor and had long billowing sleeves with frills at the cuffs. The neckline was loose with a little tie closure. What the hell was she supposed to do with this? She hadn't worn this much fabric to bed since she was an infant and still wore little footie pajamas. Well, she thought, the only alternative is sleeping naked. But she wasn't quite prepared to be that vulnerable in this creepy old house.

She worked at the buttons of her dress and eventually managed to get herself out of the dress and into the nightgown. Violet looked down and suddenly felt like she belonged in a twisted Guillermo Del Toro film. She folded her dress up as best she could and left it on the bureau before pulling back the covers on the bed and crawling in.

As soon as her body settled underneath the covers, she practically melted. Nothing could have felt more luxurious than that bed at that moment. An oil lamp on the nightstand flickered, but she was almost too sleepy to reach over and extinguish the flame. The black nothingness of sleep threatened to overtake her instantly. The fluffy pillow beneath her head was a warm cloud elevating her just enough that she could see the reflection of the cat painting in the mirror across from the bed. The cat bowed his head slightly. You and I, cat, are going to have a better conversation tomorrow, she thought, as sleep finally swept over her.

There was no clock in her room, so she didn't have a way of knowing when she'd woken up. The room was dark, but the storm raging outside offered just enough light to see ahead. Through the dark, she made out a small boy crouched on top of her.

"William?" she slurred.

He didn't say anything. The little lordling merely put a finger to his lips. Lightning flickered from somewhere deep in the clouds, casting brief glances on the cherubic face of the boy. Violet couldn't see his eyes, for the darkness of the night stole away all the color from the room, including his eyes. All she could see were black pits, and it unsettled her.

"Shouldn't you be in bed?" Violet mumbled. She tried to sit herself up, but her body was so heavy with stiffness that she couldn't move. The boy crawled up her body. It looked as though his lower body was just a shadow that moved independently of the rest of the boy. Her mind couldn't make sense of what she was seeing. Was she still asleep?

A small voice at the back of her mind screamed, and her heart tightened. She couldn't have said why, but for some reason, she knew she was in danger. Violet fought against the clutches of sleep, kicking and screaming against some horrible beast that had its claws wrapped around her throat. Or at least that was what she was trying to do. Her body refused to obey her commands. It simply lay there, frozen, powerless against the simple act of a child kissing her on her forehead.

Finally, in a moment of sheer panic, she screamed at the top of her voice, hoping desperately anyone would hear her and come to help. But all it served was to wake her up from one of the most unsettling nightmares she'd had in a long time. Violet bolted upright in bed, and her forehead was covered in the dew of night terrors.

She was alone. William wasn't there, and the door to her room was still closed.

"I guess it's just you and me, cat," she said aloud. Sometimes hearing her own voice was the only way to break the tension from fear, and she didn't care enough about what other people thought to not talk to herself. The mirror across the bed held the reflection of the painting of the cat mounted above her. She waited for the next bolt of lightning to cut away the shadows all around her. But when it did, the painting was empty.

Violet threw off the covers and turned around to inspect the painting. The gold frame, the canvas, and even the background of the painting remained the same, but the cat was gone. She pulled the framed portrait away from the wall. Sure enough, only a wall was behind it. She ran her fingers over the little gold plaque attached to the bottom of the frame with the portrait's title, *Dorian*. It felt like an old painting. None of this made any sense. Unless she was still dreaming.

"Where did you run off to, Dorian?" Violet asked no one in particular because no one else was around. Could she be having a dream within a dream? She'd never experienced a dream within a dream before.

She slumped back onto the bed. Everything surrounding her seemed perfectly normal yet absurdly bizarre. The longer she stared into the deep dark shadows around her room, the more she realized her eyes weren't adapting to the dark. Violet couldn't see beyond the bed anymore. It was as though the shadows were growing and moving in ways that didn't fit with what she knew about light and shadow. Nothing around here was consistent. Well, at least one thing was consistent. She was exhausted. The mystery of the missing cat would have to wait until morning.

Violet shimmied her way back beneath the comforting blankets. The pillows wrapped around her head again. She closed her eyes and was almost instantly overtaken by a heavy wave of sleep.

WILLIAM WATCHED VIOLET HUNGRILY. It had been a very long time since someone like her had been dropped into this hellscape. He was hungry, so very hungry. The governess never let him eat like he wanted, as he and Evelyn needed to eat. She forced them to starve while she wafted about this accursed house. He hated her. But he could taste the satisfaction of vengeance. It was close at hand.

He waited and thought. Watching the young woman sleep was giving him ideas. A wicked smile grew on his angelic face. The smile grew and stretched until it was an impossible smile, for a human child. But he had never been human, or a child, for that matter.

14

Morning came without splendor. There was no sunshine to warm this world. Violet yawned, stretched, and sat up. Outside the window of her room, the storm raged on. The room seemed to be as it was when she went to bed, except for the black pit staring at her from across her bed. The antique mercury-silver surface of the vanity mirror on the dressing bureau had been painted over, just like all the other mirrors in the house.

How was anyone supposed to make themselves presentable when they couldn't see what they looked like? A new addition to the room, though, was a wash basin full of clean water and some surprisingly modern accessories, like a toothbrush and a tube of toothpaste. Thank goodness for small miracles, she thought as she splashed her face with cool water.

Once she'd taken care of her dragon breath, she sat and picked up a silver hairbrush left on the dresser and began working out the tangles in her long hair. She didn't know what to do with her hair without a mirror. She supposed she could just throw it up in a messy bun again, but that didn't really feel suitable for the standard set around here. Violet needed some help. She got dressed as quickly as she could, which wasn't quick since she still struggled with the buttons and laces on the corset and dress. Eventually, Violet was brave enough to open the door of her room and step back into the bizarro world of this crazy place.

William was leaning against the opposite wall with one foot kicked up behind. His eyes were focused on a small object in his hands, but when her door creaked, he pulled his head up and gave her a pleasant smile.

"Good morning, Miss Violet."

"Good morning, Lord William," she said. He seemed to be pleased by her acquiescence to his title. It was ridiculous to address the child with so much formality, but she didn't want to fight him *and* the governess. Violet had the sinking feeling if she was going to find a way out of this prison, she would have to confront that woman. She wasn't looking forward to it. Lady Katherine's volatility was terrifying.

"Have you seen Evelyn?" she asked. He wrinkled up his face in detest. Apparently, he wasn't happy that she should need his sister instead of him. He bobbed his head in the general direction of his sister's room.

Violet walked down the hall until she reached the girl's room. The door was open, and Evelyn was sitting on the floor playing with one of her dolls. Evelyn pressed her dolls together, and it didn't take much imagination to understand the implication. Violet scrunched up her face at the obscenely mature play. She wondered what a girl of her age would know about such things. Violet knocked gently on the frame of the door, and Evelyn looked up and smiled at her.

"Oh, it is lovely to see you looking so fresh this morning," Evelyn said. Violet wanted to contradict the girl. She wasn't feeling very rested at all. She felt drained, sapped of energy.

"Thank you, Evelyn," she started. "I was wondering if you had a mirror I could use. Something funny happened to mine, and I'd like to do something with my hair."

"Oh please, please, please let me do your hair." Evelyn bounced up onto her feet. The doll forgotten in an instant.

"Um, all right," Violet said. What else was she going to do, anyway?

"Lovely," Evelyn said with joy. She arranged Violet on the little chair at her vanity, and the young girl set about patiently arranging Violet's hair. No one seemed very bothered by the mirror so she let the question pass, but it lingered uncomfortably in her thoughts. By the time Evelyn was satisfied with Violet's appearance, she'd lost all track of time. Time seemed to run differently here, or at least it felt like that. That might be due to the storm outside. It never seemed to diminish or move. The storm cast hazy gray light throughout the house, making it always feel like dusk, regardless of what time of day it was. The exception being when night settled upon the house. Night was different here, darker and more dangerous.

"Thank you, Evelyn," Violet offered as her hands tenderly inspected her new coiffure. Whatever the girl did to her hair, it included twists and braids aplenty. She would never be able to duplicate it, but she was fine with that. At least it was off her neck and out of her face.

"Did you want to play with me and my doll?"

"Oh, Evelyn, maybe not right now," she said as kindly as she could. "I was really hoping to explore more the house."

"That's all right, Miss Violet."

"I promise I'll play with you later, though, if that's okay?"

"Yes, please," the girl said, "I would really enjoy that."

Violet pitied the girl. All she had for company was a domineering brother and a sociopath for a governess. It had to be hard for her. I must keep my promise, Violet thought.

"Better now than later," William added from the doorway.

"What do you mean?" Violet asked.

"She's sleeping," Evelyn answered.

"She sleeps during the day?"

The children both bobbed their heads in agreement.

"What happens if you need her during the day?" Violet asked. Both children grew rigid. Good to know, she thought. The children obviously didn't want her help, and she didn't blame them for that. Lady Katherine was terrifying, but terrifyingly beautiful in some ways too. She left the children to their own devices before she embarked on her own little adventure.

There was so much to discover as she explored the house. It was full of mementos of a slower time. Despite the macabre atmosphere hanging over the household, she didn't need to fear anything. The haunting Victorian manor diminished in power as soon as Violet discovered the library. Fittingly enough, the room was on the other side of the enormous fireplace in the great hall. She'd been so distracted by her tumble through the forlorn landscape painted by Father Benny that she hadn't seen the library that shared the enormous hearth.

The fire popped and crackled in the library as it did in the great hall, but it felt more inviting. The library was a smaller and more intimate space. After skimming the shelves of the countless books, she curled into a comfortable leather reading chair and read a few chapters of *The Picture of Dorian Gray*. She loved that story because it centered on the power of art.

And even though it was a terrible cautionary tale of the atrocities humans were capable of, she couldn't help but enjoy it.

After the library, she searched for mirrors. She didn't know why all the mirrors had been covered up, but it must have something to do with the governess. It could not be comfortable for her to spend her entire existence wearing a mask, no matter how tailored it was. Violet wondered what was hiding behind it, probably something truly horrific if she went around painting mirrors in the middle of the night.

Upon leaving the library, Violet had a good assessment of the manor. Upstairs was full of bedrooms, while downstairs had the great hall, the library, and all the other usual suspects. There were quarters for maids and butlers even though none were lurking around. The long galley kitchen was built with the notion the master or mistress of the house would not cook. The attached dining room, however, was resplendent with a long table, several sideboards, and even a crystal chandelier hanging over the collection of candelabras on the table.

Violet opened every door and drawer she came upon. Other than the rooms that were occupied, everything was empty, which made the eeriness of the house only grow. Closets contained bare hangers, drawers were bereft of all the trinkets you would expect. In fact, the drawers didn't even have lint in them. She stood up after being hunched over an empty drawer, and with her hands on her hips in discontent, she looked around. As far as she was aware, only three occupants resided in the house, well, four if she included herself. But there was no food in the kitchen, nor tea in the cupboards, and not a single speck of dust anywhere.

"Weird," she muttered to herself. Violet wondered where Evelyn had found the tea.

A house this big could not be kept clean without a maid or butler. It felt old, but not in disrepair, and maybe that was because this place was really just a painting. But even paintings became dirty over time. She finally found her way down to the last two doors, one of which was the door to the governess's space that she was expressly warned to keep away from, and the other, well, she had no idea because the door was locked.

She had a love-hate relationship with locked doors. Violet cherished them for her own sanity. Sometimes, when life felt too difficult, like the walls were caving in on her, she would hide behind the locked door of her apartment. Sliding over a physical barrier against the harshness of everything outside was satisfying.

Those were the nights she wished her mom could be her mom again. She needed the comfort of her mom wrapping her arms around her, shielding her from the ugliness of the world pressing in on them. Mothers possessed a special ability to press a sense of security into a daughter's pores like a sculptor molding clay. She missed that. It was her job to comfort the child, and she felt unqualified, but maybe so did all mothers.

Her hand wrapped around the glass knob, and she gave it a twist. Nothing. She huffed in frustration. There were also times when a locked door was the ultimate curiosity. Whatever was tucked away, safely out of her reach, felt like a drug being pushed at her. Violet knew she shouldn't take the drugs just as she knew that she shouldn't press her luck to get through this door.

Age tarnished the ornate bronze plate decorating the surface of the wood that served as a mounting bracket for the door and key, but it still represented the beautiful craftsmanship of the era. Modern architecture didn't allow such ornate beauty for something so mundane and functional as a doorknob. She knelt and ran her fingertips along the relief but was distracted by the keyhole. Dim light spilled out of the tiny hole.

Violet leaned in, and closing one eye, she peeked through the little window and couldn't believe what she saw. Behind this door was a room devoid of all furnishings. Dozens, even hundreds of familiarly shaped items all covered in a mismatched collection of drapes and tarps, and even what looked to be rugs. All these flat rectangular shapes leaned up against the walls of the room, stacked one against the other.

Paintings. The room was filled with hundreds of paintings. Violet wished to pour herself through the little keyhole so that she could rip the tarps off. Even bad art had its own magic, and she had an overwhelming curiosity to know what sort of art Lady Katherine wouldn't want to look at.

Violet stood up, begrudgingly putting aside her curiosity about the paintings. She scanned the vast room. The great hall was such an odd space. The vaulted ceilings, the stained-glass windows with the storm churning beyond them, it all looked so empty. But her senses were telling her something else entirely. Shivers ran the length of her spine, and the fine downy hairs on her arms rippled to attention. She wasn't cold, though, so she couldn't attribute it to that.

Since she was thinking about it, it was strange she wasn't cold. The house was old, and with a persistent storm howling in the background, at least a draft should be flowing. The massive hearth cradled a fire popping and crackling merrily. She stepped farther into the room, her footsteps barely making any sound. Violet approached the fire, holding her hands out towards the flames. While she wasn't cold, there was a primal comfort in standing near a fire. It reminded humans of being safe. Fire could chase the terrors of the night away.

The fire offered no heat. It was a curious thing. She stepped closer still to the flames, yet she was no warmer than before.

Violet should start a list of all the things that made little sense here. As terrifying as Lady Katherine was, Violet still felt the compulsion to rely on the woman for knowledge, for any help in trying to survive this place without losing her mind. Violet stared into the golden and amber flames that leaped and curled, licking the air. The embers floated up into the air like fireflies and let everything else around her diminish.

A thought crept into her mind. It was quiet at first, soft as a whisper. Then it grew until she couldn't ignore it. *There*, it said. Violet turned around her head, her hands still hanging in the air towards the fire. Over her shoulder, she saw the door to the governess's room still closed, begging to be opened. Her eyes scanned the vast space of the great hall. She was still alone, alone with that single intrusive thought.

15

The Colorado night was cool, and the ambient light of the city washed out the black sky full of pinpricks of light. Father Benny stood on the sidewalk in front of St. Mary's and stared up at the cathedral. Its design was grand, but it was a smaller church. The buildings surrounding it were decorated in graffiti, yet the church itself was always spared. Dressed in his black suit, he could have been a shadow, but the streetlights drowned him in a fluorescent glow.

He turned away from the church and walked around to the back parking lot. Behind the church, an apartment building towered over the tall steeple. It had been built when industrial architecture was all the rage for domestic living. He used his resident key card to enter the back door. There was no fancy sign extolling luxury living, no decorative lighting, but he preferred it that way.

Ben was old, and he was beginning to feel it. There never seemed to be an end to his job. He entered the plain back entrance and entered through another door in which he needed to scan his resident card against. Sometimes he thought he would soon no longer be needed. He mused over daydreams of what would happen to him if there were no more shadows to chase down. Benny stepped up to the bank of elevators and pressed the button to call the elevator. Chlorine wafted toward him. The familiar cloying fragrance of a swimmer's delight. If he searched it out, he probably would have found a pair of lovers experimenting, teasing, succumbing to passion and lust, all while the other residents slept in the beds stacked above one another.

The elevator doors opened, but Benny hesitated. The air around him rippled slightly, and the space dimmed in brightness. No one else would have noticed. No one else's senses had been fine-tuned like his through pain and war and years. His pulse remained calm, his demeanor relaxed, but his attention was hyper-focused. Nothing gave him any hesitation, but that didn't mean much. Shadows were pervasive beasts and could hide in the smallest of places. Even a brightly lit garden had places where the sun never reached.

Ben stepped into the elevator and pressed the button to the penthouse. As the doors closed, he scanned the lobby one last time. Though nothing alarmed him, he knew better than to ignore what his body was telling him. He didn't know where exactly, but of one thing he was certain. Somewhere nearby, there was a shadow, a shadow that was more than just the void left by light.

The elevator doors closed silently on a whisper of air. Ben wondered if he'd grown paranoid after all this time hunting monsters. But it was only paranoia if the danger didn't exist. He knew all too well the danger was real. He chastised himself for growing complaisant. Ben would need to be careful. Too many unexplained inconsistencies were happening right then for him to be at ease.

The plush elevator came to a stop, and the call button for the penthouse glowed a soft red. Right next to it was a key slot. One reason he chose to live here was the security it offered. Multiple guards were patrolling the property, and it took levels of access to reach his apartment. He gave the lock a half turn, the button turned green, and the elevator doors opened once again.

Ben stepped into the small foyer that prefaced the door to his apartment. He actually owned the building, though no one currently living here knew that, which was the way he preferred it. Because of his longevity, he'd been forced to cultivate a new identity many times over. A patient man, he had accumulated wealth. Ben was grateful for the luxuries, but it was more than that. He needed to move around often, travel unexpectedly, and disappear on occasion, all in the name of destiny.

Once safely behind closed doors, he finally relaxed. He took off this persona as easily as he pulled off his false cleric's collar. Ben set the collar down along with his keys and wallet on a nearby table and was already unbuttoning his shirt as he crossed the large living space. He draped his jacket across the back of a chair in his office and made his way straight to the mini bar, where he poured himself a strong drink.

He settled in his favorite antique chair, which wasn't vintage by any means, but it was tailored and comfortable. The deeply curved shape of his Chesterfields of England Oakhurst chair was dressed in green leather, and the sweeping arch of the armrests, perfectly placed to liken him to a raven with its wings stretched out, hugged his forearms. The ice in the glass rang softly out like crystal wind chimes. He was angled toward the city, which sprawled outward and sparkled in the night with street amps playing a game of connect-the-dots through the neighborhoods. Neon signs glowed garishly, and all of it washed out the ancient cosmic light of the stars trying to sparkle in the sky.

The spire of the cathedral jutted up, reaching for heaven, and yet he looked down on it. He was no priest, but it was a disguise that offered him freedom of movement and trust.

He'd arranged the day at the museum for his own pleasure and a change of scenery. Benny loved his art even if it was meant to imprison foul creatures. It didn't matter. He was an artist, and he enjoyed precious time with his craft. But that day had not gone as planned, and he desperately needed a moment of quiet contemplation to plan his next move.

He let his eyes drift close and his head hang back as he gave his body permission to relax, to open itself up and digest all that had happened. His office was quiet, save for the usual background sounds. The ventilation system hummed as it sent a gentle current of air to twist and meander its way through the rooms. The ice in his glass cracked as it melted and occasionally gave off a loud pop. But other than that, he could focus on the rhythm of his breathing and the rush of blood in his veins.

Ben thought back to his interactions with the girl at the museum, Violet. She was young, but not intolerably so. After speaking with Mrs. Widawski, his heart broke a little for the pain that Violet had endured. Her abilities were not in doubt. She had an enormous amount of talent, and it was disheartening to see it unexplored. His eyes opened and leaned forward as he pulled the drawing from his back pocket.

He stood up and stepped over to the windows. The slight ambient light from outside cast the drawing in a strange glow. Ben stared at the charcoal lines of the drawing until he could almost imagine it moving. All the detail was there. The sun caught the subject just right to breathe life into. His finger followed the sweep of a loose lock of hair to the curve of an ear, and then the line of the jaw. Beneath his fingertip, the sweeping line of the subject's neck bent as though the crumpled page was trying to smooth itself out.

Just one twitch. He froze. Had he imagined it? Could Ben desire a compatriot so desperately that he imagined something where there was nothing? He hurried toward his desk and flicked on the lamp. Holding the drawing beneath the soft amber glow of the Tiffany lamp, he inspected every line on the drawing. He could have sworn the image moved, but nothing suggested it was anything more than what it was, a moment of longing and remorse captured in charcoal and paper.

How had his own ability revealed itself to him? Ben was very old, and he'd given up some of his memories for the sake of keeping others. He looked out the window again, lost in thought. The city night spread out, yet the very room he was standing in reflected as a hazy distortion. Ben's reflection in the glass gave him pause. His open shirt revealed the muscles of his chest. The reflection revealed his broad mahogany desk, which carried the illusion it was in water with its rippling reflection, and his bookcases.

Ben stared at the watery reflection of the bookcases. He knew the arcane secrets they contained. He always made sure to create a secret place in all his abodes. Secrets needed to be kept safe away from the world. Some secrets were too dangerous to be set loose. He turned away from the view of the city and set the drawing on his desk. With everything he'd seen that day, he needed to confirm it. He must ensure the chains of his prison creations were still intact.

He pulled a few books off the shelf to reveal a keypad installed on the wall. A familiar secret pin tapped into the keypad, and the click resounded from within the wall. He pulled the bookcase out and away to reveal a small storage closet. It was no ordinary space. The walls, floor, and ceiling were all lined with an ornate organic cage. Nestled within the cage, a collection of framed paintings. Each painting was wrapped in a unique canvas tailored specifically for each work of art, but one thing common amongst them all was the giant iron chains painted on them.

Art, true creativity, was a kind of magic few people could understand. Ben understood how art could inspire the world or destroy it. He was chosen to be a part of that magic, and although he never learned how this came to be, Ben learned his place and power within him. He flipped slowly through the paintings, recognizing each one as though they were his own children. The images painted on the stretched canvases and locked into frames weren't visible through their chained wrappings, but he knew them anyway.

His deft fingers found the painting he was searching for. He carefully pulled it out from among its siblings and took it to an empty easel open and waiting at the other end of his office. He set the wrapped painting on the floor in front of the easel, for it was too large to use the easel itself. Running his hands along the strokes of paint that forged the chain on the fabric, he broke open one of the painted links. With the forged chain of oil paint and canvas broken, he unwrapped the painting. The canvas fell to the floor in a puddle of fabric.

For the first time in nearly a century, Ben looked upon his most beloved work. It was quite unarguably the most beautiful thing he had ever painted. Infused in the paint was his love of the subject, a woman whom he'd given his heart to. The background, a brooding Victorian manor with sweeping staircases flanking the grand hall. Up on the second floor, a set of exquisite stained-glass windows cast a rich glow upon the woman at the center of the work. A beautiful woman with ivory skin and long dark hair stood wrapped in a blood-red cloak edged in celestial needlepoint.

Ben looked upon the perfect face, upon his lost love. Her large doe eyes still looking into his soul after all these years.

Her flushed full lips were forever slightly parted, always on the verge of asking another question. Ben had fallen in love with her insatiable curiosity first, but the kindness of her heart and the tenderness with which she treated even the lowest of people were the linchpins to his affection.

The paint had set long ago, but it was his tender feelings towards the woman in the portrait that caused him to never varnish it. It was dangerous to leave one of his creations unvarnished. He'd never known any creature to escape from one of his paintings, but with his victims' fate sealed by his signature, he always set the lock with varnish. This painting was just as he had left it. His beautiful Katherine at the center, but the two shadows lurking in the background worried him. Ben was relieved to see that they, too, were where they should be.

He reached out hesitantly. His fingers desperately wanted to touch her soft cheeks, he yearned to feel her lips on his once again, but there was only dried paint. Beneath his fingertips, he felt the unique texture of each brush stroke, of each imperfection of the canvas beneath, and coming from deep within the portrait itself, a single inaudible thump. Like a wave of sound thumping against his chest seconds before the crack of lightning blisters the sky, he felt the ripple of something that shouldn't be. And for the first time in a very long time, Lord Benjamin Brahm knew fear.

☠

Far beneath the fearful artist, lurking in the shadow of the church, Domn Dehanie stared up at his prey. His body moved eloquently as he shifted his gaze towards the penthouse suite. The king of monsters knew his prey. He understood the artist's power to trap shadow beasts in an unrelenting prison that starved them. But he also knew he had not found a way to kill his children. So, Domn held on to the hope that he could release the bindings and free his children. Until then, though, he would continue forging new shadows, mixing his blood with the savagery of this age of civilization to birth more children of the night.

He missed his favorites. Domn didn't love anything, any creature, save for himself. But when he created the first of his shadow children, his children with black eyes, he knew he would always cherish them. The twins, they were his first, his most powerful of all the shadows he'd created. He also knew that they had not been killed, could not be killed. But they were hungry. Domn felt their hunger deep in the rotting gristle and meat that gnashed beneath his skin.

16

Two blocks down from the little cathedral, the Lost Penny Hotel lurked. Domn couldn't think of another word for it. Once it had been a glorious example of Art Déco luxury with its steel curves and welcoming glass display windows that beckoned passersby to step through their doors. It didn't matter if they were a businessman on a trip to the corporate office or a dominatrix with a private client. The Lost Penny Hotel would welcome you in with Gatsby-inspired luxury and Fort Knox-level privacy. But time took its toll on everything. The patched paintwork peeled off the sides of the building and the welcoming display windows were cracked and hazy with dirt and grime. The residents of the hotel-turned-apartments were strange at best and dangerous at worst.

It was just the sort of place the king of monsters felt most comfortable. Domn watched the artist from the shadows for a few more minutes before he sauntered off towards the Lost Penny, happy as a cat playing with its food.

The green facade of the repurposed hotel was bathed in the garish glow of the pink neon sign proclaiming its name to the entire block. It was so dirty you could almost feel your soul tarnish as you drew closer to it. Domn slowed his gait as he approached a lone figure. He would be the first to admit he was curious as a Cheshire cat when he saw a huddled figure sitting on the sidewalk in front of the Lost Penny.

It was a woman, a woman who didn't belong. He sat on the curb next to her. She sniffled and wiped away the tears streaming down her face. Her khaki trouser and blush pink cardigan screamed volumes about her suburban life.

"My dear," he said in his lyrical Romanian accent, "whatever is the matter?"

"I think I've made a mistake," the woman said through stuffy sinuses and slurred speech. She wasn't drunk, at least not on alcohol. He felt the waves of fear and grief coming off her.

"There are few mistakes that can't be turned into something better,"

"This can't."

"Oh, I'm sure it's not as bad as that."

When that woman looked into his eyes, he gave her a friendly smile. Domn Dehanie's boyish looks always got him what he wanted. His sharp cheekbones and dimpled chin did the rest. "Go on. It can't be that bad. Tell me what you've done."

The woman sniffled some more, and Domn leaned back and took a good look at her. She was domesticated for sure, but those green eyes of hers held potential. He pulled a black silk handkerchief from his pocket and handed it to her. She took it hesitantly.

"I've left my husband," she said as she dabbed at the tears welling up in her eyes.

"Is that all?"

"He's all I have. I'm nothing without him."

Domn leaned in conspiratorially. "Was he a brute?"

"No." She shook her head.

"A liar?"

"No."

"A cheat? Please tell me he's a cheat," Domn said. She looked at him aghast, and he gave her a wink.

"No, none of that."

"Then, by all means, why did you leave him?"

"Because—because I've spent my whole life being what everyone else told me to be," she began, to which Domn nodded. "Be a good daughter, so I was. Be a good wife, so I was. I did the laundry. I raised our daughter. I laughed at his friend's jokes. And I pursued a career that his family thought was typical and conservative and could shape me into just enough of a career woman to be considered a productive member of society without being so driven as to be thought a negligent wife." She stopped long enough to take a big gasp of air.

He knew for certain he could work with her. He could mold and shape her into something beautiful, something exquisitely monstrous.

She was about to keep going, but Domn reached out and clasped her hand. "It will be all right."

"How do you know that?"

"Because you are beautiful," he said sincerely.

"What?"

"You are beautiful, dear. You have always been beautiful."

"I don't understand," she said. Domn watched her lower lip quiver through her sorrow and the unexpected kind words.

"Sweetie, you have always been beautiful. This world we live in is cruel, and it has tried so many times to crush you, to subvert you, to make you think you were wrong for having all those wonderful dreams and desires that I can see running through your heart." Domn reached out and cupped the woman's face in his hands. "Stop changing yourself for them. Be yourself. Be the woman you are when you close your eyes and slip away to your happy place."

"But what if I hurt someone?"

"They have been hurting you by making you like them."

"I-I suppose," she said, but he could still feel the hesitation in her voice. She was so close to being his. He just needed to push her over the edge.

"If you could be anything right now, I mean anything that your lovely heart desires, what would it be?"

Her eyes shifted nervously, and she bit her lip. It was then that he won her. Her watery green eyes lifted to meet his, and a shy smile pulled at the corners of her mouth.

"I'd be a ballerina," she whispered.

He leaned back and gasped lovingly at her idea. "I bet you would make a lovely ballerina."

She laughed out loud, a guffaw really. It was unladylike, uncultured, and very nearly a snort. But it was real. There she was, there was the true woman beneath the expectations of others.

"You know, there's only one thing standing between you and her."

"Her?"

"Yes, her, the real you." He leaned in again, this time so close that his lips brushed against her ear. She shivered beneath him. "You just need to destroy the interloper. Kill her."

Instead of pulling away, her back arched slightly, and her head leaned back. "Really?"

"You just need to kill the woman they created. They used you for clay, but you're in the kiln now. And all you need to do is kill the part of you that isn't real."

The woman faced him. He watched the ideas tumble over each other behind her eyes, within her mind's eye. She was his, and he could do anything he wanted with her.

"I don't know how," she admitted in a childlike voice.

"I'll tell you what. I have a friend in there"—he hooked a thumb back at the Lost Penny—"who's quite good at that sort of thing. Would you like it if I asked him to come and teach you?"

The woman was silent. She started the night lost and sad, but at that moment, the tears had stopped and she was already revealing the person beneath all the cultural and familial programming. But eventually, she gave him a smile and bobbed her head.

"Excellent, dear." He patted her knee and stood up once again. "I'll just pop in and send him out. You stay right here."

He left the woman where he found her and pushed his way through the carousel door and into the lobby. The milk glass pendants hanging from the tin ceiling cast a dim yellow light on everything. The white- and black-tiled floor beneath his feet was cracked, and the vintage Kelly green paint on the wainscoting was peeling. He glided across the lobby without pretense or hurry and approached the old-fashioned hotel desk with leisure.

The desk stretched out the width of the lobby. The once-elegant carved surface of the desk was pitted and scuffed, even polished in some places by repeated touching, and a collection of mail slots lined the wall behind the desk. As soon as Domn saw the desk attendant, he smiled.

"Gracie, you look radiant," he offered as he slid an elbow onto the desk. The drag queen towered over him. The flamboyant wig and bold makeup declared to the whole world she was the queen of her castle.

"My lord," she offered with Southern charm, a courteous bow of her head, and a deep voice that moved her Adam's apple. Domn caught the drag queen staring at his lips, her glossy lips pursing and twitching. He couldn't help but return her admiration with a wicked smile. "It's been a long time. What brings you around here?"

"I'm chasing down an artifact for my collection, but I was hoping you'd put me up in one of your rooms while I'm in town."

"Of course, it would be my pleasure to serve you," Gracie said. She sashayed along the length of the hotel counter. Domn followed her, the pair making a macabre magic mirror act as they went, and raised the bar-style counter so that the queen wouldn't need to duck. Once out from the confines of the desk, she offered the king of monsters a proper curtsy. Her strong muscular legs braced confidently in mind-bending stilettos. The new King Charles would have been honored to be greeted as such, or perhaps not.

Domn and Gracie's relationship went way back. Gracie's career was going nowhere, and Domn needed a few unpleasant tasks handled while he was on another errand. She hadn't batted a manicured eyelash at it, and as such, he'd been happy to reward her. Since then, Gracie's career had flourished. In fact, it had more than flourished. She no longer needed to do stage work or perform for anyone else. She bought the Lost Penny and turned it into her own fiefdom to collect those individuals that society had always wanted to crush and destroy.

"Anything I can help you with while you stay with us?" she asked as she pulled out a key on a room tag.

"I appreciate the offer," he said genuinely, pulling her free hand to his lips and giving it a tender kiss. "Nothing comes to mind just yet, but I'll save the fun stuff for you."

Gracie's deep voice twittered delicately at the tenderness he offered, then spun around as pretty as a dancer and led Domn Dehanie around the corner and down the stairs. Most of the residents lived on the upper floor, but she had some special rooms in the basement. She led Domn past her own rooms and to the end of the hall. One red door stood out among the dingy and worn green lacquered doors of the Lost Penny. It didn't have a number on it. Gracie put the key in the lock and gave it a decisive turn. Her long glittering nails deftly swiped away the key tag and opened the door with a flourish.

She stepped aside to allow her master to step through. He accepted her graciousness, understanding the reverence she offered him, a gift to her lord, her king. Domn Dehanie crossed the threshold and accepted the token of respect. Until he left, this would be his throne room. No one would enter or leave without his express permission. Gracie knew where she stood in his hierarchy; she knew her place in the food chain.

"Anything else I can get you?" she asked from the door.

"I'll be fine for now. Thank you, dear."

"All right, but give the bell a ring"—she nodded to the antique servant bell system attached to the wall—"if you think of anything." A bell attached to a strong wire was threaded through a system of riggers that crawled up the aging wallpaper. He nodded, and she tossed him the room key.

"Oh, Gracie, dear, there is one thing."

"Anything."

"There's a lost little lamb sitting out on your curb. You'd do well to send Dead Flamingo out to fetch her." His sentence was worded as a suggestion, but Gracie would understand it was an order.

Dead Flamingo was one of those eccentric characters Gracie collected, one of Domn's special projects years ago that didn't go as planned. He had a special ability to nurture lost souls, and he would work miracles with that suburban housewife weeping on the sidewalk. She nodded and closed the door behind her, leaving him in peace. The suite was luxurious by Lost Penny standards, but it was worn and tatty. He didn't care. He was the king of monsters, after all. He had other things to worry about.

Domn sat on the gold velvet upholstered sofa in the living room, leaning back and spreading his arms out wide on the backrest. He needed time to think. Since he finally had proof Benjamin Brahm had established himself nearby, he would have to be careful. But the only way to get the twins back was through an ugly confrontation with the artist. There was plenty of time for all that fun. He settled into his gauche surroundings, a wicked smile stretching across his lips.

17

Violet crossed the space between the hearth and the forbidden door quietly and quickly. By the time her hand was on the doorknob, the pervasive thought had won. There was no turning back. She was too curious to turn away. What she found was definitely not what she had been expecting.

She stood in the doorway staring down a flight of steps, which were unrefined and made of concrete. The walls were painted a strange sickly green, reminding her of a hospital. There was no light in the utilitarian stairwell, but down in the corridor beyond, an old fluorescent tube light created an unfriendly strobe of light and shadow. It was completely uncharacteristic of the rest of the house. The Victorian house all around her made this Gothic Noir holdout feel awkward. Why so disparate? she wondered. Why the contradiction? Violet looked behind her. She was still alone in the great hall. No one could catch her doing something she ought not to do.

She crossed the threshold from one mystery to another, wondering if the artist of the original painting had changed his mind halfway through. Writers did that, changing huge plot points in their stories as they wrote them. Perhaps the painter did the same thing. Or, she thought, perhaps it was simpler than that. Maybe she was trapped in a pentimento, a painting beneath a painting,

Violet descended the roughly hewn stairs. Overwhelming her senses was the fragrance of antiseptic, which heightened her anxiety. The memories of hospitals haunted Violet. Between the death of her father and the unexplained diminishing of her mother, Violet had spent too much time there. They never gave her good news. She took each step slowly, unsure of what waited for her in the corridor beyond.

If a disfigured ghost of a long-dead hospital patient were lurking just beyond, well, she wouldn't have been surprised at all. Instead, she stepped into the corridor lit with fluorescent tubes of light suspended from the ceiling at regular intervals. The lights flickered and buzzed, reminding her of something out of a horror film. The corridor was long and barren, and the linoleum-tiled floor and sick green walls spilled out indefinitely before her. But as the corridor stretched out like a hall of mirror tricks making it feel like it went on forever, Violet noticed there were no doors except for a single metal door at the far end.

She looked over her shoulder at where she'd come from. The steepness of the stairwell made it so she couldn't see beyond the stairs and up into the house. Violet felt a sense of isolation she hadn't felt before. Although the manor itself was strange and eerily vast for the few inhabitants within its walls, she'd never felt quite this alone.

Her steps were silent on the linoleum tiles. Other than the flickering, the only other sound was that of her own heart thumping against her chest. Violet wished it would beat a little quieter, afraid that it would give her away. Violet lost track of time as she went. There were no windows, no doors, no signs of life. But the door at the end was getting closer and the hum of the florescent lights grew louder and steadier.

Eventually, she stood before the metal door. It was out of place. It looked like the bar across the middle could be pushed in to open it. A sign mounted to the door read, EMPLOYEES ONLY. "Curiouser and curiouser," Violet mumbled. She'd gone down the rabbit hole for sure then. With one deep breath, she pushed the bar, and the metal door swung open.

And found herself in some sort of lab. It wasn't modern by any standard, but it felt familiar, almost like it could have been pieced together from her errant thoughts. There was a hint of institutionalism from the 1920s with a Gothic twist.

The walls covered in white subway tiles rose into Gothic arches that created alcoves and nooks where scientific equipment lined the work surfaces. Electrical cords were plugged into outlets, and stainless steel sparkled everywhere. A tabletop refrigerator with a clear door showcased vials of unusual liquids. Although the room lacked computers, bookshelves were built into some alcoves and were lined with dozens of journals.

An enormous stainless-steel desk was anchored at the center of the room. And just on the other side of the room, another door. Violet whipped her head around again, paranoid she'd be caught, but she was still alone. She stepped up to one workstation with the little refrigerator and opened the door. Inside were trays of vials. Each one was filled with some ungodly black substance. They were meticulously labeled in elegant calligraphy she'd be hopeless to duplicate.

Violet pulled out a vial. The black substance inside shifted slowly, syrupy and opaque like molasses. She turned the vial around and held it up to the light, but whatever it was, no light pierced through it. The substance was black as a shadow. Violet tipped the sealed vial sideways to read the elegant writing on the side.

Subject: Shawna

Notes: Volume 20, Page 86

Well, she thought, that was helpful, in a not-so-helpful way. She didn't know who Shawna was, but she felt pity for whatever had been done to her. Violet paused. Looking up from the vial, she let her gaze settle on the volumes of journals nearby.

"I wonder . . ." she said. She couldn't pinpoint when she started talking to herself out loud, but it was probably an effect of being so secluded. There weren't really many people to talk to around this creepy place. Violet set the vial down carefully and scanned one of the shelves full of journals, her finger running along the spines of the books until she stopped at one labeled "Volume 20." It felt too easy, but then she remembered that this space wasn't meant for her. It was the governess's space after all. Violet considered not invading the woman's private thoughts by going through her journals, but any clue hiding between the covers of these books that could help her get home to her mom was enough. Her worry about invading the woman's privacy washed away in an instant.

She opened the volume and scanned the pages briefly until she found the one she needed. She read, and ice crystals grew around her heart. The experiments detailed in the journal were abhorrent and cruel. Children had been trapped here and tortured. The governess went on in excruciating detail about starving them just to see how they would adapt, if they would adapt. Written in the fine sweeping curves of Lady Katherine's handwriting were studies of segregation from the other children, starvation, punishment, and so much more. Violet had finally had enough. She threw the book on the counter in disgust, backing away from it as though it were a dangerous animal.

It was the most horrifying thing she'd encountered. The world was corrupt, and it was an inevitable byproduct of humanity. Even the kindest among them was selfish, always reaching for things they don't deserve, but this was worse. This was a real nightmare. She had to get out of there and fast, but she needed evidence of what she was doing. Violet didn't know if she could take anything out of this painted nightmare, but she had to try.

She picked the journal up again and flipped through the pages until she found the entry she had just been reading. Violet ripped the pages out, folded them up, and put them in the pocket of her dress. She picked up the vial of black goo and gave it another look. Whatever it was, it was important to the governess, so she shoved it in her pocket along with the torn pages.

There was still no one else around, but that long hallway was surely too long for her to hear anyone coming. She ran to the door quietly but swiftly. Violet looked down the infinite corridor, but there was no sign anyone was coming. Violet didn't know when, or even if, she'd ever find a way out of this place, but whatever happened, she would do everything she could to protect those children.

Scanning the room one more time, Violet decided to check out the room on the other side of the laboratory. As she ran her fingers along the smooth surface of the metal steel desk, her hands shook. It reminded her of those old desks her teachers had when she was in high school. Every time she leaned on one when getting help from a teacher, they were always cold to the touch. But she didn't feel any of the expected coldness. She wondered briefly if this place had anything to do with that. The fire offered no heat, and the temperature had not chilled her.

The door was plain and unadorned. She grabbed the handle of the steel door and pushed. Beyond, the linoleum tiles continued uninterrupted in the room that appeared to be very nearly the same size, only their purposes differed. While the former was for experimentation and study, it was still a place to learn, no matter how horrendous it was. But this room was something else entirely. This was where the failures were stored. The room was simply cold storage.

Every wall was covered in banks of cold storage. Massive square refrigerator doors could only indicate one thing: This was a morgue. And at the center of the walls of coldness and death was a table, an autopsy table. Violet froze. Panic thrummed in every muscle as she prayed she didn't make a sound. The door she had entered through swooshed closed on its hinges. She cringed but silently thanked whatever god was listening that it was on a double swing hinge and didn't slam shut.

The governess lay on the table as if she were in a casket. Her fair skin made her look almost dead. She wore an elegant nightgown of black lace that left more of her skin exposed than she'd seen before. Like before, Violet couldn't see any blemish or scarring on her ivory skin. Her long shiny hair was spread out around her face in a halo of hair. It was all so perfect, almost as though she'd been staged. But just like always, she wore her mask. What could be so horrific that she'd prefer to sleep with the porcelain mask than risk anyone seeing her true face?

Violet watched the woman sleep, still afraid. She watched the governess's ribcage rise and fall in the soft rhythm of the sleeper. Luckily, her sudden appearance hadn't stirred the woman, so she took a brave step towards, and then again, and then closer still. It was a strange sensation to stand over some-one while they slept. It almost made Violet feel dirty, naughty, even. But again, Violet fell victim to her curiosity.

Violet couldn't help but wonder how the mask stayed on her face. She didn't see any ties or laces. Was it just stuck on by suction? Or could it be something else? Violet reached out towards the mask. She focused on where the soft porcelain edge of the mask met the woman's smooth skin along the line of her jaw. Her hand shook, her fingers quivering in the air. And then she brushed the mask with the softest touch she could manage. She leaned over the porcelain face the governess presented to her world and tenderly grasped either side of it. Taking a slow deep breath, she steadied her nerves before she would take that last step and give a little tug, just enough to pull the mask free without waking the governess.

"You should not be here," a familiar voice whispered from behind her.

18

Nguyen Widawski woke up to a beam of soft, warm light peeking through the break in the curtains pulled closed over the balcony doors. Her lower back was stiff, and her hips refused to obey her. But eventually, she managed to sit up. The blankets usually wrapped around Violet fell off the sofa as Nguyen stirred. She was one of the few people in that girl's life who knew the hardships she endured to keep what was left of her family together. It was cruel for a young person to struggle so early in life.

Unfortunately, she woke to no sign of Violet being home. Nguyen reached over to the nearby table to check her phone. Nothing. She frowned. Only a few times had the girl asked her to stay over, but just a handful. Violet was courteous, something you didn't see as much as you wanted in her generation, but it was always refreshing. She didn't like to burden others with something she considered her responsibility. But she'd never stayed away without calling or texting.

She stood up and stretched out her aging body before going to the bathroom to splash water on her face. Pillow creases crisscrossed her olive skin, but she ignored them. It was a price you paid for getting old, and these days, getting old was a privilege. After refreshing herself as best she could, she opened the door to Patience Brennan's room. The middle-aged woman was still sound asleep. Nguyen marveled at how normal she looked when she slept. She could almost imagine that she hadn't become sick, that she wasn't wasting away into nothing.

"Poor child," she said, thinking of Violet, wherever she was.

She padded through the small apartment to the kitchen and started the kettle. It was going to take at least one strong cup of tea to figure out what to do. The kettle hopped and popped merrily, and a stream of steam rushed out of its little spout as it clicked itself off. Just like in her own apartment, a small window was positioned over the sink, and she let her thoughts wander as she steeped the tea.

Her thoughts drifted back to the priest who had come by to talk to Violet. He was more pleasant and friendly than most priests she'd met. Could she go to him? Would he know where she might be? Nguyen didn't have the answers, but she couldn't shake a nagging sensation that something was wrong. Change was coming. Which in and of itself wasn't necessarily bad, but she usually had an accurate sense of these things and this didn't feel like it was anything good.

A soft thump coming from the other room told her Patience was awake. It would take effort to make sure the woman stayed calm once she realized Violet wasn't home. She knocked back the rest of her cup of tea and arched an eyebrow at the prospect of her upcoming battle with the nonsensical woman.

"Well, here we go," she announced to the empty room.

Almost two hours later, Nguyen had Patience dressed and fed and as calm as she was ever likely to be without having Violet to tend to her particular needs. She'd convinced the woman that a nice walk would do them good, and that was how she found herself staring up at St. Mary's. The gray stone building was imposing, but it somehow anchored the neighborhood. It was free of graffiti and mostly in good repair. It wasn't a pinnacle of the Catholic Church by any means, and seeing as it was tucked into a forgotten and impoverished neighborhood of the city, some disrepair was to be expected.

She wasn't particularly sure why she was here, though. Patience seemed to be silenced by the brooding building, but her higher-than-usual anxiety had her shifting her weight from one foot to the other. Perhaps she'd run into Father Benny, she thought. She didn't know what she was looking for, but any distraction for Patience would have been welcome. She held

Patience's hand as though she were a small child, and together, they mounted the concrete steps leading to the massive double doors of the church.

The church was everything she remembered. She didn't visit it often but had volunteered on occasion over the years, and it was somewhat comforting to see that some things in the world didn't change. Patience Brennan seemed entertained for the moment as well, shaking her head like a bobblehead as she tried to take in every detail of the cathedral. The insanely vaulted ceilings with carved statues of angels and saints tucked between the pillars holding the whole structure were enough to make anyone take a moment to absorb.

The wooden pews spread out on either side of the aisle ahead of them as they stood in the antechamber just within the doors. No Mass was going on, which she was thankful to have not interrupted, and the pews were mostly empty, except for a few parishioners kneeling. A nun stood near the front of the chapel, and Nguyen took Patience Brennan tenderly by the hand to approach her.

"Hello, excuse me," Nguyen said.

"May I help you?" the nun offered. The other woman's eyes scanned the odd couple that Nguyen and Patience were.

"Yes, please," she started, "we were wondering if Father Benny was available to speak with."

The woman gave her the most unusual look. She actually seemed to be perplexed by the question. This wasn't neuroscience, lady, so what's the deal? she thought.

"We were hoping to speak with him for a few minutes," Nguyen added. "I promise we won't take up much of his time."

"I don't un—" the nun began before a familiar voice interrupted her.

"It's all right, Sister, I'll take it from here," Father Benny announced as he adjusted his cleric collar. The nun scrutinized him even more than she did Nguyen, but he turned his attention to Nguyen and Patience.

"Mrs. Widawski, how are you today?" he asked as he guided them back the way they'd come. Nguyen let her feet follow the priest's lead, but she looked back to see the nun speaking to another nun, both of whom were glancing in her direction. Maybe today was just going to be a weird day, she thought.

"I'm a little concerned, actually,"

"I can see that," he offered with a sympathetic smile. "I haven't been introduced to your companion?"

"This, this is Patience Brennan, Father." His eyebrows raised almost imperceptibly.

"Violet's mother," he said, giving Patience a small bow of his head. But she stared at him in her funny way. He smiled kindly at her before bringing his attention back to Nguyen. "Let's go for a walk, and you can tell me what's on your mind."

As cordial as he was, it didn't sound like a suggestion. For some reason, he didn't seem to want to stay at the church.

They were out of the foyer and down the steps before she found her words.

"I'm worried, Father."

"What about, Mrs. Widawski?" As they walked along the sidewalk, Father Benny arranged himself so that he was on the street side and Patience walked between them. Nguyen appreciated that he comprehended some of Patience's needs. She looked over at Violet's mother and hoped the conversation about to happen wouldn't set her off. Patience seemed blissfully unaware of anything that wasn't as it should be.

"She didn't come home last night."

"Has she ever done that before?" he asked. Nguyen shook her head. "It'll be all right, Mrs. Widawski. I'll help in any way I can."

"Thank you."

"She's a special young woman."

"That she is, Father," she agreed.

"Are you able to tell me any more about her circumstances? Anything about what has happened to her family?"

Nguyen did her best to tell Violet's story, but it felt shallow. How did you explain the death of a father to someone? Everyone had their own sentiments about their father. Some reminisce with lighthearted joy, while others only knew suffering. The significance of fathers ran deep, especially to little girls. It's often extolled that young women end up marrying someone like their father, though Nguyen put little thought into that. Her husband was nothing like her own father.

But Violet was different. Violet and her father doted on each other. Yes, Violet and her mother shared much, but a common passion for art and creativity was not enough to forge bonds. Father Benny's face was full of compassion. His brows cinched at every pain point in Violet's young life.

"And after his passing," he asked delicately, "that is when her mother started to deteriorate?"

"Yes," Nguyen said, "like I said last night, her doctors all think it's early-onset Alzheimer's, but I think they're wrong."

"I'm inclined to agree with you. Modern science still doesn't hold any stock to the physical toll of a broken heart."

"Yes!" she exclaimed, startling Patience out of her peace.

"Where's Violet?" Patience demanded. Nguyen couldn't tell her the truth. It would crush the woman and send her into one of her fits. The last thing she needed was for Patience to mourn the mysterious loss of her daughter.

"It's all right, Patience. She just has to work."

"I want Violet. Where's Violet?" Patience stammered. Nguyen tried to calm her, but Father Benny interjected.

"Violet is very kind, isn't she?" he asked in a caring voice. His unusual accent distracted the agitated woman enough to stare at him.

"You sound funny," Patience said.

"Oh, Patience, that's not very nice."

"It's all right." He laughed. "I do sound funny, don't I?" Patience nodded like a solemn child.

"I was born in a different country. Can you believe that?" he said as though it were a shocking declaration. As they continued conversing, Patience was enthralled with the priest, and Nguyen welcomed the man's adeptness and soothing presence around Patience.

They had walked all the way around the block and had come full circle. St. Mary's loomed over them, but Patience was happy again, and Nguyen was glad they'd spent time with Father Benny. He genuinely cared about Violet and her unfortunate circumstances. The girl needed as many allies as she could get, Nguyen thought. Sooner rather than later, caring for her mother would no longer be tenable. She didn't relish that thought. It would crush Violet. And yet, that day was approaching quickly.

Nguyen and Father Benny discussed a plan for helping Violet, the first of which was to call each other the moment she came home. She also agreed to call him tomorrow if she still hadn't heard anything from her, and he reassured her Violet was a strong young woman and that she would be okay. Nguyen thanked him for his time and assistance and decided it was probably time she got Patience home.

When they reached the outside of their apartment, an attractive man dressed all in black was leaning against the wall.

"Hello," the stranger said.

If she was being honest with herself, he looked like temptation incarnate. But he didn't bother them any more than that. Nguyen put the strange man out of her mind and focused her energy on Patience.

But as she led Violet's mother upstairs, she couldn't help but feel the day carried with it a bad aftertaste. Something was wrong, and she couldn't do anything about it. Nguyen looked back over her shoulder as she mounted the stairs. She couldn't see the man from outside, but she squinted her face at him in concern. He was probably just a hoodlum, but Nguyen worried anyway. Violet's absence felt like some dark pretense of worse things to come.

19

"YOU SHOULD NOT BE here," a familiar voice whispered from behind her.

Violet nearly jumped out of her skin. She turned around and saw Evelyn standing in the doorway with a look of utter shock on her face. All the remaining color drained out of the young girl's face, and Violet froze.

What now? Evelyn gave her a twitchy sign that was hard to misinterpret. It was time to leave if Violet cared anything for her own self-preservation. She had come so close to knowing what the governess was hiding. So close and yet miles away. But something inside her told her she should trust the young girl. Maybe it was because she managed to survive this long? Maybe the girl knew something Violet didn't. Whatever the reason, she reluctantly decided she'd better do as the girl suggested. She let go of her grip on the mask, her curiosity screaming with dissatisfaction.

She slowly stepped away from the autopsy table and the beautiful figure of the governess, turning to give Evelyn her full attention. As she moved to approach Evelyn, her hand was caught. Before rotating to see what new dread had latched onto her, she could see the fear on Evelyn's face. Her eyes grew wider, and her lips quivered. With that, Violet turned back to see what she already knew. The governess's hand was wrapped around Violet's wrist so tightly that the skin around the woman's icy fingers blanched.

It didn't matter how quiet or stealthy she had been, for Violet knew the instant those cold fingers wrapped around her wrist that she'd made a poor decision on her part. She had been stupid enough to come into her space and then made an even more foolish attempt to unearth the woman's secrets. Violet realized how narcissistic that was. How vain could she be to think she had a right to this woman's secrets? Katherine had been trapped here by the same crazy magic that she had, but it was worse for the governess. Violet was certain her own entrapment was an accident. She'd only met Father Benny that day, so no malice was budding between them. But for Katherine, it had been a brutal betrayal.

Time stopped. Evelyn and Violet stood there, caught in the claws of fear, waiting to see what would happen next. Violet didn't know what to do. Was it possible to pry the woman's fingers off and make a run for it, or did she wait to see what the governess did next? Violet stared at the beautiful body lying on the autopsy table, dressed in an elegant black lace nightgown that would have made Morticia Addams jealous. Alabaster skin reached out from beneath her mask, draped taught over the muscles and tendons of her sensuous neck, following the curves of her breasts.

Her own deadly curiosity caught her, sticking her between the desire to look beneath the mask and the urge to flee. The governess's head twitched, and a sleepy groan escaped from between the lips of the beautiful nightmare. Yet Violet was still rooted to the ground.

"Now!" Evelyn hissed at Violet. "You must leave now!" Evelyn launched into action when Violet didn't move. She grabbed her free hand and pulled at the governess's fingers to release their hold on her. Once free, she followed Evelyn out of the room full of macabre refrigerators and through the laboratory. The spell of curiosity that gripped her was gone. Fear and panic rushed in to fill the void like a torrent of water bursting through a causeway.

"Please, you must go," Evelyn told her.

The two of them stood in the laboratory's doorway. The threshold between the laboratory and the implausibly long corridor beyond was a frightening tween place. Violet knelt so that she was at eye level with the girl.

"I'm not leaving you here."

"You must, miss,"

"I won't," Violet declared. She wrapped her arms around the slender child. She didn't know how to get herself home or if it was even possible. Until that day came, though, she'd protect these children from the governess. "I won't let her hurt you."

"It's all right, miss," Evelyn mumbled into Violet's embrace. "She needs me."

"Are you sure?"

The door to the mortuary opened, smooth and quiet. The motion tickled at the edge of her periphery. Doom and despair bubbled up from primal depths in the glassy reflections of Evelyn's eyes. Their heads swiveled to face the nightmare standing in the doorway. The brightly lit space, in stark contrast with the Gothic arches of the laboratory, set the alluring presence of Lady Katherine at odds with her surroundings.

"Get away from her," the governess said in a low growl.

Violet stood up and pushed Evelyn behind her, serving as a barrier between the young girl and the governess. "No."

"I was not speaking to you."

"I'm not letting you hurt her anymore!"

A gentle tug on Violet's dress caught her attention, so she turned back to Evelyn.

"She won't hurt me, miss," Evelyn whispered.

"I can't, Evelyn. I won't!"

"It is not up to you," the governess said, her voice low and beautifully dangerous.

"Stay the hell away from her!"

"Please go, miss, she won't hurt me," Evelyn pleaded.

"Are you sure?"

"Yes, I am certain, now go!" Evelyn said.

"You should listen to her," Lady Katherine said, "and stop meddling in affairs you know nothing about."

"What's wrong with you?" Violet demanded, but the governess simply laughed. It was low and sultry and made Violet's stomach twist into knots.

"You stand there judging me when you know nothing about me or what being in this place has done to me." Lady Katherine's masked face dipped menacingly. Violet was reminded of predators in the wild. The governess was on the hunt, and she had her prey in her sight.

"Please, just go," Evelyn pleaded.

Violet didn't know what to do. She didn't want to abandon Evelyn to Lady Katherine's shifting moods. There was no way these children would still be in her care if she physically hurt them, but some of the worst trauma was not something other people could see. It wasn't worn like a shirt or a pair of shoes but lurked on the inside. It slithered around your happiness and successes like possessed entrails. Violet turned around and took Evelyn's angelic face in her hands.

"You come and find me as soon as you can."

"I promise."

And with that, Violet pulled herself to her full height. She met the gaze of the porcelain mask and refused to hide her rage at the circumstances.

"If you hurt her, I'll make sure you can't ever hurt anyone again."

"Promises, promises." The governess chuckled. "You are as powerless as I am."

Violet turned her back to the governess and made her way down the long corridor to the stairs. She held her back straight and her head high, carrying all the courage and bravado she could even though she was a crying, terrified child on the inside. She wanted to run, but the way Lady Katherine laughed made her realize she was right. Violet didn't know anything about her. She only knew the small parts of the story the governess had shared with her.

She walked along the corridor in measured steps. Her fear ebbed away with each step, only to be replaced by hate and anger. The children were forced to live in fear every day, and Lady Katherine was taking out her frustration on the only companions she had. Violet hadn't been this angry since her dad died. She did not know what she was going to do, but she needed to get these children away from their governess.

Violet approached the mouth of the steep stairwell that led out of this nightmare within a nightmare. The florescent lights flickered and hummed, casting the corridor in strobes of opposing garish light and deep-set shadows. She turned back the way she'd come and wondered if Evelyn was all right. Remembering that Evelyn told her William was waiting for her, she turned back and climbed. She left behind the disjointed contradiction of the laboratory and morgue behind her. Violet exhaled Mary Shelley's *Frankenstein*, and as she ascended towards William, she inhaled *Crimson Peak*.

She could only affect what change was in her power, and right then, William needed her just as much as Evelyn did. The boy's shadowy figure stood at the top of the stairs, wrapped in the comforting glow of the fireplace behind him.

"Did she find you?" he asked. Violet nodded. "She will be safe, but you won't be if we don't hide you."

"I don't understand, William. What do you mean?"

"You don't need to understand. You just need to hide."

"But I don't know this place like you do. I don't know where we could hide that she couldn't find us."

"I do." He took her hand and laced his fingers with hers before pulling her away from the governess's space. As they walked, Violet turned back one more time to see the door close softly behind them. No one was there to close it—it just closed. Facing William, she wondered if she'd misjudged everything around her. Maybe it wasn't *all* the governess's doing. She was moody and dangerous, that much was true.

Violet let William guide her through the house, but as they took to the stairs ascending away from the great hall, she heard the metallic click of the door to the governess's rooms latch shut.

Ice trickled down her spine at the thought of Evelyn being trapped down there with Lady Katherine.

"This way," William said from over his shoulder.

"Where are we going?" Violet whispered.

"Trust me."

Violet had no other option than to trust the boy. She didn't particularly like him, but that was probably based more on his entitled attitude than anything else. Up the stairs they went, and rather than turning right to go towards all their rooms, he guided them left. When William stopped at a closed door, she was very confused.

"William?"

"She won't look in here for us," he said as he opened the door. In one confident move, he pulled her into a small closet and closed the door behind them, just in time. William pulled her down until they were both sitting on the floor. Clothes pressed against her, but Violet couldn't see them. Darkness smothered them.

"Shh," he said as the sound of running feet thundered past the door they hid behind. The space closed in on her. The candles offered so little light in the hallway, and with the storm ceaselessly raging outside, she couldn't see her hand before her face. The dim light through the gap under the door was only enough to let Violet see the shadow of a figure run by, and then another.

Good for her, Violet thought, as little Evelyn evaded the governess's chase. But there was nothing she or William could do but keep each other safe. So, she held her breath, listening to the sounds beyond the closed door, beyond the darkness. Violet hoped for Evelyn to escape the tyranny of the jaded and bitter governess.

A shriek of pain echoed through the manor. It was high-pitched, like an animal, and unyielding. Violet couldn't hide away from a sound that terrifying. She flung open the door, washing away the darkness, and stood in the middle of the hallway.

Where had they gone? What was the governess doing to Evelyn? Another scream ripped through the silence that muffled everything in this bizarre world. It was so ethereal and poignant that Violet covered her ears against it. While it hurt to listen to the pain in her voice, it was enough to tell her where the girl was. So, Violet was forced to make an impossible decision. Did she save herself, or did she run towards certain doom and save the girl?

20

So much of Violet's life had been shaped by circumstances outside of her control. The people she loved continued to be ripped away from her. How did someone decide whether to save themselves or save another? Was it flight or fight? Or was it something more sinister? Her mind floundered through all the stories she'd absorbed in her life, flipping through them like pages in a book. Violet thought about all the heroic characters and cravens alike, wondering how many times they had the choice to run away.

She didn't want to be one of those people who left someone hanging in a lurch. She wanted people to depend on her. How many other people her age would've chosen to live the life she had? Not many, that's for sure. But she didn't know how to quit. She didn't know how to abandon people relying on her for help. That was when she'd made up her mind. That was when she ran towards the danger. Towards the fear.

I must help her, she thought. I can't just leave her there alone with the governess. She couldn't save her dad, she couldn't fix her mom, but she could help this one person. The agonizing screams pierced the solitude of the manor and stabbed daggers into her heart. Unyielding was the song of anguish. The cries rose and fell like a melody of pain. She ached to save Evelyn from whatever despair Lady Katherine had in store for her.

The hallway, with its richly stained wood, elegant wallpaper, and expensive rugs, painted a portrait of wealth and good breeding. But ugliness could be covered up, dressed up. The shadows that grew and shrank in the flickering light of the candles and sconces reminded her that darkness was everywhere if she wasn't careful to stay in the light.

But Violet didn't know how to survive in the light. Tragedy had shaped her life. She ran along the hallway, towards the girl and the monster. In her wake, the candles flickered, and the shadows danced, reaching out towards Violet like leeches stretching their black bodies out towards the sustenance of blood.

Violet slammed against the door to Evelyn's bedroom and tried the knob, but the door was locked. She pounded on the door and angrily wrestled with the knob, turning this way and that, but to no avail.

"William," she called out. "William, come help me. I can't get the door open!" Behind the solid wood, she could hear the struggle. She desperately desired to reach the girl. Violet pounded on the door with her fists. "Evelyn! Evelyn, I'm here, I'm right here." Tears rolled down her cheeks.

Behind Violet, still standing near the open door to the closet where they had hidden away, William watched. His head slanted at an impossible angle. William's smile grew with his hunger as he sensed the nearness of his meal. He was so hungry. He had survived for so long on so little. He wanted to feed, to feast, to gorge on the buffet that had so carelessly stepped into their prison.

William's smile grew and grew, more and more. His lips parted, and he stepped forward, wondering if she understood how hungry he was. But the girl didn't even realize the danger she was in.

William stepped forward again, closer. He could smell her fear. It turned the air acrid and cloying. William salivated. He still remembered what it was like to feast on the flesh of humans. He was so close to having a proper meal, but she was flailing about, trying to get through the door. Evelyn was behind that door, and if the beautiful noise coming from within was anything to indicate, then she was enjoying her own feast. She was feeding while he was out here starving. William had had just about enough of that. His sister had always been the stronger one, the smarter one, but she had one failing. She was too cautious. It was time to make a bolder move, for him to take her place.

He released his disguise. Taking one step and then another, coming closer to his meal ticket, he could feel his strength returning at just the mere thought of tasting Violet's blood. Bone and tendon shattered and snapped, the skeleton within crumbling. The false form he wore melted, starting at the feet and working up as he slithered towards the unsuspecting girl, her aura bright and enticing. All along the corridor, the shadows too weak to take any form other than shadow hissed and whispered. "Feast," they called out. "Feast, for we cannot."

VIOLET POUNDED ON THE door, but she couldn't force it open. She dropped to her knees and looked through the keyhole. What she saw stopped her heart and sickened her. Through her limited panorama beyond the keyhole, she saw that Evelyn's room stretched out beyond, the dolls tossed on the floor, forgotten to fear. The governess and Evelyn were wrapping their hands around each other's throats. The two of them locked in a strained dance of phantasmagoria and pleasure. Each of their faces twisted in their efforts against death and survival.

An impossible cloud of mist and delicate blue light swirled around and between them, weaving arcs of something mystical together. It bound them in a mockery of a compassionate embrace. Their mouths were open, contorted by pain and fear and hate. The once-delicate skin of their lips was pulled back, making them look like they were snarling at each other.

The governess was sucking the very life out of Evelyn. Violet tried to understand what was happening. This prison painting was holding them captive, yes, but then Violet realized something that her mind had been trying to put into words this whole time. This place was sucking the life out of them all, herself included.

She had to get out of this place, but she wouldn't leave without the children. She pounded on the door again, but it wouldn't budge. Violet backed up and tried to kick the door. The attempt was useless with these fancy shoes. If she had her boots on, maybe she'd get past the door.

While the screams continued, Violet looked for anything that could help her. She didn't see William. Darkness had swallowed up most of the hallway behind her. He hadn't come to her calls, but she couldn't blame him. She was terrified, and William was probably still tucked away in that closet, hoping no one would come looking for him with all this chaos happening. Though, William's disappearance made it easier for her to focus on the immediate problem at hand. She wished she could hide with him, but Evelyn needed help first.

The corridor was uncluttered, other than some rugs to cover the bare wooden floors and a few nearby tables. The table nearest her was small, but an oil lamp was flickering away on it, along with a small stack of books and a bronze bust of some unknown dude with a rather judgmental expression on his face.

Approaching the table, she picked up the bust, which was heavy and solid—exactly what she was hoping for. Violet ran back to the door, and with both hands gripping it, she hammered it down on the doorknob. Nothing happened. She repeated the action again and again until the doorknob broke away and clattered to the floor. Then she slammed the heavy bust into the exposed workings of the doorknob. The action sent the pieces of metal flying into the room beyond, and the door unlatched, opening on its own. Violet tossed the bronze bust aside with a thud and shouldered her way into the room.

Behind her, the shadows screamed and thrashed to reach her, but the violent outbursts coming from Evelyn's room drowned them out. They were so hungry that they clambered over each other to get to her. They gnawed and snapped at each other, so hungry they could eat anything. The meat of a shadow was an insubstantial nourishment. It only had enough substance to kill the living. William's torso still resembled the human child he'd emulated for centuries, but it dissolved into a sticky shadow as it crawled along the floor. Bones breaking, viscera sliding around the gristle and tendons that remained. His mouth stretched open as his human form dissolved into shadow, gliding across the flooring toward Violet.

An impossibly gruesome and violent end reached out for Violet, for its first feast in over a century. But his prey stumbled into the room beyond the door, into Evelyn's room, slipping just out of William's reach. His jaws snapped, and a growl poured out of his mouth. His hunger raged. His rage churned.

William had been a breath away from devouring Violet and all the goodness within her. He vowed to himself and his far-off master he would feast on her before he spent another cursed century in this hellish prison. If he had to, he'd set this place ablaze with fury while dreaming of the decadent sensation of his teeth grinding against her bones and his tongue working at her delicious flesh. He would craft himself a throne from her bones and lick his fingertips as the fire danced in every corner of this painting.

But first, he would have to catch her.

21

Violet stumbled into the room, a tumbleweed of silk and lace. She offered no grace or composure, but at least she was on her feet. The blankets on the bed had been tossed about as Evelyn and Lady Katherine fought. Their hands clawed at each other, and they snarled and screamed as though their very touch was acid on each other's skin. If she'd understood any of the forces at play in this nightmare world, she would've been afraid, but all she saw was a child being attacked. So she reacted on pure instinct.

She launched herself onto the bed with her arms outstretched and tried to push the two enemies apart. Her anger and fear at what was happening right in front of her diminished slightly.

"No!" the governess screamed. The sound was so shrill that Violet thought her ears were going to explode.

Her body flinched at the auditory assault, but she managed to hold her ground. Violet threw her entire body into the governess, sending the woman careening off the bed. The governess slid across the floor and slammed into the wall. Though Lady Katherine lay there in a heap, unmoving, the fight wasn't over. One good blow wasn't enough to take out a woman who had spent a hundred years in this prison. She was a survivor, but so was Violet. She took the moment to turn around and check on Evelyn.

"Are you okay?" Violet asked.

"I am now," the girl answered. She should have taken a moment to really look at the girl, but she whipped back around to give the governess her full attention. Lady Katherine groaned from across the room. Her long hair had come undone and hung over her face. The lithe body of the governess twitched as she awoke from the brink of unconsciousness.

The governess unfolded herself from a heap on the floor. The soft curls of her hair against the exquisite fabric of her dress were at odds with the true nightmare she was. As she brought herself to her full height, the beautiful mask slowly turned to face Violet. She no longer wanted to know what was behind it. She'd already thought the worst. Violet's mind tumbled with ideas of *Dorian Gray* and the twisted monster revealed in his portrait, a symbol of all the evil he'd committed worn upon his body like scars.

"What the hell is wrong with you?!" Violet screamed.

"You don't understand," the governess said hoarsely.

"Don't let her get me," Evelyn pleaded from behind Violet.

The governess shuddered at the girl's words.

"You don't understand," Lady Katherine said with a gravelly voice. Her hand instinctively went to her throat. Violet would be lying if she said she didn't enjoy studying the governess's injuries, which were proof of her mortality. No matter what happened, she could feel pain. And if she could be hurt, then she could possibly be killed.

Lady Katherine stumbled forward. "She is dangerous."

"She's a child," Violet threw back at her. The governess offered Violet a laugh filled with pity and sadness. Evelyn wrapped her arms around Violet's waist.

"Get your hands off her," the woman shrieked.

"Come and make me!" Violet challenged.

It was all the governess needed. She charged at Violet in a rage, screaming at her like a banshee. Her dress flew out around her, giving her the silhouette of a bat. Hair and arms flailed about, and Violet's skin burned as nails raked across her body. She screamed but battled on. No matter how much her heart burned to protect the girl, though, she felt her spirit waning. She had no energy. The governess stretched forward, screaming the entire time for her to let go.

"Release her, beast," the governess howled. "Release her."

Violet's body twisted around the governess, pulling on the woman with all her strength as she tried desperately to get her away from the girl. Lady Katherine's hand reached violently around Violet, her hands curled into claws, the tendons and muscles in her arms and neck straining to reach Evelyn.

A sinister voice whispered along the edges of the violence, barely audible over the pounding of Violet's heart beating and her haggard breath.

"She is mine."

Violet froze. Time stood still for a heartbeat before the governess's head twisted around to face her own. Violet desired to see beneath the mask, for she couldn't tell what the woman was feeling without being able to see her expression, her eyes. All she knew in that sinking moment was that the voice did not belong to Lady Katherine. Violet and Katherine both turned to Evelyn, who sat there with such an expression of hate and something else that Violet couldn't quite place. Violet's blood curdled right there in her veins.

"What the—"

But Violet's question was cut short as something grabbed her ankle and ripped her off the bed, away from the other two.

"NO!" Evelyn yelled. The sound was so inhuman, so vulgar, that all of Violet's ideas of what was going on shattered into a million pieces. The grip on her ankle made her skin burn with pain. She thrashed around to see what had a hold of her and found herself face-to-face with a true nightmare. What was left of William's angelic young face was swallowed up by a wriggling, writhing mass of blackness. The inky pool moved in ways it shouldn't, and it hurt her mind to look at it. The shadow monster curled around her body, squeezing her and gnawing at her. William's face opened up, stretching into a mouth that could swallow her head whole.

"I'm so hungry, Sister," William replied, but the voice coming from the blackness made her skin crawl. It was wrong in every way. It wasn't human. If William wasn't human, if he was here trying to actually eat her, what was Evelyn? Was she human? Or was she something else, something dangerous?

Violet struggled against the beast as it squeezed the life out of her, its teeth gnawing on her flesh, but its grip was too tight. Its strength was unimaginable. Violet needed help, any help. She turned away from the horror of the gruesome remnants of William and the blood seeping out of her wounds. Violet tried to reach for Evelyn, but she sat still, fuming with hatred for her brother. The girl had kept up her disguise for so long, but the charade was lost in her rage. Evelyn screamed at her brother with a mouth that stretched beyond what it should. Violet wanted to curl up and pull away in revulsion, but there was nowhere for her to go. She couldn't pull away from William.

"She's mine!" Evelyn howled.

Violet had turned to the girl for help but was staring at another nightmare. There was no time to make sense of it. If she couldn't wrench herself free from William's clutches, then none of it mattered.

Out of nowhere, an outstretched hand landed in her vision. The governess had extended herself out towards Violet while Evelyn was clawing at her. What had happened? Was her enemy offering her help against the children Violet had been trying to protect? She didn't understand any of it, but she wouldn't reject the offer.

She pulled an arm free from the shadow beast's grip and clambered to reach Lady Katherine's outstretched hand. Wrist to wrist, the women latched on to each other, their very lives depending on it. As the governess pulled against the strength of the monster that used to be William and his sharp teeth, Violet struggled to free herself. The crimson against her fair skin startled her, but she persisted.

Violet turned back to the mask of the governess, hoping to see the woman's face. Even the horrific scars of whatever haunted her past would be a gift of hope in this hopeless moment. The governess's grip was stronger than she expected, lending a supernatural quality to the mysterious and terrifying woman. The two women pulled and tugged, twisted and howled, against the gnashing and gnawing of the monster attempting to drain her will to continue.

Violet lost herself in the battle to merely survive. The haunted manor around her faded into the distance, her only companions fear and pain. But nightmares were always more than just fear or simple pain. Nightmares were the truth you were afraid to see, and at that moment, she was vulnerable to the worst that this prison offered.

FOR A FEW HEARTBEATS, Evelyn couldn't decide between the tempting meal of the fresh flesh she craved or protecting her brother from losing himself to his hunger. But in the infinite space between heartbeats, Evelyn decided that blood was worth more than a passing meal.

She howled against her own rage, her nostrils flared, her temper convulsing violently, sending ripples of concussion waves through the space. A trickle of blood seeped out of the coils of Violet's ears, but she refused to let go of her grip on the governess. Evelyn screamed, reaching across the short distance, and clawed at Violet and Lady Katherine's outstretched hands.

Evelyn was different from her brother in many respects. The most important that she was patient and intelligent. She stopped fighting at the clasped hands of the two women and grew very still. William mindlessly gnawed on Violet's body, and the governess's face twitched at the sudden incongruity of Evelyn's behavior. It was just the opening Evelyn needed.

She threw her arms out at her enemy. Evelyn's clawed hands shook with power and intention, and her mouth, open in a silent scream, sucked all the air from the room.

***

Violet couldn't breathe. The air in the room was crushing her, her vision quaking, all her life force draining out of her. Her vision dimmed as her vigor was replaced with an overwhelming need to sleep. Waves of power blew outward from the monster child. Meanwhile, Lady Katherine's grip on Violet faltered.

And then something happened that truly surprised Violet. William's teeth released her flesh. Her skin clung slightly to the sharp daggers in his mouth before popping loose. It was an uncomfortable sensation, but she put that aside as she realized he was letting go.

Whatever Evelyn was doing to Lady Katherine, it was affecting her brother too. A storm howled outside the confines of the manor and within the walls of that very room. Violet's hair came loose from the ornate braids Evelyn had twisted only a few hours ago, a few hours that felt like days. Her skin hurt in the tempest, and she fought to stay upright against the wind. Yet the governess held her ground.

Violet crawled, to help in any way, but she kept slipping in her own blood. William was still mostly a foul shadow beast, pooling and thrumming against the storm. What was left of his once-angelic face examined his sister. His brows were furrowed. Was the monster worried?

But there was no more time to consider that thought. The governess was flung through the air and across the room and slammed into the wall. Her impact dented and cracked the wall, and the wallpaper peeled, draping over Lady Katherine's crumpled body.

Howling winds and pulsating air no longer pounded against all of Violet's senses. At the end of such chaos, everyone froze in place, unsure of what to do next. None of them knew what new danger lay in the silence, or the almost silence.

The only sound in the room was an ominous humming. It was an unearthly sound that filled the air with grief and fear. Violet didn't understand what it was at first, and then she saw it. There, in the middle of the room, between where the governess lay in a heap and where Violet crouched, was the porcelain mask, spinning like a top. Its pace slowed, and then, as though to settle the dispute, the mask stopped and tumbled sideways, an awkward move almost reminiscent of a fair maiden fainting. The beautiful mask hit the floor and shattered into hundreds of pieces.

22

Shards of porcelain skittered across the floor, filling the room with eerie music. To Violet's ears, it was like fine crystal rain falling on the glass roof of the arboretum. Lady Katherine stirred, groaning in pain. She pulled her arms out from under her, pushing herself up off the floor. Her long hair hung in her face, obscuring her emotion from the others in the room. The governess was halfway to righting herself when she screamed, sending a shiver rattling the vertebrae in Violet's spine.

Her screams mimicked the cries of a baby, each one having its unique pitch. There were the brief screams of being startled and the cackles of being tickled. There was joy piercing the air with a happy squeal, and there were even the screams of heartbreak warbling through the air with sorrow. But that scream, this was more. The screams of the governess were that of fear. No, not fear. It was terror. It was primal and untempered.

Lady Katherine's terror was palpable, sliding down the back of Violet's throat and leaving a trail of pity in its wake.

The woman scuttled back against the wall to get away from everyone. She buried her face in her hands. Meanwhile, Evelyn sat on the bed, relaxed with the self-satisfied smirk of a bully. She may not have gotten what she wanted, but she struck a near-crippling blow to her enemy. Her brother was pulling his form back together, and Violet tried her best to ignore the nightmarish image of flesh and shadow reconstituting itself into a passing human form. The sounds of flesh and bone and other things she couldn't put a name to churned. Her revulsion twisted, and bile lurked at the back of her mouth.

Violet panted and shook. Her body was still in the throes of a full onslaught of endorphins and adrenaline. Only a few moments ago, she was certain she was going to die. At that moment, she was completely bewildered. Her ideas of who was in charge, her protector from evil, and who her enemy was had been turned upside down. But it wasn't Lady Katherine who had her teeth buried into Violet's skin, and it wasn't Lady Katherine who had summoned a storm of vitriol and hate.

Violet gathered whatever nerve she still had and crawled along the floor, leaving a trail of bloody handprints. She stopped right in front of the governess, the woman she'd been so worried was harming the children. It was impossible to imagine that this terrified simpering creature had once inspired such fear. There was only one thing left to do.

Violet reached out her quaking arms towards the woman, pushing her fear away. There wasn't time for it anymore. Someone needed to take control, and it was either herself or those monsters disguised as children. She knew which way she'd go.

The governess quaked, so Violet touched her gently on her shoulders. The older woman flinched beneath her hands, but at least her screaming stopped.

"It's ok now," Violet offered.

Lady Katherine shook her head. "No." Her voice was hoarse from the fight.

"Please, Lady Katherine," Violet pressed, "let me help."

The governess shook her head again, but this time with less ferocity. Violet knew from her own experience that a kind voice was sometimes enough. Violet reached up and caressed the woman's wrists with the tenderness of handling a fallen chick. As she pulled Lady Katherine's hands down, away from her face, she thought the worst. Her imagination ran rampant, with the storm always raging outside, the creepy manor house, and the children who were never what they seemed—it all played into her building fear.

Violet was afraid. If she were being honest with herself, she was always afraid. She feared losing her mom to the disease devouring her true self, her personality. Violet feared what would become of herself when the day finally came to have her mom institutionalized, or even something worse. There always seemed to be something worse waiting beyond the horizon of each day. But of all the things her mind had conjured, what she came face-to-face with was nothing like what she'd been expecting.

The governess eventually quit struggling against Violet and let her hands fall into her lap. Violet pulled a tendril of the governess's hair away from her face and tucked it tenderly behind her ear.

"I'm here. I'll help any way I can," Violet said.

Lady Katherine brought her face up and met Violet's gaze. To Violet's surprise, the woman's face was beautiful. She looked like she could be the same age as Violet. Her skin was smooth and youthful and matched the porcelain color of the mask lying shattered in pieces all around them. There were no scars, no deformities, just something so beautiful that it wouldn't have surprised her if she had been the inspiration behind a Greek sculpture or a muse to humanity's greatest painters.

Violet sat back on her haunches, completely bewildered. "I don't understand. Your mask? All the mirrors?"

"In a few decades, you'll understand all too well."

"But you're so beautiful!"

"For a hundred years, I have looked the same. My skin is just as it was when I was put in this horrible place. No wrinkles to show that I've grown older. Each day I spend here seeing my unchanged reflection in the mirrors threatens to push me into insanity."

"My life has been nothing but change," Violet confessed.

"That is its own curse, I suppose."

"I was dealt one bad hand after another. All I've ever really wanted was a little stability. How funny."

"I don't see the humor in any of this."

"No, not funny like that, funny strange," Violet explained.

"How so?"

"The grass really is greener on the other side."

"Ovid," the governess said thoughtfully.

"Um, bless you?"

"Ovid, he was a Greek poet. He had opined that the harvest is always richer in another man's field."

"Oh," Violet said.

"It matters not when one is drowning in the madness of it all. I was slowly going mad. One night, I had a terrible nightmare. I had become one of the statues in the arboretum. My flesh turned to stone. Everything around me was growing and changing, but I was trapped forever to remain as I was."

"What did you do?"

"Well, I'll admit I had a bit of a fit," the governess said sheepishly. "When I awoke, I ran around the manor covering up every mirror I could find."

Violet looked at the governess, finally seeing the real woman in front of her. She wasn't some villain written into the story for the sake of the protagonist. Lady Katherine was just an ordinary girl who fell in love with the wrong guy. Violet couldn't condemn her for any of that. She wondered about her own sanity. What would she be like after a hundred years of being trapped here with those monsters?

Lady Katherine looked down at the remains of the mask she had worn to protect what was left of her mind, of her sanity. Each one of the shards was a perilous reminder this place wasn't meant for humans—it was meant for monsters. Violet heard pieces of porcelain crunch from behind her, so she whipped her head around to see Evelyn walking carelessly on the shards.

The girl joined her brother, who was still pulling himself back together into the shape of a human boy. While she lifted William up onto his feet, Violet couldn't seem to make her brain agree with what her eyes were seeing. Her heart, on the other hand, knew the right of it. It knew that in the quiet after a battle, there was still danger.

A trail of black footsteps covered the ground where Evelyn's feet had been, rather than pools of brilliant red blood. The black pools of shadow reflected no light. They absorbed it, like a black hole threatening her universe. Violet didn't need reminding that Evelyn and William were not children. The charade of innocence had been whipped away by the storm of magic that had erupted in the bedroom and the bite marks on her flesh.

William leaned on his sister. They seemed drained, but Violet didn't want to stick around to find out how long it would take them before they tried to kill her again. She stood up, hooked an arm under Lady Katherine's, and helped the woman to her feet. Katherine seemed to be wiped out as well. Violet couldn't imagine how much effort it had taken to keep Evelyn at bay. The governess leaned into Violet, and together, they faced the malevolent children.

Out of the corner of her eye, Violet thought she caught movement. But she didn't want to show any sort of weakness in front of the enemy. If she managed to survive this, then there would be time to relax, but that moment was not the time. She let her glance drift towards the movement as inconspicuously as she could. What she saw made her heart sink. The ominous inky footprints left in Evelyn's wake rippled and twitched. Evelyn was apparently just like her brother. She only held herself together better. But what the hell did that mean? Was she really the same as him, or was she something else entirely? Violet didn't want to stick around to find out.

The tension was palpable, and fear weighed heavy over everything. Just a few short strides across the room was the door. It was open. Violet bit her lower lip as she tried to think of a way to get safely away from the children without them blocking her path.

But something happened that she didn't expect. Lady Katherine turned herself around to face Violet, putting herself between Violet and the children. With her hands on Violet's shoulders to help hold her upright, she forced herself to stand tall. Her figure blocked the children from view.

"Violet," she whispered, "I want you to go to the arboretum."

"Why?"

"Something there can help."

"What do you mean?"

"Don't question me." The look in her eyes brooked no dissent. She wasn't asking. She was ordering Violet to comply.

"You'll be with me?" Violet asked.

"I will give you as much time as I can."

Violet realized what the governess was saying. She was going to literally put herself between Violet and the children, meaning she would sacrifice herself to help Violet get away. But what good was that going to do her? Violet was still going to be trapped in this place with them.

"But—"

"No, enough. You'll understand when you get there."

"I'm not leaving you here with them," Violet argued.

"Do you remember the lovely stroll we took through the arboretum when you first arrived?" the governess asked.

"What are you talking about?"

"Our salvation depends on you doing what you do best." Lady Katherine leaned in close, her soft lips brushing against Violet's cheek as she whispered into her ear, "Use your gift." Then she let her hands fall from Violet's shoulders and turned around to face the children, with Violet tucked safely behind her.

Violet stared at the back of the woman's head as she tried to understand what play the woman was going to make, but she admittedly got slightly distracted by her luxuriously long hair. She brought herself back to the moment just as the governess stepped boldly towards the children. Her dress glided over the floor, dragging shards of her shattered mask. In that moment she was no longer the same woman who only a moment ago was crumpled on the floor, hysterical about the appearance of her face. She was the governess. Lady Katherine had been holding her own against these monsters for a century, and Violet was glad she wasn't on her bad side, although she wasn't certain of what side she was on. It was all very confusing, but she would have to wait to decipher it until she survived this moment. And she had a sinking feeling that it was about to get ugly, again.

Lady Katherine owned the room. When she spoke, the universe obeyed.

"I have had enough of your miscreant behavior, children." Lady Katherine's voice was bold without her having to raise it. Violet was jealous. She didn't have that kind of confidence. What she had was a deep desire to survive so that she could get back to her mom.

Lady Katherine kept one hand surreptitiously behind her back and bent a finger, enticing Violet to follow her, or perhaps more accurately to follow her lead.

"You are nothing," Evelyn hissed.

"I am all you've had," the governess threw back. "You would have starved ages ago if it wasn't for me."

"And now we don't need you anymore," Evelyn said. William leaned against his sister for support, but his gaze drifted over to Violet with a hungry look in his eyes. Meanwhile, Violet inched toward the door. But she took a careless step, and her foot landed on several shards of porcelain.

She hissed in pain and her body twitched involuntarily at the injury. Looking down, she saw blood trickling from beneath her foot.

"Shit," she whispered. When she looked up, all eyes were on her. The momentary distraction had dissolved, and all that was left was hunger and hate.

"Run!" Katherine ordered, and Violet didn't hesitate.

Violet sprinted out of the room, fear wiping away the pain in her feet as the scattered pieces of the broken mask dug into her flesh. She had more important things to worry about. She didn't want to look behind her, afraid the children were close on her heels, but she needed to know. Without slowing down, she glanced over her shoulder. The governess was right behind her. Her long hair whipped over her shoulders, and her face was full of fear and hate and something more. Violet turned away from the beautiful woman, concentrating on getting down the stairs and beyond the reach of the children, but she couldn't stop thinking about the strange flicker of something new. There was no time to dwell on it. The children shrieked and howled in rage, which curdled the blood in Violet's veins.

23

Domn Dehanie was spread out like a bat on the velvet sofa. He'd let his head lean back and closed his eyes against all the vulgarity of this modern age. The buttons of the fine silk shirt he wore in the deepest black were open, his bare chest rising and falling with each deep breath. Since he had finished something he hadn't done in ages, he slept, and he dreamed. The gauche room that served as his temporary throne room faded away. Only to be replaced with the sounds of home.

His long dark lashes fluttered open, and the world that greeted him was fantastically oversized. The beams arching across the bowed shape of his grandmother's caravan shined in the flickering candlelight. They had been touched so many times over the years that they'd been worn to a polished shine. He pulled the quilt on his lap up to his nose, breathing in the familiar scents of his childhood: frankincense and wood smoke. He didn't want to move. Domn wished to linger there in this memory. Dressed in the finery of his Romany clan, he was surrounded by family.

He knew this memory, this place in time. It was the last time his life had been carefree. They had settled in an English moor far enough away from the city to not encourage harassment. This night in particular had been a feast, a celebration. The seasons were changing, and the autumn harvest was at hand.

He sat up reluctantly. Domn didn't want to leave the caravan. Nestled in this wooden womb, he knew he was safe, but he also knew what awaited him outside and it was worth leaving for. There was no telling how long he could stay in this dream, this memory, so he wasn't about to waste a single moment.

The alcove where his grandmother's bed was situated had been partitioned off with curtains embroidered by her own hands. The hand-dyed silk was a deep velvety blue to match the night sky, with embroidered stars over its entirety. Domn reached out and touched the constellations stitched with knowledge and patience. These were the skills that were lost in the modern world. In the waking world, there was no reverence for beauty like this. You could buy a cheap knockoff with a single click.

He separated the silk curtains, parting them with his hands, and stopped to stare at them. His hands were so small. There was a strangeness in seeing the hands of a child through his ancient eyes. It had been centuries since he'd been this young, but this night in particular was the beginning of the end for his innocence. The king of monsters left the warmth of the caravan and stepped down onto the damp, grassy earth. He wriggled his bare feet on the blades of grass and lifted his face to the deep, rich smells the earth offered. The world didn't smell like this anymore. Civilization had forgotten the simple pleasure of just existing.

The caravans had been set at the top of a shallow valley. The ground dipped down, and the moors scattered below him. From here, he could see the Romany kingdom. They brought their kingdom with them wherever they went. They weren't conquerors devouring nations for greed but were guests on this planet, content to roam and live in grace and peace. The land was rich and gracious, providing nourishment. When the sun fell, they danced beneath the starry tapestry of night. Couples danced around a bonfire, and children stole rolls of bread and ran off, cackling at their boldness, That night was going to be special. But he was searching for something more than the cheap dares of childhood boldness.

As he made his way down to the floor of the shallow valley, he searched until he located her. A short distance away from the bonfire, an ancient carved chair faced away from the flames. He had always thought of it as a throne, but it was nothing more than a simple piece of furniture. It was so old that the wood was stained black from usage. He approached it slowly, cautiously. Domn didn't need to see it to know it was decorated in cushions and quilts, not out of vanity or fashion, but because the woman who rested in it was old.

"Come and sit with me, Domn," the woman said. It wasn't a request. She was their matriarch, their queen in standing, if not by title. The Romany didn't care much for titles. That was something the city folk cared about. His clan cared about respect, duty, and loyalty. Everything they did was for the preservation and endurance of the clan. Although their future was never secure, his grandmother was the wisest among them, revered for her knowledge and years, especially for her clever-ness. Her voice was as gnarled as grit and bourbon, but it was home.

"How are you, Daj?" he asked in a seven-year-old voice. This was a dream, after all, and such things were to be expected.

"I am old, child," she answered as he came around her chair to stand next to her, "and I am tired."

Domn stood no taller than her shoulder when she sat in her chair. He leaned on the arm of the blanketed armrest. The wood beneath his fingertips was impervious to the cool night air, and its warmth permeated his flesh. His grandmother pat-ted his hand, her papery skin a comfort to him.

"Daj?"

"Yes, child?"

"Why do you face away from the fire?"

His grandmother turned her face towards him just enough that the orange glow of the bonfire behind cast her deep wrinkles in stark contrast. She didn't smile at him, but she didn't scowl either. She merely muttered, "I watch the night, Domn, not the light." She gave his hand an extra pat before turning back to look out at the shadowy landscape.

"Why?"

"The fire blinds you. I look to the night because the night teaches us about darkness and shadow."

"Why?" he asked again and was greeted with a warm chuckle.

"Don't ever let the world stop you from asking questions, little one."

When he heard those words the first time, he didn't understand. They held true meaning in the present. It was one aspect of his childhood that he'd carried with him throughout the years. He was a curious man. He wouldn't be as powerful as he was if not for his virile greed for knowledge. Some knowledge he used, while some he hoarded, secreted away in his mental cabinet of curiosities.

"Yes, Daj."

"Good boy."

Away from the fire, the moors and valley spread out before them. He stood there next to his grandmother for so long that he lost track of time. The stars moved slowly across the sky. The shadows stretched and yawned across the landscape. Eventually, his grandmother's mouth moved slightly, working at words she mumbled to the night. He couldn't make them out, but he knew enough to not interrupt her. This was her gift in action. The Romany connected with the natural world. Some read tea leaves or practiced palmistry, while others read the stars and knew more than any farmer's almanac. But his grandmother could speak to shadows. This night so long ago was the night she passed her gift to him.

This was a dream, though, and something strange happened he did not expect, something he didn't remember. The shadows twitched and vibrated. His grandmother leaned forward, squinting into the night. The hand-stitched blanket spread across her lap slipped to the ground, and her long, wiry white hair fell across her shoulder.

"What is it, Daj?"

"Shhh," she scolded. The ancient woman leaned forward still, and he worried she would fall out of her chair. Then her hair lifted in a breeze, a breeze that didn't exist. There was no wind. The night was still, but the old woman's hair hinted at something else. Domn felt it before he heard it. A massive wave slammed into him and threw him off his feet and into the air. It pitched Daj back into her chair. Her face and hair blew back as though she were caught in an oncoming storm.

Domn picked himself up off the ground and ran to his grandmother's aid. Her hands shook with the effort to stay her ground. Daj's eyes were wide and filled with blackness. The shadows she listened to filled her, and he was frightened. Then he heard it. A foul scream upon the air howled like a banshee. His ears bled from the onslaught of it. He tried to turn away, but the scream followed him. When he turned back to face his grandmother, her face was contorted. The old woman's eyes were impossibly wide, making her black eyes bulge. But it was her mouth that truly frightened him. Her lips had curled back against her teeth, and her jaw popped as her mouth opened to fit the scream throwing itself at them in the night, in the dark.

The scream that howled through the moorlands to find his grandmother made a nest in her open mouth. She turned to face him, screaming the entire time. It didn't match. The scream wasn't hers; it didn't belong to her. The scream belonged to something younger and older than his grandmother. It was then that he recognized it for what it was.

He reached out for his grandmother's face. Pain etched in every line of her stretched skin. The hands that found her face and held her gently weren't the hands of a child; they were his hands, the hands of a man. He knelt before her, holding her like a father comforting a child. This ancient woman was not really his grandmother. She was one of his children. He kissed her forehead and let himself wake up from the dream.

Domn awoke abruptly. His pulse quickened, for one of his children had reached out across worlds to find him. His temporary throne reverberated with waves of pressure hammering into him, and the bones in his chest snapped and cracked. His flesh split. As his chest opened up, he gritted his teeth against the pain. Blood and gristle separated unnaturally until his black beating heart was exposed. Every one of his children he had crafted from pieces of himself; therefore, when one was injured, he felt it deeply. Domn had hardened himself against pain and loss a long time ago, but this pain, this unique pain, he hadn't endured in over a century.

What felt like forever ago, he'd created a pair of special creatures, which gave him pride. They were something new at the time, something the world had never seen. His favorite children, the twins, nightmares that had been sculpted from the vulgar ugliness of mankind. Their bones were shaped from hunger and hate, and their veins were laced with greed. When it was time to breathe life into them, he did something he hadn't done since. Domn Dehanie, the king of monsters, opened up his chest, carved pieces off his heart, and stitched the souls of the twins. He loved them as he loved himself. But when Benjamin Brahm stole them away, imprisoning them in one of his hellish prisons, his heart shattered. He'd vowed to never leave himself vulnerable like that again.

The concussive waves pounding through the ether tore away the flesh of his chest, shredding the tissue to get at the exposed heart beating erratically. His jaw clenched, and his fists balled up so tightly that his tan skin blanched. As his fingernails dug into his palms, blood trickled from the wounds. There was a pounding on the door and a pounding in his chest. He couldn't make the world stop. He needed the world to stop.

The door to his room burst open, and the tallest man he'd ever known slouched beneath the frame of the door. He crossed the threshold and entered the room just as the scream that had pierced through time and dimensions to find him had ceased. Domn fell forward, off the velvet sofa, and onto the ugly green shaggy carpet. A fleck of spittle dripped off his lips as he panted. His chest was still flayed open wide and dripping blood onto the carpet, but at least the pain was diminishing. He sat back on his haunches and let his head hang low. With his arms draped at his sides, the wound in his chest stitched itself back together. Strings of meat and sinew lashed across the open wound, and splinters of bone and cartilage grew across the chasm.

"My lord?" the freakishly tall man said in a voice surprisingly gentle for such an imposing figure. "Are you all right?"

Domn Dehanie lifted his face to greet the tall man, though he knew who it was without seeing him. Dead Flamingo towered over him with his narrow frame. His baggy pinstriped trousers were reminiscent of zoot suits, held up by suspenders that crossed his bare chest. Incalculable tattoos were inked across his body, crawling up his neck. Though Dead Flamingo would be frightening to behold by a stranger, he was gentle and had an uncanny ability to transform lost little lambs into their true selves. No lie could blind the man. But that was also his poison: He felt every judgment against him keenly.

"I'm all right, my child. Truly, I'm better than ever."

Domn stood up. Dead Flamingo knew better than to offer him a hand. When he righted himself, his heart was once again nestled safely in his ribcage. Gracie peeked out from behind Dead Flamingo.

"What has happened?" Gracie asked.

That was a good question. He really didn't know what had happened. Whatever it was, though, it had the power to reach across dimensions and tear him apart. He was certain of one thing: The emotions behind it were distinct and familiar.

"I do believe we may be in store for a bit of a family reunion." Domn's mouth drew into a slow smile.

"What do you mean?" Gracie asked. Her over-the-top makeup was unmoving as her face knitted into a frown. Even though she didn't understand what was going on, Dead Flamingo seemed to know. He was a quiet man, but the quiet ones were always great listeners.

"The twins?" Dead Flamingo inquired.

Domn looked up at the man. Dead Flamingo's sunken cheeks and sickly pallor belied the cunning and inquisitive mind within. Domn patted the man's chest and smiled warmly.

"I believe the twins are finally coming home," Domn asserted.

Domn walked out of the room and down the corridor, the wound in his chest healed with a few last wet snapping sounds. Gracie worried at her manicure, but Dead Flamingo bowed his head in reverence to his master and followed his king.

The twins were finally coming home. Soon, Domn's family would be restored, and he'd finally have the information he needed to ensure none of his children would ever suffer in Benjamin's torturous prisons again.

24

Violet ran. There was no time to think. All she had was an overwhelming need to survive. She flew down the hallway, the fabric of her Victorian gown stretching out behind her like a kite. If only she could truly grow wings and fly herself away.

Out of the corner of her eye, she thought she saw the shadows around her writhing in ways they shouldn't be. She grabbed hold of the newel post and, without losing speed, whipped herself around and raced down the stairs. She hoped Lady Katherine was still behind her, but she didn't dare look to see.

Upon reaching the bottom, Violet ran around the corner and down the corridor leading to the arboretum. If anyone had seen her, they might have thought she was a wraith as her hair and gown flew out behind her in a blur, there one second and gone the next.

The green door waited at the end, so close yet so far away. If she could just reach the safety of the garden, maybe, just maybe, she'd have a moment to breathe. She needed to think, but there wasn't enough time.

She slammed into the door. The solid wood covered in layers of lacquer refused to yield. Violet twisted the doorknob and rattled the door with all her strength, but the door wouldn't budge. The door was fucking locked! Lady Katherine came up behind her and placed a hand on Violet's back.

"Where are they?" Violet asked.

"I managed to outrun them," Katherine said as she put a hand to her chest to catch her breath.

"You what?"

"Don't ask questions you don't really want the answers to," the governess replied with a wicked smile.

"What?" Violet asked between gasps of breath.

"I haven't felt this invigorated in decades," the governess said. An awkward second of silence hung between Violet and Lady Katherine before they both burst out in laughter. This was all too ridiculous. "Don't worry, I have the key."

Violet wanted to know why anyone would keep a garden under lock and key, but she didn't have time to argue the point. Lady Katherine dug into the secret pockets of her elegant gown, long tendrils of hair dripping off her shoulders. Violet looked back, and her heart skipped a beat. The other end of the hallway, where they had just come from, was drenched in darkness. It wasn't the sort of thing you usually saw in horror films. There was no flickering light that suddenly gave out, and the lights didn't blink out in consecutive order. This was something far more insidious.

"Hurry," Violet ordered, fear warbling her voice.

"Patience is a virtue."

"Not one either of us has time for," Violet whispered as the shadows at the end of the corridor came closer. They twisted across the walls, the floor, and the ceiling. The sconces that once offered a meager source of light bent, and the flames spat in an effort to get away from the encroaching shadows. It was no use, though. One wick after another was snuffed out by the swirling shadows creeping ever closer. "Hurry, Lady Katherine, hurry!"

The latch clicked as the governess unlocked the door. The shadows licked the space between them, and for a heartbeat, Violet wondered if they would make it into the next room. But the door opened, and they fell through.

Slamming the door behind them, they leaned back against the door as they were embraced by a momentary reprieve. The whispers of the shadows were safely behind the other side of the door, and the greenery of the gardens spread out before them. Violet and Lady Katherine were panting side by side, disheveled yet still alive. Lady Katherine spun around, slammed the iron skeleton key she used to unlock the door back into the lock, and twisted it. Then she took a deep, settling breath.

Lady Katherine stood tall and proud, and the look of determination settled on her beautiful face gave Violet enough courage to keep going. The governess reached out a hand to Violet, and she accepted it.

"Come with me," Lady Katherine said, and Violet obeyed. They held each other's hands, an invisible bond tying Violet to Lady Katherine, a bond of survival. Fear had the uncanny ability to bind people together just as much as it could tear them apart. An observer looking would think they were sisters, or at the very least very dear friends. Clinging tightly to each other, they followed the path through the gardens. Lush green vines draped luxuriously over the reaching branches of the trees that formed the impossible indoor forest. Moss grew along the edges of the path.

It was easy to forget about the monsters and fear when surrounded by nature. A few grasshoppers jumped across their path, and their presence sent a ripple through the trees, setting a few birds into flight.

BANG! Something slammed into the door of the gardens.

"We must hurry!" Lady Katherine declared.

Violet couldn't agree more, but she was still a little lost as to why the governess had come here, of all places. Did this place have some magical wards preventing Evelyn and William from entering?

"That door won't them for long." Lady Katherine said.

"What are we doing here?" Violet asked.

"I am getting you out of this hellish prison."

"How?"

"You," the governess said in a matter-of-fact tone. Violet stopped dead in her tracks while Lady Katherine continued walking. It wasn't until their hands slipped apart that the woman turned around to face Violet.

"What do you mean, me?" Violet asked.

"You are the key to everything."

"I'm not even sure how I ended up in this place, let alone how to get us out."

Lady Katherine approached Violet and looked directly into Violet's eyes. With petal-soft hands, she caressed Violet's face. There was a motherly sense to her, and she supposed it was natural. She was, after all, the older of the two, but it stirred unpleasant feelings in Violet. It had been so long since Violet had a mom of her own, and she was abruptly reminded of how much she missed that.

"Not just anyone could have fallen into one of these paintings," Lady Katherine said.

"I don't understand," Violet countered. Her voice was on edge. Hot tears threatened to spill over. She fought against them.

"I know," Lady Katherine said in a soft, reassuring voice. "The magic of this place is unique. It is only for the monsters."

"If that's true, then why are you here?" Violet's voice shook, for the fear was catching up to her. Violet didn't know how long she could keep going without losing her shit.

"I didn't tell you this before because I didn't want to complicate an already complicated situation—"

"Tell me what?" Violet interrupted.

"It has been so long since those long conversations by the fire. Lord Brahm and I, well, we'd grown very close over the time I had spent with him. He eventually confided in me the true nature of his gift." Lady Katherine's gaze drifted momentarily, and Violet couldn't help but wonder what she was remembering. "His ability to trap monsters in his paintings came with one caveat."

"What?" Violet said more petulantly than she meant to. A single twitch of one of her eyebrows was the only hint she'd registered the edge in Violet's voice.

"He needed someone to anchor the prison."

"How would someone anchor a painting?"

"A human soul needed to be a resident of the painting in order to keep the monsters contained, at least for Lord Brahm's particular skill to work correctly."

"Wait a minute." Violet's mind spun out of control as she tried to wrap her thoughts around what Lady Katherine was actually telling her. "Are you saying that unless a human is stuck in here with the monsters . . ."

"Then the monsters will escape," Katherine finished.

BANG! Violet and Lady Katherine flinched against the reminder that they still weren't safe.

"Now, listen to me," the governess began. "I have an idea on how to get you out of this place and I think it has everything to do with how you managed to get here in the first place." The governess turned away from Violet, then took her hand and pulled her along the path again. Violet had no choice but to let the woman lead her onward.

"Okay, I'm game to try anything, but you just said that someone has to stay behind to keep this place going," Violet said, but Lady Katherine ignored her and continued pulling her.

"Hey, wait." Violet yanked the governess to a stop. "Hey."

"We need to hurry, Violet. That door isn't going to hold them back much longer."

"You said that this place needs a human to anchor it."

"I did, yes."

"How are you going to come with me if someone has to stay behind?" Lady Katherine's silence shouted at her. "Oh," Violet whispered. She understood. Lady Katherine was going to stay behind. She was going to sacrifice her only chance of freedom to help Violet. She didn't like this idea, but she didn't have a better one.

"Come along, we're almost there." The governess pulled her hand again.

Violet remembered this place. She remembered the little stone bench they had sat on when Violet had first arrived. This time, the governess didn't sit down to reminisce. Instead, she knelt on the ground and reached into the foliage of the lush honeysuckle vine. Every movement she made sent out bursts of heady fragrance, and a few fat bumblebees buzzed irritably around her face. Lady Katherine paid them no mind. Violet's head spun with the strong scent, and she became a little lightheaded. She flopped down on the bench just as Katherine pulled her arm out from the vines with a triumphant smile on her face.

In her hand was a book. Not just any book, either. It was Violet's sketchbook. She lashed out, snatching the sentimental book from Katherine's hand.

"How did you get this?" Violet whispered reverently. With all the chaos that had been going on, she'd completely lost track of her belongings. She ran a hand down the leather cover of the book. The last sketchbook her father had given her was so precious to her. When she pulled her eyes away from the leather book, Lady Katherine was staring at her.

"I found it in Evelyn's room."

"What?"

"I believe that Evelyn has come to the same conclusion that I have."

"That I somehow have the ability to get us out of here?"

"Yes," Lady Katherine answered without hesitation, "the proof is right there." She nodded towards Violet's book.

"I don't understand." Violet was overwhelmed. How was she supposed to be the key to getting out of here when she didn't even understand how she got here in the first place?

Lady Katherine approached Violet and sat next to her on the bench. "Look." She reached over and opened the book, flipping through a few pages until she got to one of her sketches of Violet's mom. "How long have you been drawing this woman?"

"I don't know, ever since I could draw."

"No, that's not right. How long have you been focusing your drawing on her?"

"I don't know!" Violet hissed. She still didn't want to raise her voice, but she was tired of this. "Why?"

"Think," Katherine commanded. Her voice wasn't raised, but there was no geniality in it. Violet thought of all the times she spent sketching in her book, sketching her mom. She hadn't always drawn her mom; she used to draw lots of things, different things. The buildings in her neighborhood, headstones at the nearby cemetery, and—and her dad. She used to draw her dad all the time.

Violet looked at the book lying open in her hands. Every artist was quirky about how they worked. One of her own quirks was that she never liked to start on the first page of a new sketchbook, so she'd randomly flip to a page in the middle to start. She flipped to that first drawing. The detailed drawing of her dad sitting in his recliner with a cocktail balanced on his knee was highlighted in blues and crimson to accentuate the glow coming off the television in front of him. She was so proud of this drawing. She'd sat in the doorway to her room for hours after her mom had gone to bed just so she could finish it. Violet ran her fingers over her scribbled signature at the bottom of the drawing.

"Lord Brahm had told me once that the only work an artist puts his signature to are pieces that are complete, when the image and purpose in the artist's heart are fully revealed on the canvas."

Violet had never heard it put quite like that, but she wasn't wrong. It was the first and last time she'd ever signed one of her drawings.

"When did your father die?" Lady Katherine asked gently.

Violet understood where she was going with all this, but she didn't want to put that realization into words. If she spoke it out loud, then it was true and she couldn't take it back. Her eyes filled with tears, and when she met the governess's gaze, they spilled down her cheeks.

"When did your father die?" she asked again.

"He died that night," Violet admitted.

Lady Katherine sighed. She'd known the answer already, but there was power in owning one's truth.

"And when did your mother start to diminish?"

"No," Violet protested feebly, "it's not possible."

"Don't lie to yourself. You and I both know the world is made of more wonder and terror than most people will ever comprehend."

Violet knew Katherine was right. She didn't understand how, but she had the ability to steal a person's life with just a simple sketch. She didn't want to know how far this ability went.

BANG! BANG! CRASH! Violet looked at Lady Katherine with dread. The children had broken through the door to the arboretum. They were out of time.

"What do I do?" Violet asked.

"Draw. I need you to draw a way out."

"How do I do that?"

"Use your memories. Think of a place in your world that is real, that has substance," Lady Katherine said as she looked over her shoulder. "Draw an exit of some kind, a door, a bridge, anything! Just draw your way out of here."

"But what about you?"

"Don't worry about me," the governess said with a wicked smile. "I believe it is about time that I show these monsters what I am capable of."

Violet didn't want to think about what she had in mind, but she wasn't about to ask either. "You're sure?"

"I'm certain. Now go. Find a place to hide yourself away while you draw. I'll keep the children busy to give you as much time as I can."

Lady Katherine stood up, smoothed down the wrinkles in her gown, and let a stern and solemn expression settle on her beautiful face. In that moment, Lady Katherine was truly gone. In her place, the governess.

"Go!" she ordered Violet, and Violet obeyed.

25

Light and shadow chased each other across the broad windows of Ben's penthouse. Time ticked by. Days turned into weeks and still, Ben sat in the leather chair of his office. He waited and watched, a sentinel against the threat lurking just beneath the surface. Two weeks had passed since the disappearance of Violet Brennan, and he was no nearer to understanding how she'd fallen into one of his paintings than he was at the start of all this. He was normally fit and full of vigor, but during his watch over the painting, he'd barely eaten. He sustained himself on shame and whiskey.

The longer he kept watch over the painting, the more he was reminded of how much his life had changed since. He still dreamed of Katherine, of her kiss, and of the look of betrayal on her face. Ben still believed the temperament of the anchor, the one holding the prison gates shut, was imperative. What good was a prison if a demon ruled over it? But that didn't mean he didn't miss her. She was the only woman he'd given his heart to. Never again had he opened himself up like that.

Ben had fallen asleep at his post and woke with a start and a cramp in his neck. He might have been nearly immortal, but he was still, at his core, simply a man. His body rebuked the abuse he'd been putting it through. He stretched out, letting his bones pop and sing with the pain of being in such an uncomfortable position for so long. He rubbed at his eyes. The taut skin of his face accentuated the lines of his jaw and the depth of his eyes.

He needed to get up and move. After glancing at the painting, making sure it was as it should be, he headed for the kitchen. It wasn't until he wrapped his hands around a mug of hot coffee that he got a good look at himself in the reflection of a nearby mirror. Ben nearly jumped out of his skin, thinking a stranger was lurking in his home. But it was just his reflection. A gaunt, haggard man stared back at him. This wouldn't do. With his uncertainty about everything around him right then, that was not the time to let himself deteriorate.

There was a sort of magic that happened whilst taking a shower. The rush of water drowned his thoughts, giving him the briefest of moments of solace from his shame. None of what had happened was something he could have ever predicted. He'd been trapping beasts in his art for a very long time, and not once had anything unexpected happened. He would paint, and the beasts would fight him. In the past, when there were more shadows, they would gang up on him. Those had been challenges, but he relished them. His blood would thrum through his veins, and a smile would cross his lips.

Ben wondered what would become of him when there were no more shadows. Would he simply fade away? Would his ability to trap creatures in the oils he blended onto canvas stop? Would he become an ordinary man? He didn't feel like he was changing. But that meant nothing. A world without monsters was still a far-off thought. Would he be around to see the end? Ben didn't have any answers, but at least he had a clear head again. The shower and coffee had been just the thing to clear his mind and give him back the ability to concentrate on the problems at hand. The first being, of course, how the girl had fallen into his painting But the second was more dangerous. What was happening inside the painting?

A ripple of energy escaping the realm of paint and canvas was unheard of. Even though it hadn't happened since, it was still enough to give him pause. He must ensure the prison would hold. But to do so, he needed to know what was happening, and that was where he was stuck. How was he supposed to know what was going on within his paintings if he couldn't go there himself? While he couldn't know for sure what he'd sent Katherine into, he knew it was some type of hell.

He let the scorching water melt the tension and cramps in his muscles, finally feeling a bit more like himself. Ben swiped away the fog that had gathered on the bathroom mirror and met his reflection. He was content with what he saw. Nearly himself again, but a look of resolve had settled on his face. He wrapped a towel around his waist and brewed himself another cup of coffee before heading back to his office.

It was still early. Denver was barely waking up. The horizon full of brilliant color cast the tall buildings in halos of color. It was moments like these in which the boldest of lies were crafted. When the city was quiet and most people were still sleeping, it was easier to believe there was hope for civilization. Humanity was capable of beautiful progress when greed and envy didn't cripple it. Until people desired knowledge and experience more than wealth and prestige, humanity would remain unchanged. People believed they were creating a better world, a world full of advanced technology and beautiful surroundings. But how many forests were cut down for the sake of advancement? The crush of progress chewed up the less fortunate, and those with money and power to help sat on their thrones, criticizing laziness.

He hated the world for the way it was, but there were few surprises to be had. Sometimes it took the most horrifying circumstances to reveal the beautiful power of grace in the face of adversity. Ben had learned more about the girl, Violet, and was impressed by her grace. He wondered, not for the first time, if there was something more to the unfortunate circumstances the girl was enduring. Her struggles held similarity to his own story, though he kept his story close to his heart. Everyone was entitled to keep secrets. He'd kept some secrets from Katherine too. They were dangerous, and he shook them out of his thoughts.

Ben stared out the windows, watching the city wake up and the sun climb into the sky. In the reflection of the windows, the girl's drawing sat on his desk. It was a constant reminder of the trouble about. Some mysteries were exciting. And some mysteries were terrifying in their wrongness. He went to the desk and picked up the drawing for what could be the hundredth time. His thumb brushed against the charcoal lines and noticed something peculiar, something he'd been too lost to see before. The lines didn't smear. In fact, there was no detriment to her drawing at all, which was strange. He brought the drawing up to his nose and sniffed. Nothing.

After setting it back down, he forcibly ran his hand across the surface. The drawing should have shown signs of being handled. The corners weren't folded or creased. Artists used fixatives to prevent a drawing like this from smudging, but all fixatives lent an obnoxious odor of some kind and none of them were perfect. This smelled like nothing, not even charcoal and paper. An idea came to him. Slow at first, like trying to remember a dream, but then it solidified.

With the drawing still in his hand, he crossed the moody office and approached his painting of the beautiful Lady Katherine in her red cloak at the center of a great hall. The flanking staircases were behind her, and the children lurked in the background. It was time to see if he was crazy. Crouched on his knees, Benjamin leaned in close. This close to the canvas, he focused on the banisters of the staircases. He sniffed the canvas. Nothing. All he could see were the blended strokes of paint. As he moved his face to another portion of the painting, he sniffed again. Still nothing.

He stared at one of the beasts, the girl. Her young visage was dainty, her face emotionless. Closing his eyes, he relaxed. Ben didn't know how he hadn't noticed this earlier. Although the oils' pungent odor faded over time, they still held a particular fragrance about them. How could he have never noticed such a distinct lack of smell? He'd been a careless fool, that's how. He was angry with himself for his ambivalence towards his own gift. This newly discovered side effect of his ability would need further study once he figured out what to do about the missing girl.

Another thought rushed to the forefront of his mind. What if the lack of smell was simply because the smell stayed with the creatures trapped within the painting? He'd never gone into one of his paintings, for it would be awfully difficult to continue trapping shadow beasts if he was trapped among them. But what if he could? What if he could still lock the evil away while being in the prison itself? It was an intriguing thought, to be sure. He let out a slow sigh. It had been a very long time since he'd been this frustrated.

He opened his eyes. The painted figure of the little girl had changed, and her mouth was open in a scream he couldn't hear but could feel. Hate and rage disfigured her little face. Standing on the stairs and no longer in shadow, the girl reached an arm out beyond the banister, clawing towards something. Ben fell back and scrambled away from the image of pure hate.

From the illusion of a safer distance, he examined the painting again. It was not as it should be. The children staring down from the shadows had moved up a few steps. Katherine held her ground in the forefront of the painting. Her face was beautiful and stoic, but something was different about her. He couldn't place the difference. What was it?

And the girl, the shadow beast, how had she changed? He'd never seen one of his paintings change, ever. He leaned in close again as his heart pounded recklessly against his ribcage. He remembered the moment he trapped her—she looked as though she was losing her human form, reverting to shadow and bone. His eyes followed her reaching arm across the canvas, and he squinted at something peculiar.

On the opposite side of the grand hall was the other staircase, and beyond the staircase, around the little partition of the wall, were rooms he never painted. He wondered if those rooms existed since he didn't paint them. There was no way to know. But he did need to know what he was looking at.

Ben jumped up and went to his desk. He rummaged through his drawers, and there it was, tucked in the back. An antique brass magnifying glass he'd been given as a gift a lifetime ago. The glass had weight to it, unlike most things these days, which were made of composite materials and plastic. The weight of objects like this from the past seemed to anchor them to their time, a constant reminder of a history that no one remembered anymore.

He took it over to the painting and crouched down so that he was nose-to-nose with the shadow beast girl. Ben raised the magnifying glass, hoping for clarity and receiving much more than he expected. The beastly girl was not only reaching out for something across the great hall but also clutching something in her other arm that made his stomach knot. A horrible shadow beside her, still wearing the face of her twin, wore an expression of pain and malice. The creature barely reflected any of his human disguises. But more importantly, he didn't look like Ben had painted him.

His paintings had never changed after he'd completed them. So what the hell was going on in there? Afraid to know more but nervous about what he'd find, Ben moved the magnifying glass across the canvas, following the guiding arm of the beast.

There. Standing around the corner on the opposite landing was a figure. A portion of the figure's profile peered around the corner, directly at the girl. It was just a sliver, but it was enough. It was all he needed to know. In shadow and lace was the figure of Violet Brennan.

When he saw the leather-bound book in her hands, he understood what had happened. She was just like him. Somehow, he already knew this on some level. Maybe he was afraid to acknowledge it. He sat back, letting the hand holding the magnifying glass drop to his side. He should have felt sorry for her. Ben should have wept at the horror this young woman was doomed to experience for the rest of her unusually long life. Instead, he wept. He wept at the knowledge that he was no longer alone.

26

Behind the door of apartment 312, Nguyen Widawski stood at the kitchen sink of the Brennans' apartment, staring out the little window and waiting for the water to boil in the electric kettle. Two weeks after Violet left to go on a late-night walk, Nguyen was still here, still caring for Violet's mother. It was certainly lucky that she was retired or she would've been forced to find alternate care, and Violet wouldn't have liked that. The whole reason she suffered through the life she had was so that she could keep her mother out of a state-sponsored facility. Nguyen and Violet had sat there in the tiny kitchen talking about that option on multiple occasions, and Nguyen knew Violet's mind on the matter. The girl loved her mother so much.

All of which was why the girl's disappearance was so worrying. Violet would never walk away from her responsibilities or her mother. Although Patience wasn't well, she was the only real family the girl had left.

The contents of the kettle rumbled happily. Nguyen didn't wait for it to turn itself off before pouring herself a cup of tea. Outside the little apartment, life continued on. It didn't stop for anyone, least of all a wayward teenager.

BANG! Something in the other room fell with such force that Nguyen jumped and dropped the cup into the sink, where it shattered upon impact.

"Patience?!" she called out. The only answer to her call was the sound of violence.

She sprinted across the tiny apartment and tried to open the door to Patience's room, but she couldn't budge it. It wasn't locked. The knob turned freely in her hand, so it must be that something was blocking the door. Her imagination brought forth images of Violet's mother strewn across the floor in front of the door, and she hoped her imagination was wrong. She had accepted responsibility for the woman in Violet's absence and didn't want this to be the way the story had to go.

Nguyen wasn't a particularly large person, but she pushed with all her might anyway. Behind the door, it seemed all hell was breaking loose. She would probably spend the rest of the day cleaning up the mess, but that wasn't what worried her. Patience's howling made Nguyen want to cry. It wasn't anger or frustration coming from the woman. Whatever had set her off was heart-wrenching.

Patience Brennan wept so loudly that the superintendent could likely hear it three floors down. She pushed into the door with her shoulder, and finally, the door moved, slowly at first and then more easily. Nguyen cracked the door open enough to step into Patience's bedroom but was flabbergasted by what she saw. Patience, still in her nightgown, was flying about the room like a banshee. Her face was flushed and blotchy, tears pouring down her face. Her hair was wild and as untamed as the woman. Patience had always been on the verge of madness, but it seemed the madness had caught up to the woman.

Nguyen's mouth hung open as Patience flung herself around the room, alternating between weeping and screaming. Nguyen couldn't make any of it out at first, but it didn't matter. She needed to calm her down, and she did not know how she was going to do that.

"Patience!" she cried, but Patience was louder. This wasn't going to be easy. The woman was larger than her. Although Patience wasn't necessarily strong after years of being afflicted with Alzheimer's, madness did strange things to people.

"Patience, please stop," Nguyen begged.

"Shadows!" Patience screamed. "The shadows are coming."

Nguyen didn't understand. She'd been sleeping so well for the past few nights and wondered if maybe she'd had a bad dream.

"What shadows, Patience?"

"The shadows are moving, screaming, shadows are running." Patience howled at the universe, her words running together as though they were different thoughts all jumbled up.

"Tell me, tell me about the shadows," Nguyen persisted. Maybe if she could get Patience to explain it to her, then it would help to calm her down.

Patience whipped around. "No!" she practically growled at Nguyen. She held such a strangeness about her. In that second, the moment between heartbeats, she looked almost lucid. "Violet's in danger."

"What do you mean? What kind of danger?"

"The shadows are reaching."

"Patience, what do you mean, Violet's in danger? How do you know she's in danger?"

Instead of answering, Patience lunged at her. Nguyen fell over in a struggle of flailing limbs. Patience Brennan's strength was surprising. She pinned Nguyen's shoulders to the floor by her forearms while her head shook with the effort to toss out some violent notion or thought. Patience wasn't trying to hurt her; rather, she seemed lost in a waking nightmare. Maybe that was it. Maybe she had simply had a nightmare and didn't realize that she had woken up. It was a terrifying thought, and a shiver ran through her just thinking about it. If Patience's nightmares were indistinguishable from waking life, then what must her nightmares be?

Patience had to be calmed down before she hurt herself. To make the situation worse, someone was pounding on the door to the little apartment. Nguyen craned her head around as best she could from her pinned position on the floor of Patience's bedroom. She could barely see the door to the apartment from here, and she couldn't do anything about it. No doubt the commotion from the woman lost in her madness had woken more than a few of the neighbors. And since neighbors rarely knew each other in this modern age, or even cared to know each other, they'd sent the superintendent to check on the matter.

Patience's screams were feral, wrapped in fear and something else. When she flung her arms out, her hands clenching and unclenching, it caused enough of a shift in weight that Nguyen wiggled from beneath her. Nguyen sat up on her haunches, trying to catch her breath. Patience whipped her whole body around, and one of her clenched fists caught Nguyen's cheek.

A shroud of darkness obscured Nguyen's vision, making her head heavy and weightless all at once. She might be a scrappy older woman, but she wasn't a brawler. Through the haze and the pain, she heard someone calling out, but it had all sounded so far away. Eventually, her vision cleared, if not the pain, and after that moment of confusion, she saw Patience from a new perspective.

Patience's movements, which at first seemed like so much random flailing about, suddenly looked purposeful. Her movements held rhythm. Nguyen shook her head, trying to break the image free, thinking she'd started going mad herself, but to no avail. Patience wasn't merely having a fit—she was engaged in a fight. She wouldn't have been able to explain it to anyone else by any means, but from her haze of pain and tunnel vision, she saw that Patience was miming the movements of a fistfight.

Violet's mother was having a physical fight with an invisible person. Nguyen did not see anyone there, but Patience could see them. Whoever was at the door was becoming a damn nuisance. Nguyen had more important things to deal with than the satisfaction of her neighbors. She ignored the pounding on the door and the muffled voice calling out from the corridor.

"Patience," Nguyen called out, trying a different tactic with the woman. "Patience, let me help."

"I can't stop them."

"I can help. We can do it together."

Patience stopped moving and looked at Nguyen with puzzlement. Her head tilted slightly.

"How?" she asked.

"You tell me," Nguyen replied.

"The shadows are going to get her."

"How do we stop them?"

"I don't know." Patience whimpered. "I can touch them."

"What do you mean?"

As if in answer to Nguyen's question, the woman stared down at her hands, which were scratched and bloody. She shouldn't have been surprised, what with all the commotion she'd been causing. Lamps had been knocked over, and shards of glass littered the floor. Patience wavered and stared at her hands as though the answer to her current situation was written on them. But she shook her head violently. Apparently, she didn't like the answer she saw written there in invisible ink.

The woman howled. Nguyen wouldn't have been surprised if a pack of wild coyotes replied to the sound. Before she could get lost in that thought, Patience thrashed around again. This time, Nguyen was prepared. Since she recognized the woman was fighting some invisible foe, she avoided her wildly swinging arms.

"Patience, please let me help," Nguyen pleaded.

Tears streamed down Patience's cheeks, and both fear and ferocity stretched across her pale face. The woman absolutely believed she was fighting to save her daughter. But her daughter wasn't there. There were no terrifying shadows, either, and Nguyen was at a loss for what to do. She didn't know how to help or comfort the woman.

Patience lurched and bent in ways that made Nguyen think of an old documentary about witches. The wild reenactment of their strange moonlight dances had unsettled her, and at that moment, she was watching something like it unfold before her very eyes. But Patience grunted and screamed as if she were being hit or punched. That was the last straw. Something must be done.

Nguyen released all her worries except for one: If she let this go on for much longer, Patience would become seriously hurt. She waited for just the right opening, for Patience's back to turn towards her, before she hurled herself at the woman. Nguyen slammed her petite body into her and wrapped her arms around her as tightly as she could. Patience screamed. Her shriek was full of pain, as though Nguyen's grip on her was acid burning through her skin. But Nguyen held on, ignoring the sounds.

She tightened her grip against Patience's flailing and whipping. Her screams grew deeper and more dangerous. Patience was no longer a woman lost in a nightmare; she was an animal, and a trapped one, at that. While Nguyen considered that this attack might be counterproductive, there was nothing left to try. She held on for dear life, trying to regulate her own breathing in a desperate hope that Patience would calm down.

It was working. Patience fought her a little less as time ticked by. Her cries turned to growls, and eventually, her growls morphed into sobbing.

Nguyen hated to see the woman like this. It was not so long ago that she'd been an intelligent and caring woman. She was a good wife and a loving mother. But currently, she could barely hold herself together.

Nguyen and Patience stood there amongst the carnage. The bed had been torn apart. Pictures, photographs, and drawings had been ripped from the walls and lay scattered and shattered about the room. As Patience's muscles relaxed, Nguyen held the weeping woman in her arms, letting her know it was going to be all right. The world was as it should be, Violet was safe, and it was okay to let it all go.

They slid down to the ground; whether it was because the untethered moment had passed or if it was just because Patience was too exhausted to continue, Nguyen didn't know. They were a huddled mass of tears and cardigans, and the terror had run out of both of them. Patience buried her face in Nguyen's neck. They wept together. This was unfair. Life could be so cruel to the kindest people.

Patience rocked in Nguyen's arms, muttering to herself. Nguyen couldn't make any more sense of the mutterings than what she'd been screaming about earlier, but some words came through the tears clearly.

"Shadows—monsters—run."

Nguyen didn't know what to worry about more: the shadows haunting her friend or the feeling that they were being watched. The silence that filled the little apartment screamed just as loudly as the chaos moments before, and Nguyen remembered someone had been pounding at the door.

Without loosening her grip on her friend, she craned her neck around. Father Benny stood in the doorway to the destroyed bedroom, looking like a wraith sent from God. His black suit against his ashy pallor was offset by the stark white cleric collar tucked beneath his Adam's apple. Behind him, she saw the door to the apartment had been kicked open. The frame was splintered, and the faces of a half-dozen neighbors were pressed together on the other side. If this were any other situation, she might have laughed at the absurdity of it all, but she was deeply worried about the well-being of her friend.

This was more than she could handle. This was more than any one person could manage. She didn't know how Violet

had managed this for so long. Where are you, girl? she wondered.

27

VIOLET TUCKED THE BOOK under the crook of her arm and ran. She had never fully explored the arboretum and wasn't prepared for how large it was. If she hadn't been running for her life, she might have had time to really enjoy it. She ran through the trees, her dress snagging on branches as she made her way through the fantastical woodland nurtured beneath a glass and iron ceiling.

The storm billowed and howled above, sheets of rain cascading down the cathedral shapes. She couldn't hear the children pursuing her, but that was only because her heart was pounding in her ear. Lady Katherine had stayed behind to distract them. She'd spent a hundred years trying to restrain the evil within them, but it was too late for their redemption. The children were in the room by then, but she was too frightened to turn and look. Branches whipped her face, twigs crunched beneath her shoes, and her ragged breathing rushed into her ears. If she somehow survived this, would she ever be able to relax again? Violet wasn't sure she believed n Lady Katherine's tactics. How could she draw a way out of this nightmare? She couldn't think. How was she supposed to be creative if she couldn't even think?

Violet needed a little more time, a moment to breathe and to think. She ducked behind the broad trunk of a nearby spruce, which had to have been more than a century old. It was broad enough to hide her slim figure. She slid back against the rough bark and pulled her knees to her chest, making herself as small as she could. The last book her dad ever gave her was pulled in tight to her chest. Her breathing was labored by the exertion of staying ahead of the children trying to literally devour her. Violet closed her eyes and thought of the one thing she wanted more than anything: her mom.

She thought about all those times her mom struggled to manage the rush of the world all around them. Her panic attacks were fierce, and Violet hated seeing her mom like that. She learned over time, though, how to calm down her mom, how to pull her back from the brink. So, Violet did the same for herself. She focused on something benign, something that wasn't threatening. The tree she was sitting against was tall and broad and reassuringly anchored to the ground. She could imagine its roots going deep into the ground, twisting and reaching out, finding strength with every tendril that shot out into the earth.

Releasing her iron grip on the book, Violet gave herself permission to relax, if only a little. She let her hands fall to her sides and land on the ground. Her fingers dug into the dirt and found pine needles, then the base of the tree. Gnarled and craggy bark covered the tree, but it felt reassuringly real. Her fingertips followed the coarse path of bark, which cleared her mind. Although her fear was so close to the surface, she pushed it back and focused on slowing her breathing. The distinct fragrance of the Colorado mountains filled her, and the smell of pine and sap brought her back to memories of hikes with her dad.

Her eyes opened. Despite her constant fear and weariness, she smiled. An idea crawled to the forefront of her mind. Lady Katherine had whispered something in her ear, a last request. She desired for her to pass along a message to her lover, but Violet could do more than that. If what Lady Katherine had told her was real, if she could draw things into existence, then her idea just might work. If not, well, then she'd probably die a gruesome, painful death.

A flurry of wings breaking free from a nearby tree startled her. The truth of the danger she was in rushed back at her. Her plan would only work if she could get to where she needed to be. She didn't know this place well enough to draw it from memory, so she needed to see what she was drawing.

"Come play with us," Evelyn called out.

Her voice was that of the child she pretended to be, but her words were laced with malice. Violet definitely did not want to play with her. She wanted to go home. But first, she had to get out of this place.

"I'll play with you," Lady Katherine answered with equal malice.

Violet couldn't imagine the depth of hatred the children and Lady Katherine felt toward each other. Being trapped together had offered them something else, though: intimacy. They knew each other deeply. However, Violet didn't want to be here long enough to get to know the monsters.

"We are tired of playing with you, dear governess," William threw back. His voice was less gravelly, and Violet wondered if he'd finally managed to put himself back together. She shivered. Would she ever be able to see people as just people again? Ugh, who knew?

"I'm hurt, William," the governess teased. "After all this time, I thought you enjoyed playing games."

"We are too hungry to play with you," Evelyn countered.

"We would rather play with our food," William added.

Oh, she thought, that's what they meant. She didn't really feel like being dinner. The only alternative was to do her part and make a way out of there. There was no better way to get it done than when they were all distracted.

Violet took a deep breath before she hopped back up onto her feet and prepared to make her escape. She leaned around the broad trunk of the tree to get her bearings, hoping everyone else would keep bantering so that she could escape without being seen or heard.

"Going somewhere?" Evelyn said from right behind her.

Violet screamed in a rather unladylike manner, but her nerves and instincts were keyed up. Just as the monster child reached for her with a very hungry look, Violet bolted. Through the trees, around the massive orrery at the center of the garden, and past the grove of statues, all the while hearing Evelyn's footsteps right behind her. The creature was fast, and Violet couldn't seem to shake her.

The landscape of the arboretum changed as she ran through it. Although it was anchored by massive trees reaching toward the glass ceiling, glades and meadows and brush were everywhere. She could easily imagine herself lost in a tale of fantasy and magic. Nearly all the ingredients needed for a good book were here. Monsters, a creepy house, and a sorrowful tale of twisted love.

Vines caught her feet as she ran, and branches clawed at her face and dress. Finally, Violet ducked behind a sage bush—Russian sage by the heady fragrance of the purple blossoms. Her ears ached as she listened. Her breathing came out in a ragged stream, and her hands shook with adrenaline. Where was Evelyn?

"Come out, come out, little girl," Evelyn sang across the arboretum.

Little girl? Violet was offended for a moment but then realized Evelyn wasn't really a little girl herself. She was old and terribly powerful, something else entirely. Had she actually gotten some space between them? She knew where she wanted to draw; she just needed enough time to get there. Leaning forward as carefully and as quietly as she could, Violet peered through the tips of sage. She scanned the area but couldn't see Evelyn anywhere. Having only spent a few days here, she hadn't found the time to scout everything out, so she had no idea if there was another way out of this place. Her only option was to make her way back to the green door.

"Go, Violet," the governess called out calmly. There was no fear in her words. "I will keep them occupied, just go."

She couldn't call back to the governess without declaring her location. Evelyn might still be close, and that wasn't even considering William. Violet hadn't heard his voice for a while, which probably meant he was lurking somewhere inconvenient. Silence would keep her safe for a little while, but time was not on her side. She needed to get out of here.

Violet clutched her sketchbook in one hand and picked up the hem of her dress with the other, then bolted. Like a wraith, Violet sprinted through the forest and the glades and past the statues. She didn't look behind her, as all her thought was bent on making it to that green door. But Violet wouldn't succeed if Lady Katherine didn't do her part. So it was either run or die.

Yes! There it was, or at least what was left of it. She stepped over the remains of the green door, which had been ripped off its hinges and splintered. Sharp splinters reached out for her, but she didn't slow her pace. She poured her faith into Lady Katherine as she hoped the woman could keep the monsters at bay long enough.

As she cleared the threshold, she heard the pounding of feet. A stampede of horses could have been riding up on her, and she wouldn't have been able to tell the difference. Screams pierced the still air, then snarls. She didn't want to die at the hands of the children. She didn't want to die such a painful death.

"I don't think so," Lady Katherine said. Her voice was beautiful yet cold and full of the promise of pain.

Violet couldn't help but turn around, almost losing her balance. There, framed by the shards of the green door were the brother and sister, dressed in their human form. Only a little distance remained between them and Violet. She was close to death. Their sharp teeth bared just before their smiles slipped off their faces. Standing just behind them, a vengeful banshee on the hunt, was their governess.

The governess stood with firmness. Her long hair was wild, juxtaposing with her serene face, giving Violet a chill. Lady Katherine's eyes met Violet's, and she understood for certain that Lady Katherine had no plans to leave this place. It was as though she'd been planning her revenge for a hundred years and finally tasted victory. While the children's faces were caught with lustful hunger, they knew they'd been trapped.

The governess bowed her head almost imperceptibly as she raised her arms toward the children. Violet didn't wait for anything else. Thank you, she mouthed to the woman, who smiled in return. Violet turned her back to them all and ran, down the hallway and around the corner until she slid into the great hall.

It was an open empty space. A huge cavern of Victorian opulence and craftsmanship decorated only in a small seating area near the crackling fire and a few tables near the door. That was where she needed to be. She was exposed here, but it was the largest surface she could work with. She threw herself onto the floor in a heap of fabric and determination. Her sketchbook was on the floor in front of her with the only pencil she had on her tucked into the spine.

The huge expanse of wall surrounded the massive double doors of oak. The beautiful wainscoting and the rich wallpaper was her canvas, and all she had to do was draw. She opened the book and flipped past the drawing of her dad, past the sketches of the city she'd left behind. Finally, she found a blank page far enough away from any of the drawings she cherished. Violet couldn't explain why she felt the need to put distance between them, but that was not the time to second-guess herself.

This nightmare would come to an end one way or another. She would either draw herself to freedom or be devoured by shadow monsters. Violet closed her eyes to concentrate. She knew what she wanted to draw, but the final image was never what she started out drawing. The images would unfold like the drawing had a mind of its own. If she really had the ability to draw life into things, then what would her pencil create? Could she draw freedom, or would she be releasing another monster out into an already cruel world?

She didn't have any answers. All she had was some meager talent and a desperate desire to go home. That was it! That was the thought she needed to hold on to as she drew. The thought of wrapping herself around her mom for the biggest, longest hug ever would just have to do. Violet opened her eyes and put her pencil to the paper. She drew as though her life depended on it, because it did.

28

Ben looked down at Nguyen and Patience, and his heart broke. The faces of both women were streaked with tears. Patience was muttering and rocking herself in the other woman's arms, her wild hair clinging to tears and spittle. Ben couldn't make out all of what she was saying, but he understood enough. He didn't know how it had happened, but somehow, Patience could feel or see beyond this world and into the one that he had created.

He lowered to his knees and bent towards Nguyen. The woman was spent. She was obviously at her wit's end. Her eyes pleaded with him, though he wasn't here to help.

"I can help," he lied.

"How?"

"That's not important," he said. "What is important is that Violet is alive."

Nguyen sighed with relief. Her whole body wilted, releasing the tension and worry she'd been holding on to for so long.

"Oh, thank God," Nguyen said.

Patience raised her head and met Ben's gaze. So much pain and suffering was etched across her face, but it was still beautiful. He could see even then that she must have been extraordinary to behold before any of her personal trauma had sunk its teeth into her. Her eyes, which once must have been full of curiosity and laughter, were cloudy with fear and exhaustion.

"Violet," Patience said.

"She's alive."

"I know," she said with utmost solemnness.

Ben couldn't help but laugh. Only a mother could know with absolute certainty if her daughter was alive or dead. He reached out and put a hand on the mother's shoulder.

"Do you want to help me bring her home?"

"Yes," she whispered.

Ben smiled at her.

"Good, let's go." He extended a hand to help the ladies up. He gave Nguyen time to get Patience dressed, but Patience fought her at every step. She was too eager to help her daughter. Nguyen huffed at him until he exited the tiny bedroom so that she could close the door between them.

He ran his hand through his salt and pepper hair and turned around only to find himself staring through the open door of the apartment and at a crowd of onlookers. Sometimes he was embarrassed to be human. Certain folks had the potential to be kind and good, but people as a group were mindless, greedy things.

"Can I help you?" he asked the gawkers. He hadn't raised his voice, but he leveled a heavy threat in the accented tones of his words.

The crowd in the hallway backed off, some returning to their own apartments while muttering profanities along the way. Ben closed the door on them. Well, he did his best to close the door. He had been forced to kick it open. The sounds coming from behind it had truly concerned him, and he couldn't get any reply to his calls. He'd done what he needed to and regretted nothing, but the splintered door frame gave him grief.

He assumed he must look like a shadow, dressed in his black suit and cleric collar. He looked around the space as he waited for the other two to come out. Heated mumbling reached his ears, and he wondered what it took to keep Patience Brennan in this time and place. He let the women argue in peace as best he could.

The last time he was here, he hadn't wanted to intrude. He hadn't wanted to do anything more than learn about the girl who had somehow managed to fall into one of his paintings. Over the last two weeks, he had done his best to avoid Nguyen, but the woman was more than a little persistent. She'd hounded him, and as such, he would be the first to admit that he'd grown rather fond of the old battle-ax.

Ben wandered around the living room, examining the framed photos on every surface. None of the photos were taken in this run-down apartment. They all featured memories of a happy family. Photographs of the family at the park, dressed for Halloween, and other random moments of joy. The most recent of the photos seemed to be from quite a few years ago. He didn't blame the girl for not finding as much joy in life after the death of her father. And he supposed there wasn't time to stop and enjoy the small moments if they were always spent trying to survive.

The bedroom door opened, and Ben turned around to face the ladies. He was surprised by how disheveled they looked after having put themselves together. Nguyen seemed to read his bemusement.

"Don't say a word, Preacher," she chided him. "This is as good as we're getting, so let's go."

"Yes, ma'am."

Once in the hall, Patience became energized. She was practically bouncing on her feet, but the worry knitted into her brow signified she was still afraid for her daughter. Nguyen turned around to lock the door, but when the door wouldn't stay closed, she gave up on it. She led the way through the tattered complex and turned to face Ben once they were out on the street.

"Now what, Preacher?"

"To the museum."

"Why?"

"Because that's where she's going to be."

"How on Earth do you know that?"

"I just do, Nguyen," he said. They were wasting time they didn't have.

"I've checked the museum. I've checked with her employers. I've even reached out to some of her old friends, the ones I could find."

He understood what she was going through. He'd been through the worry and loss. Sometimes he forgot what it was like, but he saw it in her eyes.

"I can't explain it," he said. "It would take too much time and . . ." His words drifted away. He knew it wouldn't do any good. He needed to get to the painting. Ben spun around and started walking.

"And?" Nguyen asked.

"And we're running out of time," he said over his shoulder. He kept walking, ignoring the protest behind him.

"Father Benny?"

He stopped walking, staring ahead. The city was beautiful. It was full of hope and prosperity. But just like every other place in the world where humans behaved like humans. It was also standing on the shoulders of those considered disposable. The artist had spent his life pretending to be a part of both, the prosperous and the disposable, but Nguyen's voice called him back. He could wear nice clothes and own property. He had the freedom to go anywhere, to do anything he wanted, anything but be accepted.

Ben sighed. His shoulders dropped as he gave in to the woman and he turned around to face her.

"Mrs. Widawski," he answered. "Nguyen—"

"Tell me."

"We don't have time."

"Make time." She planted her feet. Ben was reminded yet again how stubborn the woman was. Violet was lucky to have a person like Nguyen in her life.

"Let's find Violet first, and then I'll tell you anything you want to know."

"No,"

"Please, Nguyen."

"No," she replied, "because I'm not entirely confident you won't disappear as soon as she's back."

"Would that be such a bad thing?"

"I don't trust you, but I have to. I need that girl back just as much as her mother does. But I don't trust you."

"You're right not to trust me."

"But I need you. Violet and Patience need you, so quit fussing around and moping and tell me what the hell is going on!"

Nguyen gripped one of Patience's sleeves to keep the woman from wandering off. The look on her face brooked no argument, and he couldn't help but smile.

"You won't believe me," he said finally.

"I think you should tell me everything and let me decide what I choose to believe."

"I'll tell you on the way."

Nguyen gave Patience's arm a gentle tug to get the woman moving, and they joined Ben. Together, they made their way to the museum, while he told them his story. Well, he told them some of his story. Some pieces of his past he kept to himself. Not even Katherine had ever learned everything about him.

Nguyen was attentive to his tale. She didn't gasp or denounce anything he said. In fact, she was rather patient with him and deliberate with her questions. He didn't know what to make of it. One thing was certain: She asked a lot of questions. By the time they made it to the imposing structure of glass and steel, he appreciated the change in subject. He'd gotten the major points across but still couldn't tell if she believed him or not. There wasn't time to worry about it.

He put his hands on the door of the main entrance to the museum and felt it thrumming beneath his hand. This was wrong. This isn't how things were supposed to be. He closed his eyes and concentrated.

"What is it?" Nguyen asked.

"Something is wrong."

"What's wrong?"

"I don't know." He didn't like not knowing. He concentrated on the feeling beneath his hand. Ben listened to it, to its rhythm, and what he heard gave him hope.

"What?" Nguyen asked.

"I think she's making her own way home."

As soon as he opened his eyes, he launched into motion. He pulled the door open and didn't wait for the women to follow. But they did.

NGUYEN TOOK HOLD OF Patience's hand, and together, they followed the preacher through the maze of exhibits. A thought nagged at her mind as they ran through exhibit after exhibit. Why was the museum open? They had just opened the door and walked right in. It was far too early for visitors. An empty museum was a strange place. It didn't feel right to be here when they shouldn't be. Either someone was going to get fired for not doing their job or it was left open intentionally. She didn't like where that thought was going.

They were going back to the last place Violet had been seen, which made Nguyen nervous. Since she'd been taking care of Patience, there hadn't been time to visit here. As she moved Patience along as fast as she could, Patience's nervousness ticked up a notch. She was constantly looking around as if she were being followed. Nguyen didn't have the time or space to calm the woman down, but it wouldn't really matter in the end. As long as Father Benny honored his promise and found Violet, everything else worked.

A black shadowy figure appeared out of the corner of her eye. She stopped for a second to see what it was, but there was nothing. She must be going crazy. When she turned around to continue following Father Benny, he had stopped as well and was staring over her shoulder. She turned around to see what he was staring at and realized he had seen the same thing she had.

"What is it?"

"A shadow," he said.

"Yes, I gathered that much, yes, thank you," she replied with less patience than she meant.

"It was a shadow I had captured previously."

"What's it doing here?"

"That's a good question," he said with a sigh. "It's not for anything good."

He turned back around and continued heading deeper into the museum until their little rag-tag group popped out into an anteroom of some kind. Exhibits surrounded the little stark piazza on all sides, but one in particular caught Nguyen's attention. She could definitely see why Violet would've been drawn to it.

Behind her, Patience fidgeted, twisting the hem of her cardigan in her fingers. Nguyen put her arm around the woman to soothe her.

"Violet?" Patience whispered fearfully.

"I'm afraid so," Ben replied.

A cold breeze blew past them, and Nguyen pulled Patience in even tighter. Ben's gaze whipped around as though he were tracking something. In an instant, his expression changed. Where it had once been filled with worry tempered by determination was replaced by panic.

"No!" he exclaimed, and in a flurry of movement, he pushed Nguyen and Patience around the corner and up against a wall, shielding them with his body as a torrent of screaming shadows drifted toward them.

The shadows had no definitive shape to them, but their coldness, their inherent wrongness, crashed over her in waves. Nguyen Widawski was a proud woman, but she wanted to run away. She was afraid, afraid as a child lost in a nightmare of darkness. The shadows slithered along the walls, jumped to the ceiling, and swirled around each other, creating eddies of hate and fear everywhere they touched. It seemed like forever before they passed. The preacher was still protecting them; from what, Nguyen didn't know, but she didn't want to find out.

Father Benny grabbed their hands and pulled them into the haunting exhibit of Gothic America, where the light played tricks on them and the horde of shadow monsters sounded as though they were being ripped apart. Deeper and deeper they went, with no time for sightseeing. As Nguyen watched the preacher move comfortably within the darkness and the flickering trickery of the light, she realized he knew darkness. Most people didn't touch darkness on this level, but here they were, walking into a living nightmare to find Violet.

Around the last bend of the winding path of the frightening exhibit, they finally came upon a little open space set up for the artist. A painting covered by a tarp rested on an easel. As the three of them approached it, the tarp moved of its own accord.

29

VIOLET TUNED OUT THE screaming battle behind her. It was merely white noise for her craft. She drew one line after another. The shape was unknowable to anyone else, but her vision was clear. She drew the lines of the doors, her pencil running smoothly along the paper to create the intricate lines of the woodwork and the shades and shadows of the patterned wallpaper. She put all her hope and faith and desperation into the drawing. Time faded away, for it was only Violet and the pencil and the paper. Everything else blew away like mist.

Behind her, the monster children fought against the most terrible foe they had ever come across. They battled against a woman who had nothing left to live for, nothing left to lose. Meanwhile, Violet fought against her own sorrow and loneliness and put it all into her art. As the lines came together, she blended them, mixing her craft with a new purpose, to put what her eyes saw onto the paper.

There was no fervor in her motions, no crazed or hectic attributes. There was no good in rushing the process. She didn't know if any of this was going to work, but she would do whatever it took to get herself back home. With patience as her guide and desire as her muse, she continued to draw.

There were no examples for her to draw upon, no how-to book to tell her what to do or what not to do. All she could do was remember what she had seen of Father Benny's work, which hadn't been fanciful. It had been the opposite. The scene he'd captured on canvas had been haunting. A lonely gravel road flanked on either side by an uninviting forest leading to a brooding manor house built of stone and shadow. Everything about the manor looked as though it had been forgotten. Behind it, a storm was building. She envied Father Benny's skill with color and brush. How could someone paint such life into clouds that looked just translucent enough to allow the glow of lightning as it traced paths through the sky and the gathering storm?

She recalled the strange details hiding in the haunted painting that seemed almost whimsical. Violet smiled a little smile as she remembered the black cat stalking its prey. The window with the soft yellow glow behind a curtain made her realize the image he'd been working on wasn't meant to be empty.

That wasn't the time for her to get daydreamy about it all. She refocused her attention on the task at hand.

As the brutal fight behind her spilled out into the great hall, Violet finished the first phase of her drawing. She held the book up in front of her, comparing it to what she saw. It was the exact same on paper as it was before her very eyes. Only a few times she was satisfied with her work. Although the style was rougher and more energetic than Father Benny's painting, it still matched. It was time to see if she really could do what Lady Katherine claimed.

KATHERINE SPUN AROUND IN a whirl of fabric and hair and claw. Behind the drawing girl, she struck out at the monsters. Pieces of living shadow flung in all directions. But she wasn't immune to the carnage. It was one against two, and the children were vicious. They tore at Katherine's flesh, not caring to devour her anymore; they simply sought to destroy her. But Katherine threw her whole being in the fight, and when one of the children would manage to get past her, she would tear at them until their rage made them momentarily forget about the tasty morsel just out of reach.

Every then and again, she would catch a glimpse of Violet, and her fears would dissipate a little more each time. The girl didn't flounder or panic. Katherine recognized that stillness. It was the stillness an artist had when they understood the task at hand and surrendered themselves to their craft. Hopefully, she wouldn't have to wait too much longer. Her own children were waiting for her to set them free, but that was her secret. That was part of her plans for after.

Evelyn lashed out, raking her claws across Katherine's face, and Katherine let loose a howl of pain. Her flesh burned, and her vision grew cloudy as blood poured down her face, but she didn't reach for the injury like some vain princess. She was a proud woman, more worried about taking more injury than she could heal from. That was all part of the curse of this place. She learned the hard way that if she were injured, the nightmare magic would repair her.

There was a time when she was so desperate to leave that she tried everything, including taking her own life. But it was all for nothing. One night, a very long time ago, she had let herself give in to despair. The memory of the sharp edge of the blade running along her wrists was still as sharp as the blade itself. Katherine had lost consciousness on the stone floor surrounding the hearth. She remembered the warm pools of blood spreading out around her. When her eyes fluttered open the next day, she wept over her healed wounds. The pools of blood had dried, black stains to remind her that she would never be free of this place.

Eventually, she learned to use that knowledge. Here she was, so close to getting what she had worked tirelessly towards. There was no denying the irony that none of this would be possible if Benjamin's new pet hadn't come here. Her beautiful mouth curled into a wicked smile, stretching the grisly wounds on her face.

Evelyn faltered at the sight of her. What were monsters afraid of? Her—the monsters were afraid of her. They would all fear the governess before she was done. This terrible, beautiful thought inspired her with renewed vigor, and she threw herself at the shadow beast with the cries of a berserker.

VIOLET NODDED TO HERSELF. The drawing was ready for the next phase. The idea had come to her when she'd been hiding in the arboretum. She had needed to make the magic of this place her own. She hadn't created it. That was all thanks to Father Benjamin. He created this hell and the rules that governed it. She didn't want to break the rules; Violet just needed to make one new rule.

Since the base image was as realistic as she could make it, it was time to add her own touch to it. Once again, she put her pencil to the paper and drew. This time, she layered a drawing over the top of the one she'd just made, adding modern shapes and textures to it. Violet didn't know if it was going to work, so she started with something small, something familiar. One line after another, turning strokes of charcoal into a familiar cylindrical shape. When she finished, Violet looked at what she'd added. There, on the floor by the door in her drawing, was an ordinary can of spray paint. It looked out of place in the Gothic surroundings, but that didn't matter. She was just as out of place here as the can of spray paint. Without moving her head, her eyes drifted up from the drawing towards the massive doors in front of her.

Lying forgotten and discarded on the floor was a can of spray paint. She sucked in a breath, startled by her own ability. Her eyes grew wide, but a smile crept onto her face. This idea was going to work after all. It was all the motivation she needed to keep going. She bent down and began the final project. She ground her pencil at odd angles against the page and used her fingers to smudge and blend with purpose.

A great rending sound growled throughout the entire house. If the devil were crawling up from hell, it would've sounded similar. Violet didn't look up, though, for she knew what it was. It was she, tearing this nightmare world apart. Her pencil strokes were wielded with purpose. She was a seamstress ripping apart the seams, cutting thread, and prying the pieces of fabric that made up this world apart. Though, she wasn't entirely certain that she could destroy it. She worried, no, that wasn't right. It wasn't a worry, more like an instinct hiding deep within. An instinct that only the original creator could destroy the piece. She could only change it.

THE ENEMIES LOCKED IN battle stopped. The sound of this world tearing itself apart was enough for them to stop and turn all their attention toward the sound. Katherine couldn't believe her eyes. She did not know what the girl was drawing, but it was massive. Around the giant oak doors that separated them from the raging storm outside, a peculiar line of paint was being drawn right before her eyes. The color leached from the flickering candles and the patterned wallpaper.

She had experienced nothing like it. The ambers and embers dripped from every flame in the house and slipped and swirled towards the girl like oil in water. A current of purpose and intention, drawing them all to her. That was when Katherine realized Violet didn't have diverse colors to work with. All she had to work with was one pencil and whatever she could use from her surroundings. Violet used those colors in her own drawing, and the drawing unfurled on the wall right before her.

IT WAS ALIVE, THE very art of it was alive. Within the center of the ragged spray-painted frame that Violet drew around the doors, the paint moved. The colors she stole from the original painting swirled together to make new colors. Violet didn't look up. She didn't need to. Imposter syndrome had plagued her for her entire life. But in that moment, she embraced the power she had. Nothing could stop her except her own mind, and she had overcome it the moment she saw that can of spray paint laying on the floor.

She ignored the sound of this world tearing itself apart. This world was changing, reshaping itself into an image of her design. And like her drawing, she, too, was reshaping. She was no longer a girl. Her childhood had been stolen from her already when her dad died and her mom became sick. She was no longer innocent. The creatures behind her were at the mercy of her will, of her desires.

Violet wanted to see the monsters behind her die, painfully. They had no idea how lucky they were that she craved something more than their demise. Home. She wanted to hold her mom again. It was all possible.

Evelyn and William were all enamored by the transformation happening right before their eyes. The children realized what was happening. An opening in this world was taking shape, and although they had no idea where it would lead just yet, anywhere was better than here. The children abandoned their fight against the governess, who had supplanted them all these years. Instead, they turned their full attention to the portal taking shape.

The children were hungry to get away. They held hands, drawing strength in each other, and advanced toward the girl. This time, they knew she was off the menu. It was alright, though; there were other things to worry about.

Katherine watched them turn away from her. If she wasn't able to stop them here, they would slip away through the very portal she had inspired. She would be damned for all eternity before she could allow them to survive while she was left here. The governess refused to be abandoned again, so she reached out with all the determination she could gather, wrapped her hands around Evelyn's face, and dug her fingers into the monster's flesh.

Evelyn howled, Katherine grimaced, and black sludge seeped out of the wounds she created. William turned away from the exit to see his sister being carved up by pure hatred as Katherine latched on ferociously and picked pieces of her away. The two creatures were locked in a fight that would end in both their deaths; he was sure of it. He refused to stay here any longer.

Seeing a way out, he decided he'd rather leave his sister to her sticky end than share it with her. He gave all his attention to his salvation, the girl with the power to tear worlds apart.

30

Nguyen and Patience clung together at the sight of something so ordinary moving in unordinary ways. Ben pressed them behind him before stepping a little closer. He had never seen anything like it. Up until right then, he had never believed the door could work both ways. The hoard of shadow beasts escaping his painting had frightened him beyond words. The only reason the three of them were still alive was because the beasts were focused entirely on their escape.

The mystical chains of the prison he crafted with paint and canvas had been broken. It had to be the girl's doing. Somehow, she had the same gift as him. He desperately wanted the girl to be okay, but he was still frightened of what was moving beneath. Ben took another tentative step towards the painting. It lurched at him. The ladies behind him flinched. It took all his self-restraint to not jump with them.

The sound of the tearing grew louder, and he heard something else beneath it. Layers of sound all jumbled together, hammering his ears. It was beginning to hurt. He stepped closer, tilting his head to pick out something buried deep within the howling sounds. Then he heard a voice—"She is coming."

Who was coming? He didn't understand. The voice, he could swear it belonged to the girl. If she was the one speaking, then whom could she be speaking of? He needed to know. He must get the girl out of the painting. There was too much at stake for him to give in to his fear.

In a burst of nerves, Ben lunged forward, gripped the tarp, and ripped it off the easel. The canvas was stretched and disfigured with the echo of some type of figure pressing against it. He stumbled away from the shadow of a grasping hand. Behind him, Patience and Nguyen shrieked. He used to think of his paintings as nightmares for monsters, but what confronted him was terrible. The surface of his unfinished painting swelled like the full belly of a pregnant woman, only that the child behind the flesh of canvas and paint was monstrous. It reached for anything, pressing itself against the surface. He didn't know what to make of it. Nothing like this had ever happened.

Turning around, he saw the horrified expression of Nguyen. The woman was confronting true evil, so it was no wonder she was having trouble with it. Beside her, the girl's mother was behaving entirely opposite of what he would have expected.

Patience Brennan was losing her mind in her attempts to reach the disfigured canvas, and Nguyen struggled to restrain her. Anyone else in their right mind would turn and run away, but Patience wriggled against the little woman's grip to break free. She was reaching out toward the painting, and as Ben turned back to the painting, he realized the truth of it. Patience was stretching out desperately for the painting, and the painting was stretching out to her.

It was the girl! The girl was trying to break through from one world to the next, but the painting was holding her back. The painting was fighting her, fighting to keep her imprisoned. Shadows were bleeding out of the painting, too, seeping around the edges, spreading themselves thin, trying with all their might to break free. He couldn't prevent them from escaping and help the girl. He needed to choose. It was an impossible choice.

Patience broke free from Nguyen's grip and leaped for the painting, and Ben only just managed to wrap his arms around her.

The woman bucked against his hold. "NO!" she screamed. The painting screamed. He needed to do something, anything.

"You can't."

"VIOLET!" There was no controlling her.

"You can't touch the paint," he begged her. "You'll be lost. It will take you."

"Help her, please."

"If I help her, the monster will be set free."

"Help her." Patience sobbed in his arms.

His early greediness of having someone else like him had vanished at the sight of the first shadow. He had a job to do, and he had to continue to give up a few if it meant protecting the world from monsters it didn't even know existed. Nguyen stood shocked at the horrific display in front of her, her hands covering her mouth and her eyes wide in horror.

Then a ripping sound tore through the air. Ben, along with Patience and Nguyen, doubled over in pain as the sound attacked every one of his senses. The invisible wall between realms was being torn apart, and there was nothing he could do about it without locking the girl into the painting forever. He hadn't signed this one yet. He hadn't declared it done. It was the only way to stop whatever was happening, because whatever this was, it was about more than just a girl.

Without ceremony, he put Patience back into Nguyen's arms and frantically searched for anything he could use to sign the painting. The last time he was there, he'd left his paints along with the painting, but they were gone. Nothing could aid him. When Ben had realized something terrible was happening in one of his paintings, he'd run off carelessly without his tools. He'd floundered about without a plan and crippled himself against his enemy. No paints, no sketchbook, nothing.

The rending sound morphed into a scream of pain and determination. Ben looked up from his frantic search to see a ghoulish broken figure pouring itself out of the paint and onto the floor of the museum. Pieces of skin and barely recognizable body parts churned as it continued to pour itself out of the painting, slow like molasses, onto the floor. A hand reached out, clawing for anything. An eye bulged from the blackness, and a wicked half-smile emerged, sharp teeth and vengeance snarling at him. He recognized it.

"William?" Ben said in awe and terror. Of all the creatures he'd captured over the centuries, this was a beast he wouldn't inflict on hell.

William coalesced, pulling himself together enough to shoot out and sink his teeth into Ben's arm. Ben howled in pain, but he knew that if William defeated him, Nguyen and Patience were in for an excruciating death. So, he fought this devil with everything he had. They grappled, twisting around each other, tearing at each other, fear and hate mixing together until they couldn't be separated.

Ben was caught off guard by William's strength. Unlike the horde of shadows that had escaped the painting earlier, he wasn't some starved echo of himself. Ben might not be strong enough to hold the beast back, so he needed something to draw with, to write with, anything that would seal the painting and lock the prison before something worse followed. His sister could not escape. The two of them were unimaginably cruel when they were together.

Tentacles of shadow and bone lashed out at him and grabbed Ben by the throat. He was buried beneath the shadow beast. Shards of broken bones stabbed into him, and he screamed in pain but refused to let the beast go. It was all he could do to prevent him from advancing on the women. Thrashing and twisting, snarling and biting, it all blended into an ecstasy of pain. His vision was fading with the beating of his heart. William had his teeth on his throat, and death was creeping in.

NGUYEN COULDN'T STOP THE grisly attack, she had no defense against the monster. Blood and shadow mixed, giving the air a metallic taste. It was all wrong, but Nguyen couldn't do anything to stop it. She wasn't the sort of woman to cry, but hot tears poured down her face.

Meanwhile, Violet's mother was still inconsolable. She didn't care about the beast shredding Father Benny apart. She was still reaching out for the painting from Nguyen's arms. Then, in a motion so sudden that Nguyen nearly stumbled over, Patience stopped.

The painting had finally given way to the struggle on the other side of the canvas. Pushing through the painting from another place, a darker place, an arm emerged. Violet? Its skin was red and raw as though the painting were clawing at her to keep her inside. But, much like the shadow monster that preceded, a being poured out of the canvas and onto the floor. Nguyen wanted to cry and scream all at the same time. It nearly broke her mind to see someone she loved appear so wrong.

The girl fell onto the floor in a heap of blood and fabric, the fighters oblivious to her presence. She stood up, raised her chin, and met her mother's crazed eyes. The mother and daughter were the calm in this storm. Nguyen didn't know what was going on, but they were speaking to each other through their eyes. Patience was calm, and Violet was haggard yet determined. Nguyen was so startled that she lost her concentration and let Patience step out of her grip. But the woman didn't run away. The satisfaction of seeing her daughter once again held Patience Brennan in place. Violet gave Patience and Nguyen a small nod, perhaps to let them know that she was all right, before she turned her attention to the pressing matter at her feet.

BEN AND WILLIAM WERE still locked in a fight that neither was going to survive unless something intervened. Violet had seen what these monsters could do but wasn't sure if she trusted Ben after everything Lady Katherine had told her. But she knew one thing for certain: He was like her and that was enough reason to save him.

Violet Brennan didn't fear the shadows anymore. She was more powerful than them. Without hesitation, she buried her hands into the wet gristle and bone that was William and pulled him off the artist.

William howled at her, throwing sticky tendrils of shadow around in a rage. He had been defeated and was throwing a fit, but Violet paid him no heed. He wasn't a threat any longer and she wasted none of her precious time on him. She knelt and applied pressure to the wounds on Ben's neck.

"Will you survive?" she whispered. He tried to speak, but blood and bile bubbled up in his throat. "Can you do it on your own?" He gave her a slow nod. *Good*, she thought. That was all she needed to know. She stroked his bloody hair out of his handsome face and gave him a weak smile before she left to hold her mom.

By the time Violet crossed the short distance to her mom, tears were already streaming down her face. Violet embraced her mother tightly. The world around them could've been burning, and neither would've cared. Blood and pain were not enough to keep them apart. The monsters knew this.

Eventually, Violet threw out an arm and pulled Nguyen into their embrace. She didn't know what the older woman had been through to keep her mom safe, but her friend was the reason she could hold her mom right then. Behind the women, Ben was pulling himself onto his feet. Most of the bleeding had stopped, but it was drying in sticky dark trails across his skin and clothes.

"Ben," Violet called out.

He turned to look at her and caught the object she had thrown in his direction. A charcoal pencil, worn down to a nub. Without hesitation, he reached over and scribbled his name on the bottom corner of the painting, and instantly, the sounds of the world tearing itself apart stopped. The storm had passed, and they were left with an unsettling quiet.

Violet turned to look for William and realized one last crea-ture had come through the painting. William leaned against his sister, who stood triumphant. Violet wasn't about to leave her mom yet, and Ben was in no shape to fight the siblings. She had no choice but to let them go, knowing something truly nasty had been set loose on the world. They looked at each other, sharing a look of worry and burden.

After the monsters slithered away, there was so much to say, but Violet wasn't ready to give up this tiny moment of peace. She turned to Ben. "I'm taking my mom home."

"We need to talk."

"I know, but give me this first." Her reply wasn't a request.

With an arm wrapped tightly around her mom and another around Nguyen, Violet walked away from the carnage left behind. She didn't care about the mess; she only cared about her family, or at least what was left of her family. They left Ben standing there alone, a pillar of black and blood, and she didn't care. All she wanted to do was go home.

Violet turned around before she rounded the corner of the exhibit. Her eyes met Ben's. An invisible line tethered them. They were connected. Forever. Violet's lips parted as she formed the words that would frighten him more than anything else.

"She's coming."

31

Katherine stood in the great hall, the massive image that Violet had drawn upon this world looming before her. The girl had taken the book with her, but the image she drew for Katherine was like a scar. It was garish and uncouth, a messy tribute to her own era. Katherine did not understand it, but an understanding of it was not necessary for it to work as promised.

She would be a liar if she said she wasn't afraid. Katherine had been here for so long that she was apprehensive about leaving. Here, she understood how everything worked. But out there, out in the world that used to be her home, things were different. Would she be able to survive there? Could she adapt after such a long time? There was only one way to find out. Besides, she owed a debt of gratitude to the girl for putting herself in danger so that she could have this opportunity.

Katherine wasn't necessarily sure the girl trusted her, but Violet at least understood her need to finish her story. So here she was, only a breath away from leaving this place, and she was having doubts. She approached the massive drawing emblazoned on the wall of the manor. It felt alive. The house was so quiet since nearly every prisoner had fled. It was in that quiet that she could hear the drawing breathing. Slow and steady, patient, like it was waiting for her. Only inches away from it, she stopped and wondered if it would hurt to travel through it. It was a legitimate question. She watched Violet press herself between worlds, screaming the entire time. It didn't look particularly pleasant. She had no way of knowing if it would be the same, but she had to assume it was.

Katherine tentatively reached out her hand toward the drawing and touched it. When her fingers passed effortlessly through the image, without pain, Katherine let out a breath she hadn't realized she'd been holding. Thank goodness for little blessings, she thought. She gave her fingers a little wiggle and nearly giggled. It wasn't just because the girl's magic worked, but because there was hope. Katherine had forgotten how invigorating hope could be.

Lady Katherine Ainsley pulled her hand back out of the drawing and prepared to step through it completely, but something happened that she had not expected. She looked down at her slender fingers and fair skin, which were deteriorating right before her eyes. A black rot was seeping through the fair skin of her hand, blooming as though the rot was on the inside and finally reaching towards the surface like spring flowers unfurling themselves from the cold soil of winter. She rolled her hand this way and that, curling and straightening her fingers. There was no pain, no loss of dexterity, but the blooming rot continued. Her blackening skin broke, and the skin festered. She watched as her skin peeled back, a weeping wound revealing the muscles and tendons beneath the surface. Katherine was fascinated.

She laughed. She had gone mad over the years as this horrible place refused to let her wither and die, but she understood that as soon as she stepped back into her world, back into time, that particular curse would fade away. She turned away from the drawing and headed deep into the house, laughing the whole way. All she could hope for was that her body would last long enough for her to do what she needed to. Her laughter echoed throughout the nearly empty house. The most wicked of witches would have been frightened by the sheer joy hanging on the melodic tones of her laughter.

Katherine needed to adjust her plans before she rejoined the world, before she offered her lover a serving of vengeance. By the time she'd gathered what she needed into a little velvet bag and made her way down to her private rooms, she was practically humming. Of all the places in this prison, her private rooms gave her permission to be true to herself. There, in the solitude, she didn't have to pretend to be something she was not. There, she dreamed of dark and terrible things.

Katherine's laboratory was an unusual space for the house. It didn't fit in the time or place, rather seeping out of something she read. She knew this place intimately. Spending eternity in a place was likely to do that. Every then and again, she would stumble across something new, a new painting on the walls or a new book on the shelves. One of those new books was like this place, like her laboratory. It was full of mystery and intrigue but also of a unique and stirring blend of modernity and something like her own time. It wasn't until she'd read that book that this place appeared. She loved the juxtaposition of it against the horror of her life, so she claimed it for her own.

The harsh flickering lights clicked on, announcing her presence. Tucked into the arched alcoves were her workspaces and she walked to the one nearest the chilling cabinet she used to keep her little experiments constrained. A white laboratory apron hung on a nearby peg, and she put it on, taking her time knotting it around her waist. Then, with a soft, happy smile, she settled onto the stool at her workspace and began the work.

The familiar buzz of the lights overhead was the background music to her craft. She pulled out a tray of vials from the chilling cabinet and let them acclimate. Next, Katherine opened the small velvet bag she had with her and gently poured its contents onto her work surface. The white shards of the mask she'd worn for so long spread out in front of her. With utmost patience, she began the tedious work of fitting them back together.

She lost herself in the work. Time continued to tick away into minutes and hours, but she paid it no mind. Her work required attention to detail and patience, virtues she had in spades. Eventually, her little experiments had acclimated. She looked upon the vials filled with the black substance Violet hadn't understood. Katherine had learned long ago that Evelyn and William were far too clever for this experiment to work. They were the original shadows, the first children of their master. Yes, she knew about their master, too, thanks to her little bees, as she liked to call them.

The other shadows in this place, the other victims of Benjamin's craft, were a different tale. She flattered them and listened to them, and after a time, they bent to her will. These shadows belonged to her, and she needed their help.

"Well, little ones, I need you now," she said to the inky vials. In response, the black viscous liquid in each of the vials squirmed and wriggled, crawling up the sides of the glass. "Excellent. Here's what I need from you." She explained what had happened and what she needed from them. Katherine was rewarded with their grateful assistance, for they were eager to prove to their mistress they could be of service.

Together, Katherine and her bees, shadows distilled and reduced to their vilest forms, worked patiently to glue her old mask back together. With the patience of an artist, she used a delicate paintbrush dipped into the vials to piece them into something that resembled their previous shape. Like everything that was once broken, the mask could not fully return to its previous state. Even though an injury might heal over time, it would never be the same as it once was. Broken people were the same. Some injuries made a person weaker, while others, she thought with a smile, made a person stronger. More hours passed, and Katherine and her little bees toiled at the job of piecing her mask together. The puzzle of shattered pieces came together slowly, held in place not by glue, but by shadow and beast and vengeance.

Framed by the juxtaposition of one lovely hand, youthful and ivory, and the other of rot and decay, the mask was finished. Every vial lay empty in front of her. She would take each of her little bees along on this next intriguing adventure. Lady Katherine Ainsley was ready to step back into the world.

She smiled the whole way back to the drawing Violet had made for her. There was the slightest tingle of fear that it would have sealed itself by the time she had finished her little craft project, but as she stood before the garish drawing, she could hear it breathing still. It breathed in slow, heavy sighs, satisfied as a lover after receiving the gift of intimacy. Katherine stepped forward and began the journey to leave this hell and step into the light once again.

32

VIOLET'S APARTMENT WASN'T THE same as she'd left it. It was still small and shabby but with evidence of violence all around her. The frame around their door was splintered, and she couldn't help but notice the damage to her mom's room. It made her angry. She was angry so much hardship should be suffered by one family. She wished all she had to contend with was something as simple as bitterness, jealousy, and grief. But she was angry at Ben for his carelessness. She was angry at Katherine for manipulating her. But more than all that, she was angry at herself for allowing all of this to happen, and the broken pieces of her life scattered around her little apartment reminded her she'd allowed her life to be violated.

The shabbiness of the place had never bothered her, but it felt more so now, after all that time she spent in the painting. There, she had been the small shabby one. But her time in that place had changed her. The universe was a much more dynamic and complicated place than she originally thought.

327

Magic was real. It was strange to wrap her head around that. She'd seen the proof. She *was* the proof. Her understanding of life had been changed. *She* had been changed, if she were being honest with herself. What was she supposed to do now? Violet had no idea. She drifted around her little apartment, a tiny paper boat lost out at sea, touching everything, remembering everything. It was all so vivid compared to the broodiness of the world in the painting.

One room away, her mom was tucked into bed with Nguyen curled up next to her. It was strange she'd only found her way back to them a few hours ago. Nguyen had tended to Violet's wounds after Violet had taken the longest shower of her life. She didn't know what she would've done if something had happened to her mom while she was gone. The old version of her would have blamed herself for everything, but that wasn't who she was anymore. Violet knew better than to keep all the blame on herself. Ben was at the center of all this, and she was glad he would share the burden. According to what Katherine had told her, this had all started with him all those years ago. None of that mattered anymore, she supposed. It might have started with Ben, but Violet was determined to put an end to this shit.

Nguyen and Violet had come to an agreement that tomorrow would be soon enough to talk about what happened to them both. For now, they relished that they were all back together, and her mom was calm and as content as she ever was. So, they'd put her to bed after a cup of lavender chamomile tea, but whatever had happened while Violet was indisposed had altered their relationship. Her mom couldn't seem to relax without Nguyen. She'd refused to be separated from the older woman. Violet had no idea how to solve that problem, but like everything else, that was a problem for another day.

She pulled the whistling kettle off the stove and poured herself a fresh cup of tea before taking it out onto the little rusty balcony. Violet leaned her elbows on the rail, cradling the warm cup in her hands. The fragrance wafted up and mingled with all the familiar scents of home. But like everything else in her apartment, even this smell was more vibrant and poignant. Her perception had shifted, and she saw her world, her universe, in new ways. It felt uglier than it had before, though it was the same as it always was. Only her awareness of it differed. All around her was poverty and sickness, greed and lust. Now, she chafed against it more.

She took a sip of her tea and embraced the warm sensation as it traveled down her throat. Maybe, just maybe, she'd finally come to terms with who she was. She was an artist. She was an artist who'd been forced to do everything but art. That newfound knowledge clawed against everyone's expectations of what she should be doing. Well, she was done with that bullshit. She had given up enough of herself to the world's cruelty. That was going to stop.

Violet closed her eyes and let the sounds of her neighborhood, of her old life, wash over her. People laughed off in the distance. An angry cat growled. But something else lurked beneath the sounds of the mundane. There, amongst all the usual noises of the city after dark, was an unusual silence. Violet tilted her head to catch the sound better. It was subtle yet tangible. She could almost reach out and touch it, as though it had shape and form.

The sound was slithering through the streets. She wondered if the sound was new or it had always been there and she hadn't been open enough to hear it. Her eyes slowly opened. Down on the street below was a figure, a shadow really, standing there. Violet wasn't surprised to see the figure in the light cast from the entrance to her building. Although she couldn't make out his features, she knew him, anyway. It was time to get some answers.

She closed the balcony door softly. Inside, the little apartment was quiet. It was amazing how simple the illusion was, that she could close a door and shield herself from the outside world. Violet, more than most, knew the cruelty of the world didn't work like that. This little sanctuary was only a mirage.

She checked on her mom, who was curled up like a child against the sleeping figure of Nguyen. Even asleep, Nguyen looked like she'd aged several years while Violet had been gone. She'd find out soon enough what she went through to keep her mom safe. In the meantime, she needed answers of her own.

Violet stepped out into the dingy corridor and closed the door behind her. She locked the door before going downstairs to meet her shadowy visitor. The key was awkward in her pocket, and now that she thought about it, everything about her life felt that way. It was all coarse and awkward. She shook her head to clear the cobwebs, then traveled down the stairs and out the vestibule of the apartment. The heat of the night was a hint of the approaching summer. Since her attention latched on to every detail, she couldn't seem to focus on any-thing. She stuffed her hands into her pockets to look a little less twitchy.

Just out of reach of the yellow light of the vestibule was the figure. Even this close, she couldn't see his features, but she recognized the way he carried himself. Confidence, true con-fidence, was difficult to fake. In a few short steps, she stepped out of the light and joined him in the shadows.

"I suppose this means you're not really a priest?" she asked even though she knew the answer.

"It's complicated," Ben replied.

"That's an understatement."

"You caught me off guard."

"Or you were just careless," she shot back, level and calm. She would not let him get out of this without owning up to his part. Her eyes adjusted to the darkness, and her perception of him changed. He was no longer something to be admired or desired. Violet had learned the ugliness about him, thanks to her time with Katherine. However, she needed answers.

"It was careless of you to have an uncompleted piece out in the open like that."

Ben's face crumpled under the weight of her declaration. "That's not fair."

"How old are you, Ben? How long have you understood all of this?" She got in his face but dropped her voice. "You could have gotten her out of there a long time ago."

"I didn't know."

"You didn't know, what? That she would suffer? That's crap. You knew what you were doing sending her in there."

"I thought she could temper them."

"You thought she could make them less evil? Seriously?" This was getting her nowhere. There was no point in arguing about the past. What was she supposed to do now? "And what about me?"

"You have to understand," he said, reaching for her, but he pulled back before he could touch her. "It's been so long since I've met anyone who could—"

"Rip people away from their lives with the stroke of a pencil?" she finished.

"It's not like that," he said darkly. Ben's anger was rising to the surface. He stepped closer to her. "What happened in there?"

It was Violet's turn to let her emotions get the better of her. She closed her eyes, but there was no escaping the memories. Would she ever escape the gruesome memories of that place? Probably not. It didn't matter. He was deflecting.

When she opened her eyes, Ben flinched. She didn't know what he saw, but it had the effect she was hoping for. "Tell me about Katherine."

Ben's head whipped back like he'd been slapped in the face. "How do you know about her?"

Violet looked at the man standing before her. She wasn't sure how she could've been so enamored with him. He kept too many secrets. He was too arrogant. "The painting."

"What's that supposed to mean?"

Violet took a step closer to Ben. The copper tang of dried blood mingled with the putrid fragrance of the black bile left behind by those shadow creatures. But beneath it all, the scent of his natural musk lingered. She looked up into his astonished face and raised an eyebrow at him.

"Don't tell me you didn't know about her."

"There's nothing to tell," he barked. "She died." Ben stumbled back and ran his hands through his hair. Was his hair grayer than it'd been before? "She died a long time ago," he said resignedly.

"You don't know, do you?"

"Know what?"

"Nothing dies in that place."

"Don't be so dramatic," Ben threw back at her.

"Don't be an asshole."

"You're only really just a child. You don't know what you're talking about."

"I met her, Ben!"

"What? That's not possible."

"If that were the case," she said as she closed the distance between them again, "then how do you explain me being able to come back, huh?"

Ben froze. His lips parted before he spoke. "Your situation was different."

"How so?"

"That's not important."

"That's it, right there," Violet hissed. "Unless you can own up to your mistakes, then how are you going to help me with any of this?"

"It's not that at all."

"Then go on, tell me what the hell is going on." Violet was sick and tired of being left in the dark.

"You're like me." Ben opened his hands like they were holding an imaginary book, like an offering.

"I'm nothing like you." Violet spat each word, lacing them with venom. She didn't need his problems. She was different, and she had learned that the hard way. Ben wasn't the one who taught her how to use her ability. That was thanks to Katherine. If it hadn't been for Katherine's help, Violet would probably still be stuck in that hell, a hell of Ben's making.

"But you are. You find the life in everything you draw." Ben reached into his pocket and pulled out a neatly folded piece of paper. He extended it to Violet with a reverence that she didn't understand.

She took the paper from him and unfolded it. It was the last drawing she ever made of her dad. Violet ran her thumb across the scribbled signature in the corner and knew what he was trying to tell her. She had the same ability he did, to control the fate of other creatures with a swipe and a scribble. But she already knew this. She understood her ability more than he did.

Violet brought her eyes up to meet his. "I did this on accident," she said softly, "but you, you do this shit on purpose."

"To protect people. You've seen them. What do you think happens when those creatures are set loose on the world?"

"Who are you to decide who is the villain in this story?"

"They are evil. They rampage. They devour." He grabbed her by the arms. "Nothing good comes from them."

"You threw her to them knowing they were going to feed on her."

"I gave her up because she was the strongest, kindest person I knew." He struggled with the next words. "I needed someone to anchor the painting or else they would all escape."

"You could've just signed it. That would have locked the painting," she said. The longer he struggled with his emotions, the more she understood. He had loved her, truly.

"I—I couldn't."

"Bold enough to throw her to the wolves but not enough to make sure her suffering was for something good."

"I—"

"No, you don't have a say in this anymore. I don't know why I was given this ability, but I sure as hell am going to use it better than you." She shoved the drawing of her dad back at Ben. "If you're not going to help me, then what's the point of you?" She'd decided; she was going to have to find her own answers. Violet was going to have to do this like she'd done everything else in her life. Alone.

She spun on her heels and walked away from him. After everything that had happened because of his carelessness, Violet was more than happy to leave him in the shadows.

"Wait," Ben called out after her. She stopped. "There's so much you need to know."

"You're right." Violet turned around. "There's a lot I don't know. And at the beginning of all this, I thought you were going to be the one to help me."

"I *can* help you," Ben implored, each word tangled up in need, in his desire to have a partner. He believed he could help her, but he was lying to himself. That lie could bring them both down, and she wasn't about to let that happen.

Violet put as much space between them as she could. There was plenty he could teach her about whatever the hell was wrong with them, but she couldn't trust him. How could she? After everything she'd been through and everything Katherine had told her, there was no way she could put her life in his hands. She could do it on her own but wished she could soothe the knot in her chest. The encircling loneliness threatened to overwhelm her. She had to get control of her emotions, or she was going to drown in them. In this ocean of heartache, she was drowning.

The streets were quiet, as though the neighborhood was holding its breath, waiting for something to happen. Soon enough, she would put an end to all of this.

"I don't think so," she said.

33

Ben walked through the museum in a daze. His injuries were healing, but he was covered in gore. He didn't care. His world had turned inside out, and he hadn't had a moment to process anything. Time had been the one thing he always seemed to have plenty of, until then, it would seem. He'd just witnessed an army of beasts he'd spent his entire life capturing escape into the world, and he nearly didn't survive the experience.

The museum was silent as he made his way through. The silence shouted at him. He thought his skull was going to shatter with the pressure of it all. He needed to get out, to get away. Ben let his feet take him away while his mind worried at Violet's words. "She's coming." Who was coming? But he knew. He knew who it was. His heart knew. It broke afresh. The scars that webbed throughout his ancient heart cracked, fissures of pain and sorrow, and guilt overpowered him. So, he walked aimlessly, without seeing, without caring.

His grief and fear were so overwhelming that he almost missed the tinge of metal in the air. But he'd hunted monsters for a long time, and Ben's instincts were finely tuned. He stopped outside on the sidewalk. The museum entrance behind him cast his silhouette on the dark street before him. The street was devoid of traffic, and the only sign of life was a homeless man digging through a nearby trash bin. But the sickly metallic taste of wrongness hung in the air, mingling with vehicle exhaust and animal urine. He looked around, cautiously noting his surroundings and momentarily setting his grief aside. There was work to do.

After all this time, he was surprised true evil wasn't always something grotesquely disfigured. Quite often, it was beautiful and intriguing. The human condition was attracted to it. Little bees to pollen, humans swarmed and gawked at it, not realizing evil was contagious. It was far more contagious than goodness. Ben had seen it all throughout his years walking the Earth. True goodness was a rare thing. Humans were beasts. They craved power, and worse of all, humans were conquerors. There was no end to what even the lowest of humans could destroy in the vain attempt to have superiority over anything and everything.

He followed the alluring scent of evil down the street until he reached a nondescript, dark alley. Ben hesitated. A strange sensation wriggled in his stomach like a worm. He hadn't felt this sensation in over a century. Fear squirmed and tugged at his insides. The jagged shards of the museum cast long shadows and blocked out most of the stars in the velvet sky. A neon EXIT sign glowed red against the deep blues and purples of the shadows. The light of a nearby streetlamp couldn't reach the mouth of the alley, and he wondered if he could be wrong about what he felt. He ran his hands through his hair before stepping into the shadows.

The concrete walls and patchwork cobbles insulated the place against the bustling sounds of the city nightlife. His footsteps landed softly. Ben had spent his exceptionally long life in and out of the shadows, so he was familiar with the ugly side of humanity that civilization tried to hide behind modernity and progress. Yet there in that place, old monsters still lurked. Each soft step he took felt as though it echoed, announcing his presence with a shivering scream. Detritus piling up against the walls reminded him the alley might very well be home to some vagabonds of the city. A blue dumpster was pushed haphazardly up against another wall, which was covered in graffiti that glowed eerily in the dim light.

At first sight, it seemed like he was alone, but the hairs on his arms rose to attention and alerted him to another presence. Something was here, out of place in that time and space.

The alley was not long, and it had a dead end up ahead. A luxury apartment building, the Museum Apartments, butted up against the angles of the museum. He approached the wall at the end of the alley. There was no door or passage, which was unusual. Why connect these buildings in such a haphazard way? His mouth twitched, threatening to smile. Maybe that was what his senses were trying to warn him about. Perhaps that place was wrong intentionally. Perhaps if he offered it a little patience, it would reveal itself.

Ben embraced the neon shades of night, oblivious to the noise of the city. The velvet sky was out of sight, washed out by the city lights. A rat scurried along the trail of trash that accumulated against the walls. A breeze funneled in from the street and swirled in small eddies around the giant casters of the dumpster. His hands pushed back his black jacket, and he stuffed them into the pockets of his trousers. He didn't know how long he waited there, and it didn't really bother him. He was a patient man, and his patience was rewarded.

The concrete slab before him was covered in sloppy graffiti that was dripping. However, its carelessness suited the environment. What little light made its way there cast the paint in an array of glowing blues, greens, and purples. The empty places between strokes of aerosol were pitch black as if the night had swallowed up the empty places. The deep dark places of the night claimed the forgotten for its own, which Ben understood. He was, after all, a creature of the night, a monster to monsters. He was most comfortable in the dark and was never afraid of what hid in the shadows. But there must be balance. Monsters couldn't be allowed to roam the world free of consequence.

The colors of the paint shifted as though caught in a beam of light. He tilted his head, and a subtle beam of iridescence cascaded across the wall, shifting unnaturally against the curves of the graffiti. Ben took a step closer. While passing cars were casting beams of light, the glow of the streetlights out on the sidewalk wasn't strong enough to penetrate the darkness of the alley. Then one spot of paint undulated, slowly at first, then quickening. The rhythm mimicked that of an expectant lover. It pulsed quicker and deeper until it dipped impossibly into the concrete and sprang back as though a tiny pebble had been dropped into a pond.

Curious, he thought. It was a familiar effect, but he had never come across another creature capable of manifesting such a thing, other than himself, of course. The ripples spread slowly as honey across the vertical surface of the cracked and peeling wall. This was not his doing, so how was this happening? The girl had returned. She'd gone off with her mother, so this couldn't be her work, or could it be? He'd never known anyone to come back. It was a frightening prospect to think that the monsters he had captured in oil and canvas could escape their prison, but he'd seen it with his own eyes. He didn't want to even think about it, but the question was begging him, How did Violet return? And was it possible that whatever door created could still be swung wide open?

The very molecules of the wall shifted and writhed in a way so unnatural it made his intestines lurch. The strokes of careless graffiti were rearranging as though an artist, in a fit of displeasure at the state of their own art, had thrown some mineral oil at it and begun reworking the piece. It was disconcerting to watch, but he could not look away. He wondered if this was what it was like to watch him at work. Ben's curiosity was impossible to deny, and he reached out towards the paint crawling across the wall reorganizing itself into something new. But his hand lingered in the air.

Colors shifted, shades swirled, mixing to create new colors that hadn't been there before. He wanted so badly to touch the paint, to feel life being threaded through it, but he might very well be pulled into another world, one possibly not of his making. And that was enough to temper his curiosity. He stepped back and admired the work of another artist as he waited for the piece to take shape. It wasn't long before a gilded frame filled his vision. Layers of paint spilled and tugged at each other to create texture and depth. The rich texture of damask wallpaper in alluring shades of aubergine and shadow poured from the top of the gilded frame.

Something familiar nagged at him. Was it simply a case of déjà vu or something more? Ben's lips parted, and his pulse quickened. It had been a very long time since anything had intrigued him to this extent, and he was eager to introduce himself. A new color bubbled up from the center of that inspiring magical painting, then a pool of red paint leaked out onto the center of the burgeoning canvas, spreading out like a puddle of blood. Before him was a hooded figure cloaked in red, a hint of the side of a woman's face. The embroidery along the edge of the rich cloak was of a fine and elegant celestial design. I have seen you before, he thought, as the youthful lines of a woman's face turning away beckoned him closer.

His body was pulled closer to the exquisite portrait unfolding before him. The gilded frame loomed over him as the figure of the mysterious woman looked more real with each passing second. His hand rubbed at his chest as his heart pounded against his ribs. He had been alone for so long. The painting on the abused concrete wall was nearing completion. Watching this masterpiece unfurl itself was intoxicating. Witnessing a power to rival his own was erotic, and his body responded in kind. Then he saw it.

The fabric of the cloak moved subtly, softly, with the very breath of the woman. He caught the barest hint of her pale face, pristine as porcelain, before the woman turned around. The perfect flesh of her face was not hers at all, but a mask. It was simply the most beautiful face he had ever seen, but his heart ached to see that it had been shattered. It was covered in infinitely elegant lines, filled with a familiar black substance that absorbed light. The Japanese art of mending broken items by piecing the cracks together with gold, *kintsugi*, was also a way to admire the history of an item. He had always believed that people were the same. Only those individuals who turned their damage into beauty were even worth his time and attention. This was something more than traditional *kintsugi*. Instead of being stitched together with gold, the mask was held together by shadows. The effect was haunting.

The figure was petite. Although the gilded frame was huge, it mostly showcased a dark manor as the backdrop. It was familiar, like an echo of his own work, and beautiful, but it couldn't hold his attention as the mysterious figure could. He leaned forward as though an invisible string tethered him to the woman, but he forced himself to resist. He hadn't confronted a figure like this before. The shape beneath the hood tilted its head at him. He wondered what he must seem to it.

He didn't sense any fear from her, but something more than curiosity lingered there.

She stared at him from across the impossible barrier of concrete and paint, of time and magic. Time was of no consequence to creatures such as that. He paid time no mind until the figure stepped up to the side of the gilded frame. Ben's blood threaded through his body as he became anxious and eager to reintroduce himself. Although his power was abstract, built on imagination and creativity, he was still a physical creature. He had physical desires, and the visage before him had reawakened them.

The woman hesitated at the edge of the frame, reaching out a slender ivory hand. An invisible barrier pressed against her perfect skin, and he wondered if she was trapped. Her head twitched gently, and he was reminded again of something familiar. The feline-like movements were slow and deliberate, exotically patient. It stitched together a memory that twisted around the warm viscera of his body.

Ben recognized her. His heart recognized her, but he couldn't admit to it. It couldn't be, he thought, realizing finally that the brooding manor in the painting was that of his own creation. How was it that someone else could conjure his art, his magic? He knew the answer, though. Somehow, that was Violet's work. Ben's curiosity grew as he watched her push more firmly against the barrier, her hand breaking through the magical canvas and out into his world. Like all magic, however, there was a consequence, a price to pay to keep the balance between worlds.

The porcelain flesh of her slender hand resisted, tugged, and shriveled, aging right before his eyes. The more she pushed against the unseen force, the more her flesh rotted. Her body glitched against the magic. She stepped out of the brooding manor behind her and set her feet in the dirty alley.

They faced each other in a manner of speaking. His hair moved slightly against an icy breeze accompanying the figure cloaked in red. The fine fabric hugged her form, breathing with her. Ben desired to touch her. The tease of mystery brought a smile to his face.

The woman's hand reached for her mask. Where the flesh had once been perfect, it sloughed, falling in small chunks to the ground. Sinew, bones, and tendons showed. The mechanic movements of her hand were on horrifying display, yet he could not look away. He needed to see who this was even though his mind knew this answer. Ben was astounded by the aching beauty of the mask, a carved replica of the woman he'd fallen in love with so long ago. The eerie glow of magic cast iridescent shades of blues and purples. The exquisitely delicate lines of shadow that had repaired the once-shattered mask caught the light. It gave off the impression of something moving. But it was more than a simple illusion of light and color. Ben recognized the face of the mask. It was a face he remembered. The face of the only woman he ever found himself able to love.

Ben knew by the ache in his ancient heart the woman standing before him was none other than Lady Katherine Ainsley.

"Katherine?" His rich, sultry voice caught on the grief of his memories and guilt. His lips parted when the mask was drawn away, and for the tiniest of moments, the beautiful ivory face he longed to see again appeared. The rot in her hand was crawling up the flesh of her slim neck, seeping over the lines of her jaw, her blushing lips eroding. The flesh fell away as a slow, sinister smile spread across her lips.

He had once loved her. Then he'd trapped her. And in that moment, he feared her.

"Hello, Benjamin."

34

The alley smelled of urine and rotting garbage, but Ben hardly noticed. He only had eyes for Katherine. Right before Ben's eyes, the delicate skin of her face withered and molted away. Desiccation crawled across her skin, slow and ethereal as an autumn fog. He had clung to his memory of her petal-soft lips, but that memory faded when her lips curled and stretched into an exaggerated grin. Katherine's smile was chilling. The wet tendons and muscles working beneath the rotting flesh glimmered in beams of light cast by passing cars. That smile was the very essence of nightmares. Ben was truly frightened but not by the decay before him.

He'd learned long ago to see past appearances. Something else entirely turned his blood to ice. There, for anyone to see, was an expression of pure satisfaction. Like a Cheshire cat, she stood there serenely watching the rolling shock and awe cross his face. She'd achieved something extraordinary, a goal she'd been striving toward, and whatever that goal was, he didn't know. He *did* know she'd survived more than a century surrounded by wicked creatures, and he feared that sheer act of survival more than anything.

It would have been better if she'd died in there, of this he was certain. Over and over again, he'd tried to convince himself she had died years ago. Death would have been kinder. It should have been something beautiful. He'd even managed to convince himself it had been a poetic death, that there was something Shakespearean about it.

Instead, he desired to reach out and touch her. But it was a dangerous thing to do. He took a tentative step forward, and she didn't move. Her mask dangled casually at her side as the rot continued to spread. A thought bloomed in his mind. Was the rot only skin deep? Or had her very essence been corrupted? Could she be redeemed?

There was something else, too, another thought crawling through his mind. Her skin blistered and peeled as though invisible maggots were eating away at it. His body ached just looking at her. It had to be painful. She shifted slightly, and the tendons and bones popped and snapped. Despite all this, he still sought her touch. He *needed* to touch her. He hadn't realized how much he needed her to forgive him for what he'd done all those years ago, until what was left of her lips parted and she spoke to him.

"Hello, Benjamin."

"Is that really you?" he asked.

She shook her head gently. It was as though she were judging him as a child who had done something foolish.

"You look older," she said.

"You look—" He had only known her loveliness. He remembered her curiosity and compassion, and he covered her desiccation in a blanket of memories. But he would indeed be a fool if he tried to ignore the gory consequences of her escape from his painting.

"Don't hurt yourself, Benjamin. I'm no silly young woman eager for compliments from the dashing lord of the manor. I've grown beyond those trivial needs." Her words sounded light, but just beneath the surface, a current of venom pulsed. "In fact, thanks to that very interesting young woman you sent my way, it would seem that most women have grown beyond the need for male validation and affirmation."

"I don't understand how."

"You used to be quicker than this, Benjamin."

"How are you here?"

"How did I manage to extricate myself from that hell, you mean?"

The temperature between them dropped. A flood of unexpected emotions threatened to overtake Ben, and tears broke through the dam of stoicism he'd built to protect himself against heartache ever since he'd condemned her to something much worse than death.

"I would say," Katherine continued without paying his anguish any mind, "that it was no thanks to you, but if it weren't for you and your continued carelessness, I would never have met Violet."

"It was her, then?"

"Of course it was her," she mocked. "You really do seem to be struggling, dear."

"I am so sorry."

"No."

"What?"

"No," she repeated. "You don't get to apologize for what you've done. There is no sufficient apology that can undo what you've done." She spoke calmly, but her words held tension. Her time with monsters had changed her irrevocably.

"Katherine, I—"

"Benjamin." His name escaped the ruins of her mouth like rancid butter, dark and watery. "There is nothing you can do to make this right."

"I must try," he begged.

Lady Katherine Ainsley stepped closer to him. She was so close to him that he could feel her coldness. She held no warmth, and he wondered, Had she died in there? Was she, in fact, just a talking corpse?

"Benjamin, dear," Katherine began, her voice bored, "the only thing I need from you is your eternal suffering."

Her words pierced him. In his unnaturally long life, he'd learned to decipher lies from truth. Lies were easy and comfortable. Truth, on the other hand, was awkward and painful. Invisible strings that had lashed around his heart the moment he'd met her, binding them together, cinched tightly at her words, her truth. Her words came out with barely restrained revulsion. How could he ever hope to make this right if her time in the painting had changed her so completely?

Her words cut into his heart and nearly doubled him over. He'd sent his lover into a hellscape hoping she could change the nature of monsters, change them into something less evil. Although he'd thought he was guarding against his own arrogance by sending her, he'd only given proof to this fallacy by sending her in his place. He never had the power to change the nature of such creatures. Benjamin Brahm had been playing God to defeat demons, but in the end, he only created a devil terrifying enough to ruin him.

All the things he'd cherished about her had been corrupted by time and circumstance. While Katherine had once been warm and endearing, she was cold and indifferent. Her kindness festered and turned to poison. Her tenderness was cold, but something more akin to granite rather than ice. This woman, this creature, was something new and very dangerous. She had found some truth on the other side that gave her the strength to endure. Here she was, back where she should be, with experience and vengeance to keep her warm. Benjamin didn't doubt her. He felt her desire to see him suffer and knew it would inevitably come to pass.

"Now," she said with a lazy rotting smile, "if you don't mind, I have things to do."

He still needed to prove she was real, to feel her against him. Through his tears, he could see her awareness of his desires, which brought an uncomfortable stretch to her cold smile. The physical distance between them was negligible, but he wasn't so naïve to think it was just an empty space between them. There was an infinite cosmos of betrayal and suffering filling that void. The warmth of his tearstained kiss on her rotting flesh couldn't fix that. His lips couldn't press against hers hard enough to keep the rot from spreading. The damage was done. Now came the consequences.

Katherine lifted the mask back into place. It must have shattered during her time in the painting because its pieces were held together by something black and sinister, not glue or paint. She tilted her head. No, it was held together with shadow and malice. The delicate rippling lines were so black that even the night sky would be jealous. Had she somehow managed to piece her mask together with her own hatred?

"Katherine, please." He hadn't meant to sound so needy, but he couldn't keep the desperation out of his voice. "Please, the world has changed. You'll need my help to survive here."

"No, Benjamin," she said cooly, "I don't need your assistance with anything . . . yet."

Benjamin shook. He was a mess of desire and shame, and he couldn't do anything about it except watch the object of his shame turn away from him and begin to depart. Twice in the same day, a woman walked away from him. An unfamiliar sensation bubbled up. He was unaccustomed to rejection, and it unnerved him. He'd always thought of himself as a problem solver, fighting and capturing monsters for God's sake. He had a destiny. But here he stood, alone, the very picture of a problem. It was his fault that any of this happened.

"Oh, and Benjamin—" she said, with a look over her shoulder.

"Katherine."

"I look forward to our next encounter."

"Likewise," he returned, even though he wasn't at all sure about it.

"I'm sure," she said.

She seemed to understand the hesitation in his voice. He was lost. In a few short weeks, his life had been turned upside down and inside out. He'd managed to lose everything that mattered. He couldn't seem to get his bearings. What was he supposed to do now? How could he fix this? Ben drifted aimlessly through an ocean of pity, wallowing in the defamation of his ego.

By the time he pulled himself back to the present, she was gone. The tiniest ember of his hopes for something good to come out of all of this was snuffed out, and tears coursed down his face. He refused to weep, but the tears came unbidden. He would not forget his former lover's chilling smile, but the rest was lost to his grief.

35

THE LOBBY OF THE Denver Art Museum was a broad open space. An open gift shop was positioned to the right, with low shelves surrounded by glass cases that reached the ceiling. The white walls and white shelves glowed with backlighting. To the left of the main bank of doors at the entrance was some exhibit space, but it was all overshadowed by the terrazzo staircase of the Sturm Grand Pavilion. The composite material only softened the scale and shape of the exquisite terrazzo staircase in ivories and creams. It was the perfect backdrop for Domn Dehanie in his tight black jeans and open black shirt. His golden skin and short dark hair contrasted with his white surroundings.

He descended the stairs leisurely, a trail of black writhing shadows trailing behind him, each stumbling over the other to lick his boots with viscous tendrils. The horde of shadows that had escaped from Lord Benjamin Brahm's twisted prison had caught their master's scent and swarmed him in eager relief.

He welcomed them back home individually, addressing each beast by name, their coos of gratitude and pleasure like gargled rocks.

Domn stepped into the main welcome center with a sparkle in his eyes. He was happy to have his children home, but something was amiss. Not so far away, an imposing security guard stood out starkly with his stiff posture and folded arms.

"You look unhappy, Walsh," Domn said. "Whatever is the matter?"

"The girl is back."

"How did that happen?"

"I don't know, but . . ."

"But?" Domn asked. A hint of impatience hung in his sultry voice.

"I don't think Benjamin did it," Walsh finally said.

Domn stopped moving. His figure was tall and strong. Broad shoulders and a muscular chest carried him along through this mortals' playground, and his persistence and passion kept him entertained. He leveled his cool eyes at the security guard.

"What do you mean?"

"He looked surprised," Walsh said, his voice fluctuating.

"It wasn't the old painter," a voice from behind Domn said.

Domn Dehanie wasn't surprised often, but his face froze in a beautiful arrangement of surprise and wonder. He was a calculating man. His kingdom had survived this long even with treacherous bastards like Benjamin Brahm removing his children from the board. It was purely because he anticipated his enemy. Dehanie turned around slowly, savoring the reunion. Walking into view from around the base of the spiraling grand staircase of terrazzo and ingenuity were his two favorite creations.

"Evelyn?"

"Father," she replied, filling that one word with all her longing and anger and fear, "it was the girl. She has his gift."

A king never begged. It was not in his nature to show weakness. So, Domn opened his arms wide, inviting her home, rather than going to her. Like most children, she didn't care either way. Evelyn was simply glad to be free of her prison. She approached him slowly, her brother still clinging to her for support.

"Father?" William called out as his master wrapped the two beasts in his arms.

"I'm here, William," Domn comforted. "You're home now."

William was barely able to maintain what he could of his human form, and at the first touch of his master, he dissolved into a vicious shadow. He melted into Domn, in and around him, so that, at times, there was no distinction where one ended and the other began. Domn let his children relax as they were welcomed home. They had been gone so long and craved the comfort of their own kind. Evelyn alone, of all Domn's creatures, maintained her shape. It did not escape his notice.

Domn pulled William away from him, tenderly, lovingly. Tendrils of nightmare and shadow stretched and kneaded as the two of them separated. The last of William to pull away from his master was the twisted remnants of the child's face. The horror of him brought a smile to Domn's face.

"You're a very good boy," Domn said, and William gurgled and cooed with satisfaction. "Now run along." Smiling, he looked out upon all his children. "All of you, please, go and feast. You'll need your strength for what's to come."

The horde of shadows shrieked as they swirled around the museum's visitor center, a great tide of malice sweeping out around Domn, Evelyn, and the uncomfortable security guard.

"Do you think it's a good idea to just set them loose?" Walsh asked.

Domn ignored the man. Instead, he soothed Evelyn. She was the smartest and strongest of all his creations, but she held some uncertainty. He wondered what it must have been like in Brahm's prison. He pulled her back gently so that he could get a good look at her. Still, in her human shape, she looked up at him with hunger, but her hunger did not match the others. She wasn't hungry for a meal. Evelyn was hungry for something else. It took a moment before Domn's brows furrowed in displeasure. He realized what she was craving.

His most beautiful creation had grown a taste for power. She had been trapped in that painting for so long that she'd grown accustomed to not having a master. In there, she must have been her own master. His creation had designs of her own, and this displeased him. Looking at her youthful face, he saw the evidence. Of all the shadows that emerged from their prisons, she alone was strong enough to hold her human form.

Domn crooked a finger under her chin and raised her face to meet his gaze. Her young cherubic face was healthy, well, within reason. Nightmare children could never really mimic the flush that blood offered. They had no blood. Their bodies were made of the detritus of this world, pieces of corpses tangled together with his own dark dreams. They were never alive, but they carried his purpose out into the world.

"You look well, child."

"I've stayed strong for you, Father," she said, but there it was, just behind her black eyes. He could feel the determination set in her jaw.

He uncurled his fingers and wrapped them around her jaw. Evelyn's stubbornness grew bolder as she continued to meet his gaze. That was, until his grip on her jaw tightened. Her expression flinched at the strength of his fingers as they continued to tighten.

"Father—" she started, but her mouth couldn't move anymore. Tighter.

"Domn?" Walsh asked tentatively, but Domn paid him no attention. He was busy.

His grip on the girl's jaw tightened, drilling into her stubbornness. At the sound of the first bone snapping beneath his grip, Walsh took a step back, and Evelyn barely managed to open her mouth in a silent scream. Domn closed his fist around her jaw and ripped it off her face.

Evelyn crumpled to the ground, nothing more than a whimpering fool. Domn let her jaw fall to the floor before walking away from her. Walsh dug out a wrinkled handkerchief from his pocket and handed it to Domn, who took it and wiped the black mess from his hands.

"When you're feeling up to it, Evelyn, you'll tell me about this girl," he called out over his shoulder. "I think she might be just what I was looking for."

"How so?" Walsh asked.

"She just might be able to get under Brahm's skin, and that's something that I can use."

"You don't think she'll have an issue with that?"

"I think that if she's seen what he has created, then she just might have an issue with him, more than me."

"If you say so," Walsh said skeptically.

"A lie told out of love is still a lie," Domn added.

A gargling sound from behind Domn made him pause. He turned around to see his creation pulling herself back to her feet, the remnants of her jaw in her hands.

"Were you trying to say something, dear?"

"He's weak," Evelyn struggled to say.

"I've known that for quite some time."

"More than you know."

"How so?" He approached her once again. She flinched but stopped herself from taking a nervous step back.

"The governess will be his downfall," she said, her head held high confidently in defiance.

"Who is this governess?"

"It's her, Father," she said with loathing, "his lover."

Domn's face wrinkled in confusion. At first, he didn't understand. He didn't know what she was talking about. He pulled tendrils of memory from the back of his mind until the realization hit him. His eyebrows raised a notch at that singular notion.

"Are you saying that Lady Katherine Ainsley had been trapped in that prison with you?" Domn asked.

She gave him a singular nod. A slow wicked smile grew across his delicious mouth. "How positively wonderful."

Domn grasped his creation's face and pulled it toward him. He placed a gentle, loving kiss on the crown of Evelyn's head, and the tension in her body drained. His thoughts seductively focused on the future. "Oh, what exquisite nightmares I can create from this."

36

Katherine walked away from Benjamin and away from her past. She had not been lying about her desire to see him suffer. She wasn't the young, innocent thing he had met all those years ago. There was no mistaking that she'd endured suffering no one should have to endure, but here she was, a stronger woman for it. Over the years, she dreamed up so many ways to make Benjamin suffer. It kept her sane. At least, that was what she told herself. She wasn't so deluded as to ignore the possibility that she'd gone mad ages ago. It didn't really matter anymore. She would have fun, regardless of her circumstances. While Katherine was more than eager to implement her plans for Benjamin, she had to acclimate to the new world.

The last time she had walked this world, it had run on horse-drawn carriages and locomotives. It had already been a time of marvelous change. This, however, was altogether another level of change. The first horseless carriage that screamed past her caught her off guard. She very nearly yelped. It had been a long time since she was out of her depth. She could think of no better way to understand this new age of mankind than by experiencing it firsthand. So, Lady Katherine Ainsley headed toward downtown Denver.

A few people were out and about at this late hour, but those she came across stared at her. Katherine knew on some level she was a spectacle. Her apparel alone was a contradiction. Her gown and cloak stood out starkly against the torn trousers made of something resembling serge de Nîmes. Shirts with large primitive graphics printed on them also seemed popular. She didn't even know what to make of the various coiffures she'd seen. She had been raised in affluent circumstances and understood one's own appearance told a story to those one interacted with. A person could control that narrative by changing the way they dressed.

Either she didn't understand the narrative being told or one's own appearance no longer counted as much as it used to. Or perhaps it was something else entirely. Perhaps the judgmental attitudes derived from one's appearance had been overcome. There certainly was plenty to be concerned about without having to worry if the hem of a dress was appropriate. There was something liberating in that thought.

The streets were a cluttered mess of lights and signs, but they held some order. The distinct lack of beautiful architecture caught her attention the most. Everything was square and cold. It was a shame to lose the beauty of form and function. Surely, there were beautiful things to be had in this age. She would have to be more intentional about seeking it out. Her porcelain mask gave an impossible shiver that brought her to a stop. The soft white of the porcelain pieces practically glowed against the contrast of the impervious black holding them together, and each piece moved, miniature tectonic plates rubbing against one another. Her children were restless.

"What is the matter, little ones?" she spoke. A nearby vagabond stopped rifling through a trash bin to stare at her. Katherine listened to the wordless language of her children. "Oh, I am so sorry, how thoughtless of me. You must be starving."

Cutting across the bitter tang of petroleum fumes and urine, the sour perfume of this place, a scream pierced the night. It was shrill and filled with terror. Katherine didn't know much about this time or place, but she recognized the sound of another woman in peril. "Let's see what we can discover, little ones." Her tone held a note of sincerity. The black seams of her shattered mask writhed and wriggled in anticipation.

Less than a block away, a scene of horror from across the street played in front of her, of a shop whose glass front was barricaded by an iron gate. There was no hiding the criminal elements even from someone so out of step with this time. All the buildings had been vandalized in some fashion. Graffiti or shattered windows taped back together; it didn't matter. It might look a little different, but vandalization was all the same throughout time.

Katherine's red cloak rustled slightly in a stale breeze winding through the streets. The air was stifling. The night was oppressive, though she didn't mind. It was the burden of a dying season. Summer would soon give way to autumn, and with the change of season came a change of energy. She looked forward to it. Until then, she would need to take care of herself and her children.

Across the street, a brute of a man had a woman pressed against the metal gate shielding a storefront. His hands groped her, violated her. None of this surprised Katherine. Men held the illusion they were at the top of the food chain, and for the most part, women allowed them to continue in this belief. There was power in womanhood. There was power in the combined ephemeral knowledge of women joining forces, but the ever-present patriarchy was persistent in continuing to pit women against women. She was interested in changing that narrative, but she was also wise enough to know that she couldn't accomplish that without help. She needed an army.

The woman screamed out again. Yes, he'd do nicely. Katherine stepped off the curb and crossed the street. The streetlight overhead changed from red to green, but she paid it little mind. She was the very picture of a woman on a mission.

Meanwhile, the brute persisted. He didn't seem to notice Katherine's presence. She approached him from behind and waited patiently for him to acknowledge her. The man's victim, on the other hand, noticed Katherine right away. The woman's eyes grew at the sight of her masked face. The woman stopped fighting, caught by the fear of something new. Katherine wondered if the woman could put a name to that new fear, but probably not. This new age might be full of technological and scientific advancements, but from what little of it she'd seen, it had lost valuable earthly knowledge. The knowledge of women from ages come and gone. This world had lost touch with the knowledge of the hedge witch, the wise woman, and the power of the circle gatherings when women shared advice and experience.

This abused, frightened woman would be the perfect start to creating an army of women who could take back control from those who forced their will on everything and everyone else. Katherine tapped the brute's shoulder.

"I'm busy," he growled.

"I can see that," Katherine replied coldly.

The man pressed a forearm against the woman's throat before he turned around to get a look at Katherine. "I said I'm busy, ya freak, but maybe I should get my freak on with you instead."

"You could try, but I don't expect that it would go very well for you."

"Dumb bitch," he said as he relinquished his hold on the woman he'd been assaulting. "I think it's 'bout time someone teach you a lesson." He turned around and wrapped his meaty hands around her upper arms. Katherine tilted her head curiously at him. "It's a bit early for Halloween, bitch. Why you wearing a mask?"

"You're about to find out," Katherine said. Her voice was low and full of honey. How else did one catch a bee?

"Oh yeah, go on, show me what you hiding underneath that freakish mask you got on." His words came easily, but the longer he stared at her mask, the more his words slowed. Katherine recognized the effect. He was finally paying attention to the details of her mask, the pieces held together by something otherworldly. The brute was facing something he probably thought shouldn't exist, but he was enchanted by it, nonetheless.

She raised her forearms slightly and rested her hands on his barrel chest. "My children are very hungry."

"Your what?" he mumbled distractedly.

"My children," she replied. "They're hungry."

"Okay," the brute slurred.

"And you look perfectly delectable." Her words became an intuitive invitation hungrily accepted by the congealed shadows holding her mask together.

Pieces of porcelain fell from her mask like snow as the shadows released their grip on the mask. The impervious shadows stretched out, spanning the short distance to the brute's dumb face. Their blackness absorbed light as they moved. They stretched and wriggled, crawling across each other to swarm the man. His previously vacant expression twisted in agony as Katherine's shadows devoured him, burrowing through his flesh, burning the viscous fluid of his eyes, and feeding upon him.

The man's screams were memorable but short-lived, more like the animal he was than the man he pretended to be. Her shadows made quick work of him. The creatures feasted until they were full to bursting. Satiated and content, they slithered up her figure and collected the pieces of her mask before resuming their places. Her shattered white mask reformed to cover the grotesquery below.

"You know . . ." a sultry voice said from somewhere behind Katherine. The accent was European but familiar. "You probably shouldn't leave such a mess behind."

Katherine wasn't frightened, but she didn't like being unpleasantly surprised. "So you say?"

"The local constabulary is a tad more sophisticated than they used to be." The man emerged from a nearby shadow dressed all in black. There was nothing but confidence and charisma in the man's face. Here was a man who was used to getting his way. Katherine looked at the bloody mess left behind by her children. She supposed he wasn't wrong. Someone was bound to stumble across it.

"Any recommendations?" she asked. He smiled. It was a lovely smile, too, full of appetite and patience.

"I'm bursting with ideas," he said as he took a few steps toward her.

"I would love to hear them." Her voice dropped with curiosity. As she stepped closer to him, she realized they had met before. What Katherine didn't know was if he recognized her as well.

He bowed slightly. "Domn Dehanie," he said in a sultry voice, "at your service."

"Lady Katherine Ainsley," she answered with a hint of a curtsey.

The king of monsters held out his arm to Katherine, and she accepted it.

"You know," he started as they walked away, "I'm staying at a local place, The Pink Penny. I'd be happy to make an introduction for you if you're looking for a place to stay."

Katherine scrutinized the handsome man from behind her mask. He looked at her eyes with no awkward hesitation. He appeared as youthful as she remembered him, and she knew he was accustomed to the more inhuman aspects of existence. She should be wary of him. He was obviously not all he appeared to be, but sometimes, allies came in unexpected packages.

"I would appreciate that very much," she answered politely.

The two of them left the bloody carcass behind. Meanwhile, the neon signs threw shadows off the nearby buildings, splattering the streets with vulgar pinks and greens. But not all shadows were made from the absence of light. Some shadows were the absence of goodness and stretched themselves out curiously.

"You know," Domn said coyly, "I believe we have a mutual acquaintance."

"Oh, really?"

"Indeed."

"Whoever could that be?"

"I'm sure you remember Lord Benjamin Brahm."

"Yes," Katherine said, unable to hide the iciness in her voice, "I am familiar with Lord Brahm." She felt the gentleman's eyes on her, but she refused to turn to him.

"You, too, I see." The king of monsters patted Katherine's hand. "I think we're going to be great friends.

"Indeed." Behind her mask, the grisly wreck of her face stretched into an eager smile. "Indeed, we shall."

Epilogue

Violet stood on the tiny balcony alone. The night was quiet. She didn't know what happened to Benjamin after she left that alley to go find her mom. He had changed, but to be honest, she really didn't care. She wasn't particularly sure who the real villain in all this mess was. Katherine had been put through unimaginable torture and didn't deserve to be abandoned in that prison for monsters, but she understood what Benjamin had been trying to do. His paintings were filled with pure evil, and he desired to temper that evil with goodness. But she wasn't convinced that good could actually overcome evil. If she had learned anything from her experiences lately, it was that the universe really didn't give a shit about good or evil, right or wrong. The universe did whatever the hell it wanted and left broken people in its wake.

She looked out at the city unfolding around her. It was like origami, each fold revealing or concealing some other part of it. She could probably live a thousand years and never understand the shape the city would take. Everything was changing, changing all the time. Violet wanted to scream at the world, at life, to just stop moving. Not forever, just for a minute. But it never listened to what she wanted.

The velvety black sky of night hovered above, and the street-lights connected the city. Cool night air whispered across her cheeks, and a gentle breeze fluttered the tendrils of hair framing her face. The air smelled of diesel and despair. Among the countless forgettable neighborhoods wrapped within the bosom of the city, Violet couldn't have guessed at the nightmares lurking just beneath the veneer of civilization. These people around her were not privileged. Civilization chewed them up and spat them out. How much of their suffering was because of the machinations of evil?

She had confronted true evil, but it wouldn't be the last time. Benjamin had explained it all to her, but it hadn't really sunk in yet. She didn't want this gift, curse, or whatever it was. She just wanted to be an ordinary girl. The thought of going shopping with her mom or going on a hike with her dad were the little things she craved. But she wasn't destined to have any of those things other people took for granted. The one thing she had that she could find any joy from, her art, had been corrupted by powers beyond her ability to understand.

Violet hadn't adjusted yet. And to make things worse, time had run differently out here than it had inside the painting. She'd been gone for two weeks. Violet had lost so much precious time she could have been spending with her mom. But apparently, time was the one thing she suddenly had too much of. Benjamin had said that she more than likely shared his extraordinarily long life. How the hell was she supposed to get a grip on being nearly immortal? She didn't want more time if it meant watching her mother continue to wither away. She didn't want to live forever if it was only in the service of hunting monsters. Violet wanted it all to go back to the way it had been before.

She turned around and leaned against the wrought-iron railing of the balcony. It felt strange being back home. Her belongings in the apartment were all where they should have been, well, except for the mess in her mom's room. After Benjamin had left, Nguyen stayed with Violet. Multiple cups of tea later, Violet couldn't thank her friend enough for caring for her mom. Nguyen was a good woman, and it wasn't her responsibility to take care of her mom, something Nguyen had tried to point out to Violet too. She had reminded her it wasn't Violet's responsibility to care for her mother like this, but Violet still wasn't ready to hand her mother over to be institutionalized for the rest of her life. After everything she'd been through, it was the hope of getting back to her mom that had pushed her through.

Violet wondered if being back home was a good thing for her mom. Was she really the right person to be taking care of her? Was she even capable of giving her a fulfilling life? Violet couldn't answer those questions. Could a doctor even answer them? Debatable.

She left the little balcony and returned inside. She stood in the quiet living room. Her blankets were folded up on the chair, waiting for her to make her bed on the sofa. The dishes had been cleaned and dried and put away. Everything looked normal. But the truth was, nothing had ever been normal around here.

She made her way through the tiny apartment with the dingy paint and threadbare carpet until she reached the closed door of her mom's room. Carefully, quietly, she turned the knob and opened the door. Violet tiptoed inside to not wake her mom, who slept soundly. Violet loved watching her mom sleep. It was the only time that she could see her mother as she was when she was healthy and vibrant.

After everything Benjamin had told her about their abilities, she understood the truth of what had happened to her mother. She wasn't sick or had Alzheimer's. The truth was more insidious. She had stolen her mom's life from her. With each drawing, every stroke of charcoal, and the purposeful blending of light and dark, Violet slowly leached the very essence of life from her. It wasn't malicious, she hadn't meant to do it, but it happened, nonetheless. Benjamin had told her she could not return what she'd stolen, though she wished she could give it all back. Everyone wanted to be special, but being special came with a price. What was the point of being special if there was no one to share it with?

She supposed she had someone to share it with. She had Benjamin, and Benjamin had her. Violet felt bad for him on some level even if he were to blame for Katherine's suffering. The man had been alone for so long. She could see it in his eyes when he told her about her own abilities. The problem was she didn't trust him. She'd spent too much time with Katherine to see him as blameless. Violet was going to have to learn more about this life of hers. There had to be rules. There were always rules. But there would be time for that later. Right then, she just wanted to watch her mom.

A dim night light plugged into one of the electrical outlets cast the room in a strange blue glow that was too bright and yet not bright enough all at the same time. Lately, she found herself thinking that everything around her seemed to always be too much and not enough of something. She had too much time and not enough time. She had too much power and not enough power to save the ones she loved.

The deep rhythm of a sleeper's breath made her mom's chest rise and fall. Her face was relaxed, and the stress of the harsh reality closing in on them evaporated. Violet wished she could take away the world's cruelty. She wished she could bring her mother joy instead of sorrow and loss, but that was not in her power. To lose someone so dear to you left a scar that never truly healed. It had started ages ago when her dad had died. Her heart ached for her family to be whole, but there was a pit at the center of her heart that would never mend. Everything she'd been through recently just exasperated the damage. Cracks and fissures were spreading across her scarred heart.

She could eventually become strong like Benjamin, but she couldn't imagine herself drowning in guilt and remorse. The guilt of what she'd done to her parents was already weighing on her. She hadn't known what she had done at the time, only that she was a kid who loved her parents very much. Violet wished she could turn back time. She couldn't, but there was something she could do.

Exiting the room, she shuffled around the apartment until she gathered everything she needed. A few minutes later, she settled in the doorway to her mom's room with her favorite sketchbook and a stack of pencils. The light from the living room spilled into the bedroom, offering just enough light to work with. Violet turned the pages of her sketchbook until she found the drawing of her dad. She ran her fingers across the image and her scribbled signature at the bottom.

Violet missed her dad so much that her heart contracted tightly every time she thought of him. His sandy hair and rosy cheeks framed his bright blue eyes that twinkled when he laughed. He had been genuinely content to spend his life with his two loves, his wife and daughter.

She had drawn him on the right page, which had been a habit of hers. Having an unused page touching one of her drawings kept the drawings clean. One of her high school art teachers taught her that trick. She hadn't learned yet that she need never worry about her drawings smearing. That was one of those peculiar tricks Benjamin had taught her about their gift. The medium would never smear unless the artist intended for it to do so.

She thought about that word: gift. Her memories resisted it. A gift was something you wanted, something treasured. This gift had already stolen one life, so Violet didn't know how to think of it as a gift. It was a curse. Was there anything worse than a curse? If so, that's what this was. She looked up at the sleeping figure of her mom. There was only peace on her face. Violet hadn't meant to steal so much from her mom, but she could end her suffering. Looking back at her book, Violet smoothed out the nonexistent wrinkles on the blank page facing the drawing of her dad.

The blank page gave her pause. Was she really doing the right thing? It didn't feel wrong. In fact, of all the things she'd been through lately, it was the only move that felt right. It was time and wouldn't get any easier putting it off. So, she set her mind to the task.

Violet closed her eyes and cleared her mind. She took a long, slow breath through her nose and held it for a long time before she let it out from between her lips. All her thoughts of the harsh world outside their little apartment faded away. The broken love of Benjamin and Katherine dissipated like an autumn mist as the morning sun burned it away. Even the tatty apartment she lived in faded into the background.

Violet opened her eyes, found her starting point, and then set about to her task. Hours passed by. The night grew long and the shadows stretched all around her, but she had no mind for the sounds of life beyond this moment. One stroke after another, she drew the sleeping form of her mother. She put her grief in every stroke. The tears that fell from her cheeks mixed with the charcoal on the page, emphasizing the dark spots. Violet put more care into this one drawing of her mother than she had put in hundreds of sketches and doodles. She wanted to remember everything about her mom. This moment would never happen again. Violet would never get a second chance. She had to make every line and smudge and pause count. Violet drew the waves of her mom's hair and the downy hairs along her hairline that would catch the sunlight just right when they would walk to the park. Every wrinkle in the blankets tucked up under her chin and every eyelash was crafted with love and sorrow on the page.

As the skyline lightened ever so slightly, with the hint of dawn not far away, Violet applied her last few strokes. Her neck was stiff and her hand had cramped up a few times, but it was done. She'd added a little color to it, like she'd done with her dad's drawing. The deep onyx lines from her charcoal were accentuated with lemon to catch the streetlight coming through the window behind her mom's bed. She added the blues of the ocean and forget-me-nots to change the menacing shadows into something sweeter.

Violet put the pencils down in the center of the sketchbook to hold her place while she leaned back and stretched out her body. There was only one thing left to do, but she wasn't ready, not just yet. She stood up and set the book down on her chair before crossing the small room. As she sat down on the edge of the bed, her mom didn't stir. Her breathing was shallow and sparse. Violet leaned down and placed a tender kiss on her mom's forehead.

"I love you," she whispered.

She stayed there for a little while, committing every curve and freckle of her face to memory. But she couldn't put the inevitable off any longer. She picked up her sketchbook and turned around to face her mom one more time. With a flick of her wrist, she signed the drawing and closed the book. She didn't need to know if it worked. Violet already knew. The fragile tether keeping the mother and daughter bound snapped.

She set the book back on the chair and returned to the living room to retrieve her phone. Violet flicked her thumb across the screen, and the bright display burned her tired eyes. She stared out the door as the sun began its ascent in a blazing crimson, then dialed the numbers. As she listened to the ringing on the other end of the line, she fiddled absentmindedly with the little glass vial she'd brought back with her from hell.

"Nine-one-one, what is your emergency?"

Turn the page for a sneak peek of the next book in
The Governess Trilogy

1

Colorado State University, which had been founded well over a hundred years ago, was nestled in the heart of Fort Collins. Like any college town, it was a contradiction of city life and student life. The city always had delusions of grandeur and its residents wanted the modern conveniences of the metropolis, but they were unwilling to relinquish old-fashioned ideals. The people were loud and obnoxious and, above all, rude. Therefore, Lyle Owen preferred working at night. He was too old to put up with that kind of shit.

The radio hanging on his belt squawked, startling him so badly that he dropped the paperback he was reading.

"Lyle, will you head over to the art building," the facilities' superintendent barked.

"What's up?" Lyle asked.

"I've got a noise complaint coming from one of the offices over there."

"Do you know which one?"

The silence on the radio stretched a little too long, and his heart sank.

"Uh, your favorite."

Lyle shrank in his chair. Professor Chandler's room. He was an arrogant ass, fond of reminding everyone he worked with he was better than them.

"I'm on it," Lyle said with a grumble.

Although Lyle was sixty-eight years old, he couldn't yet retire, thanks to his ex-wife and her attorney. He moved his tired body into motion, with slow and laborious movements, making the heavy set of keys on his belt jingle. Since he was small and frail, he wondered how the keys didn't push him over.

The school year had recently started, so students would be running around, even at this late hour. In a month or so, the kids who couldn't handle the demands of the semester would thin out. He'd never been to college himself. That was a privilege for rich kids. He'd managed well enough working with his hands and never seemed to have trouble finding work. It wasn't hard to get a job if one was willing to do the crap jobs most people didn't want.

The Colorado State University campus was full of trees, and even though the surrounding city was too crowded for his taste, it wasn't a horrible place to live. He could always be somewhere worse, like Florida.

Lyle made his way across the campus, crossing paths until he reached the visual arts building. It was low and spread out in a dysfunctional fashion, with pops of color from sculptures that made little sense. It was like a puzzle no one finished putting together.

He entered a side door that should've been locked, although it didn't surprise him. The students often worked late into the night, some of whom had access to the building after hours. His black shoes barely made a sound as he traversed the corridors of green-tiled floors and the occasional fluorescent light. Glass cases showcased the art of students and celebrated the school's awards. It made no matter to him. Most of the art was abstract and beyond him. He thought it all just looked like noise. He was only here to do his job.

Professor Marcus Chandler's office was at the far end of a corridor lined with classrooms. The bulbs were off, with the only light peeking in from adjacent corridors. The frosted door to the professor's office was closed. Lyle expected nothing else. It was way past the professor's usual office hours. What he wasn't expecting was for the light in the office to still be on. Something about the place felt odd. He was an old man, but he wasn't stupid.

Although everything surrounding him held an eerie quality, he had to get the work done. He listened hard but couldn't hear anything. Then he realized the whole place was still and quiet. And it wasn't the type of quiet he was used to. A sleepy campus had a special sound to it, but this wasn't like that. It was more like the type of quiet when the power went out, devoid of the white noise of the electronic gadgets people were accustomed to.

He shook his head at his nonsensical train of thoughts and forced himself to get going with the job. Lyle unhooked the keys from his belt and flipped through them until he found the master key, all while his wrinkled face was only inches from the window. But he saw movement. He was suddenly nervous. Who knew what sort of misbehavior went on behind closed doors? Maybe the strange noise was nothing more than another disgusting example of the abuse of power.

Lyle knocked on the door. "Professor Chandler?" Lyle's voice was papery and thin, an echo of his age. He listened at the door, but there was no response. "Professor Chandler, I'll be coming in now."

He waited again. Still nothing. With that, he slid the key into the lock. The tumblers clicked, and he twisted the doorknob. He swung the door open and stepped cautiously into the office.

"Apologies, sir," he announced, looking to the side. Lyle didn't want to catch anyone by surprise, and he *definitely* didn't want to see anything he'd be forced to lie about later. That just wouldn't do. "There's been a report of an odd sound, and I'm just here to investigate."

At no response, Lyle turned and nearly choked on his own tongue at the gruesome horror confronting him. The professor was poised like a caricature from a dime store horror novel at his desk. His swollen purple tongue was protruding from his mouth, contrasting against his ashen, waxy face. Professor Chandler's hands were flat on his desk with two elegant fountain pens stabbed clean through each and embedded in the wood.

Lyle Owens tripped over his feet in an attempt to get away from the nightmare he found himself in. Even the pain of landing hard on the floor wasn't enough to break his gawking stare. He screamed. The shrillness of pure terror cascaded through the otherwise empty building. There was no one to hear him scream other than the corpse pinned to the desk.

Lyle scrambled backward, and his hand brushed against something on the floor. He was already too frightened to maintain any semblance of composure as the shock of it sent him screaming again. But when he looked down, grateful to have something else to look at, he saw a drawing. But it was unlike any other. It pictured the ghoulish scene in the room exactly, right down to the putrid gorging tongue. Lyle picked up the drawing with shaky hands, the page crinkling, and stared at the fine lines and exaggerated colors. He couldn't make out the scribbled signature in the lower corner.

A horrible thought pierced his fear. Someone had taken the time to sit here and draw this macabre scene. Had they watched the man die? Had the artist been the one to do this to him? Lyle struggled at the thought a man could do this to someone. Yes, there were evil people in the world, but it was one thing to believe in evil and another to be confronted with it.

His insides squirmed, and he wretched at the gore. A gargled choking sound, not his own, brought him back to the scene in front of him. He looked up at the corpse. It opened its eyes and, in the gruesome silence between them, begged for true death.

About the Author

G. H. Fryer is a nerdy Pisces who writes about mischief, mystery, murder, and the occasional dash of magic...mostly because society frowns upon enacting them in real life. Her debut novel was the contemporary murder mystery, *The Arsenic Box*. Fryer lives in a small northern Colorado town with her husband and daughter. When you're arranging clandestine affairs with her, please remember that she can be bribed with coffee, tea, wine, and chocolate.